School of Night

Also by Alan Wall

Jacob
Curved Light
Chronicle
Bless the Thief
Lenses
A to Z
Silent Conversations
Richard Dadd in Bedlam & Other Stories
The Lightning Cage

School of Night

A Novel

Alan Wall

THOMAS DUNNE BOOKS
ST. MARTIN'S GRIFFIN ✠ NEW YORK

THOMAS DUNNE BOOKS.
An imprint of St. Martin's Press.

www.stmartins.com

Library of Congress Cataloging-in-Publication Data

Wall, Alan.
    The school of night : a novel / Alan Wall.—1st ed.
        p. cm.
    ISBN 0-312-28778-X (hc)
    ISBN 0-312-31628-3 (pbk)
    1. Literary historians—Fiction. 2. Raleigh, Walter, Sir, 1552?–1618—Friends and associates—Fiction. 3. Shakespeare, William, 1564–1616—Authorship—Fiction. 4. Secret societies—Fiction. I. Title.

PR6073.A415 S36 2002
823'.914—dc21   2001048996

First published in Great Britain by Secker & Warburg,
Random House

First St. Martin's Griffin Edition: May 2003

10 9 8 7 6 5 4 3 2 1

To Monsignor George Tancred

lifter of burdens

Acknowledgements

I would like to thank the following for their help:

Bob Bass, Elizabeth Cook, David Elliott, Marius Kociejowski, Anita Money, W.S. Milne and Bernard Sharratt.

Thanks to Ann Denham for everything.

Philip Byrne was, as always, invaluable for his detailed critique, and for his friendship through difficult times.

Anthony Rudolf kindly shared with me his insider knowledge and much else besides.

Ray Leach restored first my house and then my good humour.

David Rees employed his bibliographic know-how on my behalf.

Thanks to Mike Goldmark and Fiona for their heartening response, and for the hospitality at Uppingham.

I am grateful, as ever, to the staff of the London Library for their assistance.

I would like to thank Eileen Gunn and the Royal Literary Fund for their generous support.

Lastly, but a long way from least, my agent Gill Coleridge and my publisher Geoff Mulligan supplied more active solidarity over the last year than any reasonable writer could normally hope for. The final shape of this book owes much to both of them. Not forgetting Lucy Luck and her mighty labours on my behalf.

Blessings on all their heads.

The oddest thing about the School of Night is the irresolvable effect it produces in regard to memory and analysis, one not dissimilar to that of the synoptic gospels, and which might be described thus: how something so luminous in its brilliance, its sheer intensity of life, is in all crucial respects neither provable nor disprovable, but must remain a matter as much for faith as science.

THOMAS BRIDEWELL, *Ralegh's Secret Circle* (1926)

The hue of dungeons, and the School of Night

WILLIAM SHAKESPEARE, *Love's Labour's Lost*

Part One

Come to this house of mourning, serve the Night

GEORGE CHAPMAN, *The Shadow of Night*

1

Five days ago I stole the Hariot Notebooks. From the university library where they had been put on display. Two buckram-covered volumes, only recently discovered, in an archive not long before acquired. Thomas Hariot was the scientist of genius who spent much of his life providing Walter Ralegh with intellectual companionship in the Tower of London, but because he does not currently have the fame he deserves there wasn't much security in the room, merely one of those wooden cabinets with a slanted glass top and a Victorian lock, which was more decorative than it was secure.

I'd come to see the notebooks the week before. I knew Hariot's script well enough to be able to transcribe what was written on the four pages displayed, though the enciphered passages were as unintelligible to me then as they were to everyone else. Only once I'd arrived home and spent a day going through the transcription with my code books did I realise what I was looking at. Even then, it wasn't until I'd returned from my last trip to see Daniel Pagett that I sat down and, for the first time in my life, planned a crime.

What I had deciphered, you see, in amongst the cryptic stresses and inversions, the algebraic signs and equations, was a single phrase, 'the School of Night'. I didn't really need to look since I knew the passage more or less by heart, but still I took down my old copy of Thomas Bridewell from the shelf and flicked through its chapters until I came to the paragraph I had marked twenty years before:

> *We have only ever located one reference to the School of Night, and that is in Shakespeare's play,* Love's Labour's Lost. *The discovery of another, which might confirm the speculations constituting this little book, would be something of an event in the world of literary and historical scholarship.*

I still find myself asking one question: would I have found the courage to carry out the crime I'd planned if Dan hadn't tempted and taunted me in? The following morning I went out and bought the heavy screwdriver. (But it was always my father who did all the stealing in our family, so why did I do it? What pushed me over to the wrong side of the law, after a whole lifetime spent so timidly obeying it?)

Five days ago I stole the Hariot Notebooks; the evening before, Daniel Pagett had died. Daniel, who was not my brother, and yet was the nearest thing to a brother I have ever had. Did his death unhinge me? I don't feel unhinged. If anything, my mind for this last week has brightened with unexpected clarity. My thoughts have grown sudden – electric eels signing their gloomy element with rapid and sinuous traces. The blackness in my heart, that fetid ditch of sorrow and suspicion, is now being burnt away. I think I might be seeing the light at last, though it's certainly taken long enough. I've spent most of my life in the shadows; that's where I'd chosen to live.

Dan's final words are buzzing still in my head. I am now a criminal. The present has not yet noticed, though the past is in a mighty uproar: one of its beloved crew has been rescued at last from the salt of oblivion, from four centuries of incomprehension and obscurity. The testimony of Thomas Hariot is now being resurrected through a loving act of theft.

I don't often smile these days, but I can't help smiling briefly at my location. Here I am in a tower, looking down on moving water. I can't see it, of course, in the anthracite darkness out there, but I can hear it. The sea is a medley of turmoil and patience, washing away mountains, swallowing its guests in fluent mouthfuls. I am here because later today, once the dark makes way for dawn, Daniel Pagett will be taken from this place to a furnace and burnt. Daniel Pagett, my friend Dan. Only at night are heavenly bodies at their brightest, even as they fall. That was the wisdom of the School of Night.

How I wish I could start at the beginning, then I might write a book as memorable as Dan's life. But I can't start at the beginning because I don't know where it is. Anyway, if twenty years spent editing news for the BBC taught me anything, it is that the beginning of any story is simply wherever you start to tell it. And the end comes (or could you still be listening, Dan?) when you run out of breath. So I think of this, which is, I suppose, a kind of beginning. Two boys, both twelve years old. An asphalt playground, severely slanted because the school is built on a steep hill outside town. The boys know little of each other except names.

Their homes are in the same town, but one of them (Sean Tallow, me) lives with his grandparents on a council estate, and the other (Daniel Pagett) lives with his mother and father in a detached millstone-grit house on the other side of town. This is in the north of England where Dan's father owns a chain of grocery stores called Pagett's General, thereby indicating a precise economic and social gap that could be measured in inches with a pair of steel callipers; reason enough in itself for the pair of us to keep our distance.

On this particular day my constant tormentor, Mark Scully, has decided to make a feast of my fear. Not content with the usual kick in the shins and slap round the back of the head, his persecution is growing noisy and a crowd is gathering. He jabs sharply with his right fist into my mouth and then follows with a straight hard punch. As that one lands, the bone tenting the flesh of my nose thrills with electricity; tears scald my eyes. The boys are shouting, 'Hit him, Tallow, hit him.' I don't, though. I could never bring myself to hit anybody, one of the reasons I'd become such a focus of attention in the first place. Scully is growing enthusiastic for his work now and a grin fills his over-large face as he moves in for the finale. He taunts over and over again. 'Tallow's dad's a tealeaf, Tallow's dad's a tealeaf.' He stinks of victory, and I am merely praying that this humiliation might be over and done with quickly when something unexpected happens. A figure muscles through the swaying ring of spectators – Daniel Pagett. He pushes me away, squares up to Scully and belts him hard in the gut. Astonished, Scully buckles and as he comes back up for air, Daniel hits him in the face, first with one fist then the other. Thud thud thud as Scully lets out a whimper, a cry for mercy, but by now the little crowd has sensed the fall of a playground tyrant and they start spitting at him as he reels and stumbles. Daniel lands a couple more blows, then leaves it to the other boys to spit, copiously and accurately, until Mark Scully is covered from head to foot in great gobbings of phlegm and saliva. A whistle blows, everyone runs except for Scully, bent over in the corner by the railings, howling in the invisible tunnel of his grief now that the end of his reign has at last arrived. His fingers are frantically raking through the gluey substance his clothes are smeared with as the teacher walks quickly towards him, but the rest of the boys have already scattered.

And that evening, when I mounted the school bus and saw the vacant seat next to Daniel Pagett, I went and sat down. Not a word passed between us all the way into town, but before he stood up to get off at his stop in the centre, Daniel breathed on the windowpane and wrote a single word. It was already fading, leaving only ICKEN but I didn't have much doubt that the vanished first letters had had been a C and an H.

That was how we met nearly thirty years ago. I looked courage in the face and realised it had a name. Now it is about to become no more than memory and ashes, buried in a little graveyard by the sea, leaving me here inscribing that name painstakingly on the glass, then watching it fade as the mist of my breath disappears. Daniel. Daniel Pagett. Dear dead Dan.

2

Maggots are clean as cats, but they do sweat. Any place that contained them was soon pervaded by a lingering and slightly suffocating smell, as though the air itself were being subtly eaten away.

They were kept in big green plastic tubs and they squirmed and wriggled over each other like dwarf anaemic worms. When they split open, what came out was acrid milk. We would hand over our cloth bags to the owner of the fishing shop, who scraped up our sixpenny portions in a silver scoop.

In my memory Daniel Pagett and I are still sitting at the side of a canal waiting for the rain to pour out of a blackening sky, our luminous floats upright in the dead, unmoving water. From time to time we reel in, rip the drowned maggot off the hook and carefully attach a new one, the juiciest we can locate. We thread the hook's point between the tiny beige freckles of those embryo eyes, as the maggot wriggles between thumb and forefinger. There is a creamy spurt as the barb cuts through, then our lines are flicked smartly back over the water. And we wait.

The symmetrical windows of warehouses and mills stare

down at us and now and then a narrow boat chugs along between the locks, seeming to take an age before it arrives, its vivid paintwork freakish against black water and black stone. Occasionally there might even be the wet flapping miracle of a fish, a roach perhaps or a perch with its poisonous dorsal. You had to press it down flat like a fan so it couldn't sting you. But not the pike we always talked about; that was to remain only a gleam of menace in our darker thoughts. Then back home again on the top deck of the bus, with a stale sensation in my mouth of smoke and sour metal, a taste like the word futility on my tongue. Did Dan feel that way too? Was that why he always said, 'A maggot's life, Sean, is it really worth it?' I surface from the memorial contamination of these murky trawls and wish I could ask him. I think I might have left it too late. Before many hours have passed I'll watch his coffin rolling slowly through the curtains in the crematorium chapel. I could ask his wife, I suppose, but she is in another room below me, sleeping.

Daniel Pagett, whose dying wish was to bequeath me that portion of his life he couldn't stay around to finish for himself. Shall his gift be a curse or a blessing? Only by following the thread of the days that lie ahead will I ever get to the heart of the matter and find out.

It is December and the weather is dirty. I stare at the notebooks lying open before me. I have already decoded most of their names, the members of the School of Night: Christopher Marlowe, Thomas Hariot himself, the Wizard Earl, Thom Nashe, Lord Strange, George Chapman, Matthew Roydon. Every now and then the names of John Dee and Giordano Bruno appear, brilliant reflections that glitter on a shifting surface. And always and everywhere Walter Ralegh, who lived like a star, a light that blazed even in the eyes of those who hated him. These men entrusted to one another thoughts so startling and illegal that each held the life of the others in his hand and on his tongue. A few words in the wrong ear could mean death for any one of them. Another reason for them to congregate only when the lights had gone down. Creatures of darkness, one and all.

If you could see me out there from the far side of this glass, which nobody can, you wouldn't notice anything unusual in my appearance. A little over six foot tall, thin, my dirty yellow hair just about neat enough, at least for my occupation. I am obviously not a businessman; I lack any precision of grooming or dress. Even in new clothes, which I very rarely buy, I retain a mildly dishevelled look. But I have acquired a certain appearance of public confidence, however misleading the persona might be. I even have a deep tan, which could make me stand out in these sunless regions. You would certainly not guess from my expressionless face tonight what loathing once filled me at the spectacle of my own body. It was this self-directed disgust, not so uncommon perhaps in adolescent boys, which made me wake every morning and think of Daniel Pagett.

These days when so many memoirs recount the late discovery of an occulted sexuality, it might be as well to make something plain: I never wanted to have Daniel Pagett, indeed I could not properly have imagined what such a possession might mean. I didn't want to have Dan, I wanted to be him. I would have preferred to inhabit his body and his mind, and would have been only too happy to relinquish my own in return. But instead I would lie on the sheets in the early morning and look down: the ribs protruded clearly underneath my skin and all I could think of as I stared at myself was the turkey at Christmas being gradually picked clean, a hull's skeleton emerging slowly through the sand.

I was taller by a good two inches, but painfully thin, while Dan's body seemed somehow more serious, solid all the way to the ground and built for business. As the years passed, this contrast grew more pronounced, with me finally breaching six foot, all bony, stooping hesitancy, and Dan there beneath me taut and trim as a sail. I would stand on the sideline, in reserve, and watch him slick down towards the goal. Any comparison of bodies led swiftly to despair, so I thought I'd better concentrate instead on the matter of mind.

Dan had never communicated with me since that day in the playground, not even by writing another message in the mist of his breath on a windowpane. Once, when asked by Crawley which category of man he found most despicable, he had answered without hesitation, 'The coward'. I watched from the other side of the class as my contemptuous saviour raised hands and answered questions, passed examinations, received the incessant praise of those in authority. Then, ill at ease in any case out on the streets around my home, I took to the library.

It had risen over the previous year, a great tower of concrete and glass in the city centre, a tribute to the north's wary respect for learning. Our sons and daughters, it announced in solemn tones, will suffer no impoverishment in matters of the intellect. As for the wariness, that was easily explained, since whenever its sons and daughters started to distinguish themselves in any intellectual field they left town by the next train.

Here, on the seventh floor, I began to read and discovered, contrary to so many experts I've encountered subsequently, that intelligence could be acquired and enlarged; that the innate part was no more than the ghost of a chance with which to get started. As I read books in greater and greater quantities, I felt the minds that fashioned them entering me, bringing new words and sensations, opening up unexpected reaches inside which I'd never imagined possible (I even discovered that the vast territory of nameless dread was not one experienced by me alone). My hand went up in class too, and as I was rewarded with encouraging nods and even an occasional smile from Mr Crawley, I began to answer as often as Dan. An unexpected fluency issued from my mouth; the dead had taken to speaking through me. If that sounds grand, I can't think of a more mundane way of putting it. I certainly hadn't spoken that way before and I hadn't learnt it from anyone at home, so how else can I describe what was going on?

In the end-of-year examinations when we were fifteen, Daniel Pagett and I shared first and second place in a number of subjects. This astonished everyone, but no one as much as me. Dan and I still didn't speak though, and if I closed my eyes I could always see his finger writing the word CHICKEN on that school bus window. But then Mr Crawley formed his little group.

There was a question often in my mind in those years and it was this: can you be popular and yet have no friends? This seemed to be the case with Daniel. Everyone thought highly of him (with the possible exception of Mark Scully) but he was close to no one. In the days when only policemen and soldiers had short hair, Dan's was cropped. Its spiky bristle

formed an appropriate thatch above his large brown eyes. His
nose was firm and secure, not like mine, which was thin and
fragile, almost inviting someone to come along and break it.
Daniel didn't seem to blink much either and his beard,
which arrived early, was dark. When mine came years later at
university it was fair and furry, hardly worth the trouble of a
razor. Dan was one of those boys who seemed ready for the
world from the word go; after that he simply grew readier
and readier. And yet even when he was smiling, his full-
fleshed lips turned down at the edges with a permanent hint
of contempt.

Crawley's subject was history. History with him was an
unceasing obsession, and it was Crawley's group that finally
brought Dan and me together. Its purpose was to get people
into Oxford, Crawley's old university. Each Friday night
during term he held a seminar at his house, which was half a
mile away from the school. One of the boys would read out
an essay and the others would be expected to comment upon
it intelligently. We had been chosen for signs of maverick
intelligence, little rogue sparks flying unexpectedly from the
steady flame of the curriculum. Increasingly Crawley came to
focus his attention on Daniel and me, and increasingly I
found myself speaking, over a whole variety of subjects,
words which had leeched into me from my hungry reading.
Sometimes I even startled myself with how precise and
articulate my working-class tongue was becoming. And each
Friday night, as we left Crawley's little house, Dan and I
would be carrying more borrowed books in our arms than all
the others put together. Dan had taken to listening carefully
whenever I spoke and then at last he started talking too. I can
still remember that day as clearly as any in my life. It seemed

I had been forgiven at last for my lack of physical courage; that the new-found clarity of my thoughts might make up in some way for the incoherent fog where all my actions disappeared. Or was Dan merely curious to know who and what I was? Whatever the reason, he spoke.

'Would you like to go fishing tomorrow, Sean?'

The next day we sat for the first time on that towpath, waiting for something under the water's dark surface to make contact.

3

Four decades of cowardice: can I now be really shaking free
of it? Dan had put the matter with characteristic pungency:
what some might have called my resignation, my patience in
the face of all misfortune and adversity, he called cowardice.
By which he meant that I accepted whatever life put in front
of me without demur. I never answered reality back. I did
not engage in that tough quarrel with the given that the
Greeks called dialectics. I had learnt to put it differently: I
never tried to push against the river. But the first truly
dialectical manoeuvre of my life was undoubtedly the theft I
committed the day after Daniel died. At long last it seemed I
was reclaiming my identity, following in my absent father's
footsteps.

I can see the navigation lights of a boat out there, a
luminous smear like a snail's progress across the dark and
shifting acres. I can't fathom any clues as to what happens
next though, in the sea's traffic and the wind's bluster. Who
else but Daniel Pagett could pursue me like this from the
grave? And he's not yet in the grave. I think he is here now,
in this tower. Those might even be his thoughts entering the
woman who sleeps alone downstairs. Dan's last woman. His

last woman and his first. The line I've just decoded in the Hariot Notebooks is this:

Sir Walter said today: Is that the sin against time then, to lament it can never run backwards?

When Dan finally came home with me, I felt uneasy about letting him in. I had never been to his house, but I'd heard enough about his very different circumstances. And it was true that, on entering my grandparents' small and crowded front room, he looked about him initially as an anthropologist might on discovering an unknown tribe, but it hadn't taken long for him to make himself comfortable. Very comfortable.

'I think I'll come to Blackpool with you this year,' he said one day as we walked through town.

'But you haven't been invited.'

'Get me invited, then, Sean, or what would be the point of keeping you in service?' In saying this, he placed a little more emphasis than usual upon another quality that distinguished him from those about him: how nicely spoken he was, in a region where the pronunciation of an aitch was thought by most to be a waste of breath.

Two months later we sat in Yates's Wine Lodge as my grandmother told stories. I'd already heard them all at least twice, but for Dan they were undiscovered country. She was talking of some of my grandfather's more notorious misfortunes while out drinking.

'One Saturday night he was so blotto he didn't realise how thick the fog was until he'd left the pub. He knew his way all right, but the drink must have affected his compass. He made straight for Horton Park Pond. And fell in. Well, the last time anybody saw anything alive in there was before the war, but there's no shortage of slime. In fact, come to think of it, there's a lot more slime than there is water these days.' My grandfather had returned to the table with drinks from the bar. He gave his wife a sceptical look, his green eyes suddenly piercingly precise. Despite his years of boozing, working on the bins had kept him lean.

'Not that one again,' he said. She shook her white head at him, though it shook slightly all the time by that stage.

'You go outside, you, if you don't want to hear. Anyway, he got himself out of the pond finally, but he brought half the slime with him. He was covered from head to foot, and he'd left his keys in there for good measure. He managed to get back to our house, though God knows how, and started banging on the door. I went down and looked out through the letter box. All I saw was a green man and I thought, he's not coming in here, whoever he is. He ended up sleeping on the doorstep, though he'd done that before.

'In the morning I took out a bucket of water and cleaned him down, and there he was, good as new.'

'Nearly died of bloody pneumonia,' the old man said, though without apparent rancour.

Each day we walked along piers, pressed coins into slot machines, ate hot dogs, hamburgers, candyfloss and toffee apples, drank beer then fell asleep swiftly on the beach with the gritty tang of hot sand beneath our skin. There were still some mill girls about in those days, even if their skirts no longer billowed out like hybrid roses, as they'd once been framed in Bert Hardy's famous Brownie. Blackpool is the least liminal of any seaside town – its only lethal edge is the one between the workday and the holiday. Towards the end of the week, Dan and I set off alone to the South Shore. Within an hour, Dan had picked up two girls. I say he had because I had nothing to do with the operation and was convinced that it was Dan they were both after anyway, even the one who linked her arm through mine later as we walked along the promenade. I had been trying to remember how much it would cost for us all to have a ride on top of one of the open-air trams that were clanging past. Not that there was any money left in my pocket, but there still seemed to be plenty in Dan's.

'Are you here with your parents?' said the blonde one, Jane, who was now holding Dan's hand.

'No,' he said gravely, 'no, you see, Sean and I are orphans.' My girl, Susan, giggled at this, and after sticking her tongue energetically into her ice-cream cornet she said to him, 'You're not an orphan.'

'How do you know I'm not?'

'I just know, that's all.' She had started lavishing her tongue once more on her whipped vanilla. Dan stopped dead and we all came to a ragged standstill around him. He stepped in front of my new companion and squared up to her as he had once squared up to Mark Scully in the playground. I thought for a moment he was going to hit her.

'Why do you eat ice cream all the time, love?' he said, as she continued giggling. 'Is it to make your tits bigger? It's working anyhow. Soon you'll be able to put them both in your mouth.' Susan silently unlinked her arm from mine, just as I was growing used to the freckled warmth of it, and said to Jane, 'Come on.'

So that was the end of our holiday romance. In bed later it

struck me how I wanted to be Daniel Pagett a little less than I had at any time since first setting eyes on him. Only a fraction maybe, but that was the first unit of subtraction in my esteem. Next day I brought the subject up.

'Why did you have to talk to her like that? She only said you weren't an orphan.'

'How could she know?'

'But you're not.'

'How do you know? Maybe I'm a changeling.' We had been studying Jacobean drama. I spent the next minute or two pondering the fact that since I'd never met either of his parents, for all I knew, maybe he was.

When we arrived back home my grandfather's roses were splashed all over his wall, red, yellow and white ones; they had flared into life while no one was looking.

4

Nothing much is flaring into life out there tonight, though I suppose the eating and the being-eaten continue apace. I find myself reading over and over again these litanies of names. Could I be the first person to understand them since Hariot wrote them down? Here are the definitive lists of the Elizabethan illuminati, who felt the time had come to get to the heart of things; who wanted to know what kept the stars shining and the skies dark. Even to think some of their thoughts, and then utter them, was a criminal act.

How hard I seem to be finding it to keep my mind off dead Elizabethans, while Dan, who is now as dead as any of them, keeps flicking in and out of this room. It's as though he's not decided yet whether it is really time for him to go. Maybe the gravitational force of a lifetime's memories is holding him here a little while longer. Hariot once said he felt Ralegh's presence, his physical presence, circling around him for weeks after the axe had fallen.

My grandparents' red-brick terraced house was provided courtesy of the city council. I'd been born there, with the local midwife in attendance. My grandfather was a dustman and even though he was the driver, he prided himself on sharing all the work, hoisting bins on to the leather patch on his shoulder and ditching the dribbling contents into the van's stinking maw. In those days there were no lorries with cantilevered mouths to crunch and gobble the garbage. He drove a light brown Karrier Bantam. Each side of the vehicle had three convex metal doors that slid open and shut, and the refuse was tipped in with a smelly clatter. Then on to the next point down the lane, the opening of another narrow snicket, where the bent and battered bins would stand askew in ragged rows along the cobbles.

During the war he had been a driver in India and, although he never saw combat, he had been torpedoed twice on his way out there and watched his best friend dying slowly in the water. He had driven for thousands of miles on India's high hills, had his arms and chest tattooed with tigers, elephants and snakes in purple and vermilion, sampled the Asiatic beers and developed a lifelong aversion to the smell of curry. My grandmother said that after he was demobbed he was so thin, so dark-skinned and so tattooed, she had nearly closed the door in his face after his years away. Only when he spoke did she realise.

On the fireplace stood a row of elephants, their black teak and ivory tusks brought back with him from the subcontinent. He would sit in his armchair in the evening, smoking and reading the racing pages while Daniel and I debated Crawley's assignments, spoke of history, of peace and conflict, of the hot war and the cold, while my grandmother put the kettle on. By then we had already given up on fishing. Despite so many dead hours at the side of the canal, and whole days spent attending the seething menace of the perch-crammed reservoir, the pike had eluded us. In the local museum, mounted in a glass cabinet on the wall, its enormous eyes still stared out with an intelligent promise of ferocity. It seemed calm enough, only waiting for the return of its watery kingdom. Don't ask me why I always found the sight of its pale belly so repellent.

The reason I lived with my grandparents was simple: my mother had managed to vanish from my life by lying in the bath in midwinter and having the electric heater fall from the shelf above into the soapy water. Death had been instantaneous. Given how cold that bathroom could be and the jungle-mist of condensation moistening the stone walls whenever you turned on the hot-water tap, her need to warm the place is easily explained. But there was always a rumour, one that never entirely disappeared, that my mother had simply had enough and called it a day a little earlier than most. Could she really have abandoned me like that, before I'd grown to the size of a decent dog? There would have been a ready explanation if she had.

My father, you see, was a petty criminal of spectacular ineptitude. A single example of his crimes should be sufficient to capture the flavour of the man. In one of his rare intervals of non-imprisonment, he announced that he had acquired a job as a redcoat at Butlin's holiday camp in Skegness. This was so implausible an occupation for him that everyone assumed it was merely a euphemism for low-grade criminal activity further afield. But he *was* employed as a redcoat, jollying along the campers to sing in strangled voices out of their blushes. However, the requirements of ceaseless good humour and early rising must have reminded him too much of his national service, thus prompting his second desertion. And as he made his way cross-country, he dropped off at various shops and off-licences to steal his basic provisions – dressed all the while in his hunting-red jacket. By the time he arrived back at the house where I now lived with my grandparents, he had slept rough so often that the jacket was punctured and torn in several places. He might as well have mailed the police his itinerary. They arrived a few hours after he did, while he was proudly presenting photographs of himself by the seashore. My grandmother saw them opening the gate and spoke to her son-in-law gently.

'You'd better get your things, love; looks like they've come for you again.'

The police could hardly keep a straight face as they booked him. My grandparents had been ashamed. Years later they could still barely bring themselves to speak of it.

Back he had gone once more to Armley, that squat stone fortress in Leeds with the dirty barred windows. His sentence this time was thought by some to be excessively long, given that he was such a no-hoper as a villain, but at least he was well used to the place by then. He managed to instil in me a contempt for, and a sickening fear of, the life of crime. How curious then, to think that crime's the life I've finally chosen.

5

My training has been as a historian and during these bleak hours now on this bleak night I find myself wondering if my apprenticeship might have been an utter waste of time. I've been landed at last with this solitary task: to become the biographer of Daniel Pagett, archivist of his triumphs and tantrums, his loves and hates, his melancholy and his laughter, and I'm far from sure I'm up to the job. I fear I may lack faith, not to mention intermittent and equivalent shortfalls of hope and charity.

The hook first went into me one evening at Crawley's, the hook from which I've dangled ever since. I suppose the reason so many people become obsessed with the writings of the Elizabethans and Jacobeans is simple enough: they seem to have more to say to the present than the present can intelligently say to itself. I run my hand gently along the spine of one of the Hariot Notebooks. The secrets I've been searching for all my life are contained inside them, enciphered and displaced in code though they may be.

Crawley had a little astrolabe on his fireplace and was fond of taking it down, turning it over in his hands and talking about its relation to the stars.

'It works pretty well, whether you believe in Ptolemy or Copernicus,' he would say. 'Given its date, there's a fair chance that it was used by people who moved from believing one to believing the other. Moved in their heads, that is. The stars and planets all carried on as before and I doubt the navigation improved much as a result. It is a curious thing about the paradigm, that it can be utterly mistaken and yet generate so much close and detailed observation as to remain extremely useful.

'Now you, Sean, have effectively said that our signature, our character, is always to be found in our expressions; that anything read scrupulously enough, with sufficient intelligence, must to some extent reveal the nature of its creator. You do believe that, don't you? You think the impersonality of the artist, for example, is a myth.'

'Yes.'

'Then read this page to us, and tell us what you deduce from the words about the author.' He handed me a copy of *The Tempest*, open at a page in Act One, and I read out the following:

> Knowing I lov'd my books, he furnish'd me
> From mine own library with volumes that
> I prize above my dukedom.

MIRANDA: Would I might
> But ever see that man!

PROSPERO: Now I arise:
> Sit still, and hear the last of our sea-sorrow.
> Here in this island we arriv'd; and here
> Have I, thy schoolmaster, made thee more profit
> Than other princes can, that have more time
> For vainer hours, and tutors not so careful.

'So, Sean, tell us what you would deduce about the man from the words?'

'That he loved books,' I said.

'That he loved books, perhaps even excessively,' he said. 'And what else? Given that these words were written at the very beginning of the seventeenth century?'

'That he had a particular interest in the education of girls.'

'It does look like that, doesn't it?' Crawley said smiling. 'When people make a point which doesn't move the action of the play on at all, and make it with such eloquence, you would suspect a personal interest. But here's the interesting thing. There's not much about William Shakespeare of Stratford that we can state with any certainty, but two things we know for sure. First, that when he died he left no books in his will, not a single volume, and in those days books were a valuable commodity, carefully detailed in inventories and testaments. Second, that his daughter Judith was completely illiterate. She couldn't even write her own name. So where's our signature gone, Sean?'

'Maybe he had a different way of signing off.'

'Maybe,' Crawley said. 'Or maybe the paradigm's wrong. There is something very worrying about Shakespeare: let's call it the chasm that appears whenever we attempt to match what we have of the works with what we know of the life.'

And that was how I started pondering the problem of who and what William Shakespeare was. By the end of this story I should have found the answer, but it hasn't come cheap. It's going to take a few more days to decipher the Hariot

Notebooks fully. That's the only excuse I can offer as to why I had to steal them.

One of Crawley's theories was this: if history can be told then life has a meaning, and if it can't then life is an uncharted asylum and we, its inmates, are all criminally insane. In those days I thought he overstated this, now I'm not so sure. So can I recount this little chronicle? Or have I finally arrived in the house where your wits come astray?

Perhaps if I had spent more time in daylight I wouldn't remember as vividly as I do. But that last summer before university still shines inside me with a rotting phosphorescent flare, as brightly as if it had ended last week. We had taken our Oxford exams, had our interviews and both been accepted. All we needed now were the required A-Level grades. I thought I'd better earn a little money. I suppose that was the first time I'd seriously looked up from my desk to see what was going on outside the window. The giant humming of the mills around town had been falling silent and they were now the last place to find a job – they had been laying people off by the month. There was a bread factory two miles to the north and I'd heard that they were asking for casual labour. So that's where I went.

The first thing they taught you at Rumbold's was to drink a pint of juice with added salt at every obligatory two-hour break. The place was so hot in both summer and winter that the body pumped out all its natural liquids and the salt along with them. Then you worked in disciplined frenzy to match the pace of the conveyor belts as they delivered up four relentless lines of sliced white loaves on to your level. You had to pick them up five or six at a time and arm them over on to eight-tier trolleys. You only needed one thing to go wrong, an absent trolley, or a mis-timed swing, and you were in chaos. I stuck this job for five weeks and then one day somebody, either by mistake or out of mischief, doubled the speed of the conveyor belt. We were already drenched in sweat and hunched in self-absorbed labour, and now the loaves were gathering and colliding all about us, ludicrous shifting hills of glistening greaseproof packets. The small bald-headed Pole I worked opposite went berserk. He jumped on to the central alley, took two loaves in either hand and threw them down the gap into the level below; after that he took the wooden trays out of a vacant trolley and threw those down too, yelling at the top of his voice some Polish curses that I couldn't understand. And then he walked out, as the cries of complaint started to rise from below, blending with the moans of halting machinery. No one ever saw him again. At the end of that week I decided to follow suit. By then, in any case, I wanted to get back to the graveyards.

I don't know why we so often ended up inside them, Dan and I. They were free, I suppose, for the living if not the dead. And there was always somewhere to sit, eat sandwiches, prop our bicycles; even a porch to crouch in if necessary until the shower was over. But Dan didn't want to come any more. So now, on my own, I made for them again. Without intending any disrespect to Daniel, I began to find they were even better without a companion, those scattered stone lectionaries for the departed.

There weren't too many churches belonging to our own Roman Catholic faith, with their buried Michaels and Theresas, but there was no end to the ramshackle tabernacles of nonconformity. Those who lay around there, in the riches of this industrial earth, had become my study. That, I suppose, is how my historical work began (and maybe where it will end too, with the interment of Dan's ashes). So many loom weavers and drystone wallers and factory hands. Their labours had built the new world. Their hands had smelted the iron as the air turned cellophane-yellow and the age wrote in black italic script across whole conurbations. I whispered their names and tried to imagine hearing them spoken in the fellowship of the chapel or the intimacy of the bed. How we summon faith out of the air and gather round about ourselves a cloud of witnesses.

I noticed that the old stones were cut deeper than more recent ones, often more crookedly, but deeper. So deep that even lichen wouldn't colonise the incisions. I loved the precision of the names, places and dates; this was that craving for hard information that Crawley so frequently mocked in me as the veneration of data, my worship of testaments and tallies. The reason I sought such chiselled facts is probably obvious enough: I felt life might be secured by them. Death too. We needed those stones with their hard inscriptions to stop ourselves sinking under the surface of uncertainty, the tepid swill of imprecision. Just as we need the words of Hariot that lie on this table before me to resolve four centuries of speculation and doubt.

Dan didn't have his bicycle any more, even if he had wanted to join me: he had bought a car. Or rather his father had bought a car for him. He'd ended up with a second-hand Ford Anglia, which for some reason he found ridiculous.

'Note its lines of comic domesticity, Sean; don't you see, it's basically an enormous American car that's shrunk from being left out in the English rain. But enjoy for a moment the razzmatazz of its cut-back roof. This car's a joke.' He drove me over the moors, seeing how hard he could corner. He was denouncing, with some passion, the ratios of its gears, when I asked him if he would mind slowing down. He turned and looked at me in wonder.

'Sean, cars don't actually *go* any slower than this.'

We pulled over at a lay-by. Dan walked round and round, from chrome bumper to chrome bumper and shook his head as he kicked one of the tyres.

'If my old man weren't such a penny-pincher, he might have upped the ante a few bob to get me something better than this. Three hundred more and I could have had the MG. *You should start at the bottom, same as I had to.*' The booming tone of command in Dan's voice was presumably in imitation of the father I'd not yet been allowed to meet. He had turned away and was looking over the moors. 'They want you to come to dinner, by the way.'

'Who?'

'Mother and Father want you to come to dinner. Two scholars on their way to Oxford, a farewell evening prior to the life of learning that awaits us. All that crap.'

'So you do have some then.'

'What?'

'Parents. It's just, what with you being a changeling, I thought there might be a lonely gypsy caravan on the wasteland . . .'

'Saturday night. Seven o'clock. Bring your deaf aid, but make sure the batteries are flat before you arrive.'

On the opposite side of town to where we lived lay the valley. The prevailing wind ran down it towards the centre, and for this reason they said the mill-owners had built their houses out that way. They obviously wouldn't have wanted the smoke from their mills following them home – 'Only the money,' as my grandfather remarked. Whether there was any truth in this or not, the valley road was blessed with large houses on either side, set grandly in their spacious gardens. And the Pagetts lived in one of these. I caught the bus there that Saturday evening. Dan had given me directions and when I reached the gate I stopped briefly and looked up the long, immaculately mown lawn to the big house. Another of my grandfather's remarks ran through my mind: 'I tell you, lad, one half doesn't know how the other half lives.' It seemed that one half was about to find out.

I knocked and a woman opened the door. I said nothing for a moment as I stared at her slim figure, swept-back black hair and pale, beautiful face. She wore a wide shiny belt with an enormous gold buckle, fastened tightly over the pullover that hugged her breasts and trim waist. She permitted me a few seconds of appreciation and then, without smiling, finally spoke, and I couldn't help noticing that her accent was a lot closer to mine than it was to Dan's. She shared the unmanicured vowels of my kind.

'You must be Sean then,' she said. 'I'm Dan's mother.' The intonation flat, unshaped by any affluent tuition. She opened the door wide and I walked in.

I suppose the house had been built around the middle of the nineteenth century. There was a particular local style which never changed much, the windows hardly adapted at all from the stone mullions of Tudor times, the door frames still carrying their rudimentary block lintels, the dimensions simply growing bigger as the money poured in from the industrialisation going on up the road. I liked the manner of these houses: they appeared oblivious to changing fashion. They had an air of ageless strength about them. It was this impression which made all the more startling the condition of every object inside.

The contents of our own home were neither tasteful nor tasteless, they were simply cheap. Many of the objects had come, in any case, via unorthodox routes, being discards from those who could pick and choose. I had even grown fond in my own way of the huge luminous fish on our sideboard, its entrails a kaleidoscope of twisted coloured glass, though I doubt that Ruskin would have appreciated it much; fond too of the endless shells – *A Present from Blackpool* – which served my grandfather for ashtrays, and the little metal towers that I used as paperweights. What was startling, in Dan's parents' mansion along the valley, was how gleamingly new everything appeared. Things shone with novelty as though in a department store. From the thick-pile fitted carpets to the polished chandeliers, every single item looked untouched by human hands, and so, by the way, did Dan's mother. Her black hair hung down six inches beneath her shoulders and glistened like sealskin, as she stood carefully in profile against the French windows and lit a menthol cigarette. The minty smoke drifted across to me; on my tongue a moor fire started to turn acrid.

Dan was in the garage outside and Mrs Pagett suggested I go and see him. He was leaning into the bonnet of his Anglia. I tapped him on the shoulder and he surfaced looking oily.

'Seen the house, have you?'

'Yes.'

'If you do need to buy any of the items on display, sir, the lady in the black top will be more than happy to help you.'

Dan's father arrived back an hour later. One of the enormous Jaguars that were fashionable at the time swung smoothly into the drive. I was standing at the window with Dan when his father climbed out. His red hair and red moustache certainly made his appearance striking.

'Here comes trouble,' Dan said wearily. Around the room hung photographs of Mr Pagett in his RAF days, standing in front of aeroplanes or sitting in their cockpits. The moustache had been more flamboyant back then, with curly wings spread right across his cheeks, two decorative serifs to garnish his broad smile. The man who came in still had the smile, though it was no longer as fresh and open as the one in those photographs (is it possible to smile impatiently?) and the moustache had been trimmed now to fit the requirements of civilian life. His face was a vivid crimson. He held out a hand.

'So you're the other chap, are you? How Dan got in's a mystery to me, given how little work he does. They've obviously lowered the standards at Oxford since my day.'

'Did you go to Oxford?' I asked innocently.

'No. Too busy fighting Germans. Then after that I was too busy building a business.'

'Never mind, you can go at the end,' Dan said. 'They'll probably be taking OAPs by then.'

'My son finds the subject of the war and my life in business a joke.' Dan looked out of the window at the beautiful lawn stretching all the way down to the valley road; you could hear the distant burr of the cars beyond.

'I applied to the University of Life, Dad, you know that,

but I failed the entrance exam; so I'll just have to make do with Oxford.'

I found myself staring at what appeared to be a picture of Wharfedale, made out of some luminous fabric. Dan's face suddenly appeared in front of me.

'Lovely, isn't it, sir?' he said with a garish grin, as though we actually were in a shop. 'We did consider the nineteenth-century watercolourists, as you would expect, but mother thought the frames were dust traps.'

'You'll have a beer, Sean?' Dan's father shouted from the kitchen.

At dinner, which we ate at a grand smoked-glass table edged in chrome, there was desultory chat about our forthcoming life at Oxford, but the conversation only began to engage me when Mr Pagett reminisced about his time in the RAF. Then he moved on to the period after the war and Africa, where he had built his first general fruiterer's business. A business, it became apparent, he would have been more than happy to continue building. But on a visit to England he had met Dan's mother and they had been married three months later. Then Mr Pagett had discovered the snag. He faltered in his narrative and Dan stepped in.

'Mother wasn't prepared to go to Africa because she didn't want to have to touch black men.' As he said this, his mother underwent an involuntary shudder.

'Still don't,' she said.

'So there we were,' Mr Pagett said briskly. 'Had to make alternative arrangements.'

'Might as well have gone to Africa,' Mrs Pagett said quietly, half to herself, 'given what it's got like round here these days. You must be old enough to remember the smallpox scare, Sean.' I was. I could still recall the endless queues of shadows shuffling along in fog outside the hospital, waiting for vaccinations. A cloud of sinister potency covered the town, and everyone's mouth was covered with a handkerchief, as though trying to keep out the word *epidemic*.

'They were Asians, Mother,' Dan said quietly, 'not black men.'

'Well, they certainly weren't white men, were they?' she said, her voice rising with sudden passion, the first she had shown since I'd arrived. Mr Pagett's face became one degree pinker. He flicked his fingernails rhythmically and incessantly against his heavy wine glass. I found myself looking intently at his wife's mouth each time she spoke. Her lipstick was some strange dark blue I couldn't remember seeing on anyone's face before. Then I turned and looked at Dan. Of all the expressions of contempt I had seen on his face, and I had seen many, the one he now directed to his mother had about it a chilled disdain which was unique.

'Anyway, Father decided to become a general fruiterer in England instead of Africa, didn't you, Dad? And although perishable goods have always been his first love, he has broadened the stores to include universal provisions.'

'Only way forward,' Mr Pagett said, leaning across to replenish our glasses. 'Won't be able to do it for ever, of course, which is why I'm hoping young Dan here will look seriously at entering the business after Oxford.'

'Dad . . .'

'Things might appear a little different when the time comes to discover that money isn't just the stuff that comes out of your old man's pocket. And there's nothing wrong with that Anglia either. Performed very creditably in the rallies.'

At the end of the evening, Dan offered to drive me home, and asked his father if he could borrow the Jaguar.

'You're not driving anything,' his father said. 'You've been drinking.'

'So have you.'

'I'm used to it. Come on, Jacqueline, get your coat on, we'll have a little wander out and take Sean back.'

So Dan and I ended up in the back seat, with his mother and father in the front, and as we drove across town Mrs Pagett remarked, in a tone of incredulous hostility, at the change in the appearance of so many neighbourhoods now that they had been colonised by Commonwealth immigrants.

'Just look at the colours they've painted those houses,' she said, though she must have seen them a thousand times. They were certainly bright, like the narrow boats Dan and I had watched while sitting on our towpath.

'Cheer the place up a bit anyway,' Dan said morosely.

'Well, it doesn't cheer me up, Daniel. Cheer the place up! Never heard such codswallop in my life. I gather your father's a dustbinman, Sean.'

'No,' I said, 'my *grandfather's* a dustbinman. My father's a criminal. A pretty lousy one, actually.' Jacqueline Pagett then fell silent again.

As we approached my grandparents' house, Dan gave directions to his father. Finally we stopped and his parents looked out of the car window at the house of my birth. I think Mr Pagett's expression probably said, It's going to be a long way from here to Oxford, my boy, so you'd best start preparing now. But there was something in Dan's mother's

face that I recognised, an emotion there I knew only too
well. As I climbed out and said my goodnights, I realised
what it was: panic. Mrs Pagett was having a good look from
the inside of her husband's Jaguar at where she had once
started out from and it was evidently a place to which she had
no intention of returning. As the car pulled away I noticed
Dan breathing on the window and writing something, but I
couldn't make out the letters.

The following week, we received our A-Level results. I
had the grades I needed for Oxford. Dan didn't.

6

It had not seemed possible, so no one had bothered to consider it. Dan didn't fail. I could not remember him failing at a single thing. Until now. What a moment to choose. Then it started me thinking. For the past six months he had ceased to answer questions in class, but I had put that down to no more than boredom: Daniel was very easily bored. His decision no longer to accompany me on my rides across the moors and to distant graveyards had hurt briefly, but I had put that down to boredom too. Besides, I had something else on my mind by then: I had fallen in love. With Sally, the assistant librarian on the seventh floor. I no longer woke in the mornings and thought of Daniel Pagett; I woke and thought of a young woman in a sky-blue municipal nylon coat. I could still hear the whispering whistle it made as she walked past my reading table in her high-strapped sandals, with her blonde hair falling to her shoulders. I even started to think of what might be contained inside the sky-blue nylon coat, but then excitement ended in hot confusion.

So I wasn't jealous of Dan's absences. If he had struck up with a new companion somewhere, I suppose I might have been, but the only new character he had been seen with was

Billy Lister, so jealousy was as impossible as curiosity was inevitable. The Lister Family were a fixed feature of our otherwise peaceful northern town, like the Alhambra Theatre or the moors that surrounded us in all directions. I had first heard the name when I'd looked on astonished at a boy of ten, who had been kicked by a pony which he'd approached from behind, and had then leapt back at the creature in a frenzy, swiping at its legs and neck with a rough stick while the pony bowed its head and took its punishment.

'Who's that?' I had asked.

'A Lister,' my companion replied, as though nothing more needed to be said, as though he had simply directed my attention to one of the forces of nature. They lived in various parts of town, some of them in council housing from which it was said they could not be evicted, some in ramshackle buildings they had claimed as their own, and always and everywhere in complete squalor. You didn't go too near the Listers unless you particularly needed a stay in hospital, but I had once made my way quickly down by their terrace alongside the railway line. Assorted debris cluttered each room while ragged children ran about and yelled. At one window I stopped and stared. There in the front room, happily truffling about amidst the scattered newspapers, was a pig.

The accounts of their doings had become one of the locality's legends. Every so often a rent collector, a hygiene inspector or a truancy officer would venture into their domain, on the foolish assumption that the law might still obtain where the Listers had planted their ensign. They paid no rent, their children rarely went to school and no one, it seemed, could ever persuade them to do anything they weren't minded to do. The representatives of these various agencies would be sent packing, with curses ringing in their ears, sometimes even with a wound to show for their pains. They were a sort of collective crime, this extended family, but certainly not an organised one. The menfolk travelled in and out of prison with a regularity other people reserved for their annual holidays. Crimes just happened to the Listers, they didn't need to organise them. They didn't organise anything.

And there was only one possible reason for Daniel, of all people, to be seen in the company of Billy Lister: Billy was dealing. His name had already appeared in the local papers and he had some time before received a lengthy spell of probation, after working his way through a number of chemists' shops in a thirty-mile radius about the town. They had been broken into on successive nights. Dough moulded into the crude metal bells of the burglar alarms meant that their buzzing wouldn't have woken a slug. I remember thinking to myself with surprise as I read about it that the strategy was really quite intelligent. My old man had never tried anything as cunning as that. I also remember thinking that it wouldn't be too long before Billy Lister was checking out the facilities my father had known so well at Armley, though I believe an overdose a few years later saved the prison service the trouble.

Between the end of the school day and the pubs opening was Billy's time around the cenotaph. I had been there once, looking about warily. I can still remember someone called Suzy in her hallucinating colour combination, who at the beginning of that year was laughing a most beguiling laugh, but by the end was wired with some constant electricity that

twitched every muscle in her face. Here Billy Lister had
returned, with renewed credibility, soon after his probation
order, to dispense delight from his pocket pharmacopoeia.
All different sizes and colours of pills; uppers, downers, and
those they said took you off to somewhere else entirely.
People even spoke of the stuff which squirted out of needles,
but separate and discreet arrangements had to be made for
that.

I had complained once of exhaustion during revision and
Dan had slipped me three black bombers, saying I wouldn't
feel tired if I took those. I didn't either. I stayed up all night,
my mind accelerating far ahead of its own thoughts into a
region of exhilaration and instantaneous comprehension.
First taste of the nocturnal life to come. But I discovered the
next day what any devoted amphetamine-user soon learns:
each speeding of the mind's process is matched by an
equivalent erasure. Usually of memory. So I declined Dan's
kind offer of any further supplies.

What remains of that summer? We had four weeks of
uninterrupted sunshine and Dan was suddenly around again,
seeming to gaze upon me and my curious family with fresh
attention. We drove for many miles, at weekends taking my
grandparents too. I can still remember the sounds of
Wharfedale frothing in the morning, or the buzzing factories
along the Calder; still remember sitting on benches outside
moorside pubs, staring at my grandfather's face through the
aquarium murk of his upended beer glass, or listening to
mill-races sucking on their wooden slats. I remember
discovering with delight that in Wensleydale the young
shoots of grass that start to form a green mist over a hayfield,

soon after the first crop, are called fog by the locals. Millstone-grit outcrops; canals with skins untouched by anything except their own weeded memories; the welcome vinegary stink of fish and chips wrapped in the *Telegraph and Argus*. One day, weirdly, a wrecker's yard void of personnel, where we stumbled about amongst shattered heaps of cars mounted perilously on one another's bodies, as though they had all died in a scream of metallic copulation. Sometimes I still see the shy ghosts of those days, part of a snow of images in an antiquated cinema, along with rusting advertising signs on old shop walls: Bovril, Oxo, Lifebuoy, Senior Service.

I had prepared myself for Oxford as best I could, spending a little money on clothes. I even did something I have a superstitious dread of: I peered in the mirror. Only the once, and I have largely managed to avoid it ever since. A gangling, mottle-faced youth peered back. I didn't want to look at him; I've never gone bathing in those silver pools. Maybe my repugnance came from that evening when I had seen my mother floating just beneath the water in her bath, for I was the one who'd discovered her. No, if Narcissus had had the same allergy to his reflection that I had to mine, he'd never have drowned.

Dan insisted he would drive me down. He was staying on for a third year in the sixth form to resit his examinations. He could have gone to another university with his grades, but decided to stick to the original plan.

'You can suss it out for me,' he said. 'Get my bed warm.' He turned up in his Anglia. I put my suitcase in the back, said goodbye to my grandparents and we were off.

As we headed south and the counties began to blur one

into another, he suddenly started talking about his mother and the evening I had gone to dinner.

'You kept looking at her,' he said.

'What was I supposed to do?'

'She could pass for thirty, couldn't she?' He paused then. 'Did you want to?'

'What?'

'You know what. Did you, with my mother? Assuming you hadn't known who she was, would you have?'

'Maybe,' I said truthfully, I who had never done 'it' with anyone. I thought of Sally.

'I wouldn't want to,' he said, with a vehemence I wasn't expecting. 'I might have come out of those soft doors, but believe me I've never wanted to get back in. Freud was completely up the spout about that one.' Then we drove on in silence as we left the north further and further behind us. Finally he spoke again.

'It's called Indigo,' he said, more to himself than me.

'What is?'

'My mother's lipstick. That dead dahlia stuff she smears on all the time. Everyone always wants to know and don't say you weren't looking, either. Seems to be something about her mouth does things to men. I just wish she'd seal it up with cement. She gets it from Paris, her Indigo, not that she goes there herself these days. Not at any price. You can probably guess why.'

'Black men?'

'Well, anything that's off-white really.'

'Unless it's pink presumably,' I said and Dan finally unclenched for a moment. There were dark bruises under his eyes that furrowed as he laughed.

'You've been unfaithful, Sean.'

'How come?'

'You've been seen in the company of that librarian on the seventh floor.'

'Sally,' I said and smiled at the taste of the word in my mouth.

'I'll keep an eye on her for you while you're gone.'

7

Hariot's Notebooks recount a number of incidents concerning Walter Ralegh at Oxford: the magnificent rebukes, the flashing displays of wit, the coruscating diatribes against anyone who tried his patience, which was not very hard to do. Already he was gaining the reputation for arrogance that would cost him dear later in life. Alas, it was not so with me. An alien seed planted amongst the wheatstone pinnacles and towers, that's how I felt, but I suppose I was far from being alone in that.

'How are you finding the food down here?' the Master's wife tipsily asked me, at the first wine-and-cheese party I attended. She was evidently intrigued by my accent, in pursuit, I daresay, of the latest collegiate exotica. I thought I should give her something to think about.

'It's the first time I can remember eating a vegetable.' She looked at me solicitously. 'It's been difficult, you see, the last few years up north,' I said, with the flattest intonations I could summon.

'Really. Why's that?'

'They've been putting up traffic lights finally, but the horses that pull the carts have never been trained to distinguish between the red lights and the green, so the roads have been jammed solid. The food supplies just haven't been getting through.'

'I didn't realise,' she said, a look of bewilderment briefly crossing her delicate but sozzled features. 'Now, isn't your town the one with very high immigration?'

'No, it's an optical illusion. One of the industrial side effects of the coal we keep in the bath.'

The bursar, who had been standing behind me in silence, now gave my sleeve a tug. I turned to look at him. A solid, four-square sort of man. Ex-army. Everything about him was polished. He was smiling, but it was a warning smile, as though to say, However squiffy she may be, however rudimentary her demography, the Master's wife is permanently off-limits. So watch it, sonny.

One evening in the college bar I was sipping my pint when Charles Leggatt came in with a woman. Charlie was a prominent college radical, the most exquisite revolutionary I have ever met, his radical impulse seeming to arise primarily from his profound distaste for anything which might, however remotely, be described as petit-bourgeois. Sadly, he seemed to find the general tenor of revolutionary politics at least as absurd as he usually found the oppressive manoeuvres of capitalism. His interventions in the Junior Common Room debates never took long before they swerved off into sharp-tongued irony. He was valued on both sides for his withering sarcasm, but it was hard to believe that he represented too much of a threat to the system. He was very tall and even thinner than I was. He wore round wire-rimmed glasses and a goatee beard, which made him look like a miscegenation of Trotsky and S.J. Perelman. His

eyebrows always arched above the top rim of his glasses, two
tiny thatches to roof his pitched, sardonic smile. Now he
introduced me to his companion, Becky Southgate. I stared
at her spiky corn-coloured hair, her bright liquid eyes; she
had the quivering demeanour of a hungry young bird
throttling for food.

Charlie seemed to like me, probably because I exhibited
not even the most petty of petit-bourgeois traits. Soon we
were all talking, then we were arguing. And before I knew
where I was, Becky was upbraiding me for my paternalistic
view that it wasn't necessarily a liberation for a woman with
children to have to go to work. I kept seeing my
grandmother's buckled legs, after forty years of charring at
five o'clock in the morning.

'I suppose you think we should all be locked in the home,
carrying out the domestic chores God appointed for us in the
Old Testament.'

There was something in the tone of Becky's rebuke, in the
confidence of its delivery and its long-vowelled intonation,
which produced in me a silent fury. I was still trembling with
rage by the time she left. Charlie came back alone to the bar.

'You shouldn't let Becky Southgate upset you, you
know,' he said in his curiously high-pitched and fluted voice.
'The main thing to remember about her is that she's a
hysteric and a liar. Do you know that a few months back she
actually accused me of deliberately putting my hand on her
breast after one of our party meetings? I mean, if I'd needed a
tit to maul, there were plenty of others I could have picked
on apart from hers, however heroic its dimensions. Sometimes I actually have them *placed*, in my hands, while I'm
trying to concentrate on something else entirely. All I was

doing, as a matter of fact, was to help her on with her coat –
all part of my residual bourgeois inheritance, according to her
– but she insisted it was molestation. Harassment. Sexual
exploitation. The works. I was brought up before the
Disciplinary Committee, Comrade Protheroe to you, the
bloke at the top of the new block, reading PPE. He was *very*
disapproving.' He gestured to the barman to refill his gin and
tonic. 'Hysterics, in my experience, always make good liars.
My mother's one, so I should know. They can summon tears
from the air. They grow so used to donning the mask of
emotional turbulence that, after a while, they can no longer
say whether the expression on their face is feigned or not.
Have another drink, Sean.' I nodded. Once again, I was
impressed by the way he could reorder without speaking. A
hand was waved, a finger pointed. There was an air of
command about it all. He continued: 'A certain restraint of
the mind is required to establish the truth, you know; a
certain withdrawal from the clamour of emotion. Since the
hysterical state abolishes any such restraint, and replaces the
veridical with the theatrical, it's soon emptied of all truths but
the purely gestic. Sadly though, it's far removed from the
welcome silence of the dumb show. There's panic and
unease even in their breathing, believe me. When dear
Becky is speechless, which isn't often, admittedly, you can
still hear the sharp words growing even sharper an inch or so
beneath her tongue. Always ticking on towards the next
explosion.' He sank his drink and once more motioned for
his glass to be filled. 'Nice tits though, it has to be said,
simultaneously ample *and* firm.'

   I decided to stand my ground and flattened my honest
vowels an inch closer to the earth, presenting those people

with the simple fact of myself as something irrefutable. But the truth is that I've never much liked confrontation. So mostly I retreated into the corners of libraries, bookshops, coffee bars, certain pubs where the lights were low. And when at last I retreated into the fastness of my college room overlooking the old quad, I summoned all the spirits that attend the mysterious powers of remembrance to bring Sally, her voice and her flesh, back into focus.

I remembered our first evening out together, listening to her short flat words. Her accent was much the same as mine, despite her job in the library. We had ended up sitting on a wooden park bench cocooned in the aroma of her perfume. At the end of the evening she had let me kiss her, and my hand had brushed accidentally against the cashmere mound of her breasts. My fingertips retained the unimaginable softness of that prospect for the whole of the next day.

I wonder what it would have been like if Dan had been there to lead me about. But he wasn't. In the meantime, my tutor, affable, unworldly, largely bald but with truant strands of hair straggling his dome, took great delight in unfolding his aged canvas maps of historic England on the floor, then crawling across them on all fours, his pipe occasionally emitting gobbets of flaming ash, which I had to try discreetly to stamp out.

'We can't talk about the Elizabethans at every tutorial, Sean,' he said one day. 'Your interest in the matter is in danger of turning into something of a compulsion.'

But still I took comfort in the evenings by examining that preoccupation Crawley had managed to plant in me: the enduring question of authorship, the aristocratic claimants, the Shakespeare cryptogram. He'd been right, I was sure enough of that: something in this paradigm was entirely mistaken. And why was it, exactly, that Shakespeare was so utterly obsessed by crime?

8

Why history anyway? Why spend so much of your life pointing backwards? Henry Ford thought it bunk; others seem merely to recollect whatever it is that calls for recollection, using the process as no more than a utile aid to existence. Only a few are infected entirely with the virus of remembrance, that disease which taints the blood and plants poisonous seed in the brain, the heart, the bowel. Such remembrance aids nothing, facilitates nothing, except perhaps for further acres of remembrance. It is, as faculties go, tragic. Therapists and counsellors queue up to help ease the pain of it, this thorn that flowers into life and yet roots ever further downward towards death. Thus Crawley: Mnemosyne loves Thanatos — only death gives her the hard edge necessary to finish off her tales. Well, Dan's dead enough, unless he's about to grow phoenix feathers in his mariner's graveyard, but I still haven't got to the end of his story. Or the beginning.

Uniquely in Oxford at the time, our Master insisted on meeting every undergraduate individually each year. This interview was dreaded by all the students and I soon found out why.

His room was at the far side of the college from mine. I stood outside at the appointed hour in my gown. Mortarboards, the invitation had stated, were not required. When the fellow before me came out he raised his eyes theatrically to heaven, and then the voice of authority sounded from within.

'Come!' it said, and I did.

Sir Nigel, so I had been told, was once an eminent surgeon at the Radcliffe, but had long since been retired from his post there. One would occasionally see him hobbling about the quad with a pair of walking sticks. Both hips had been replaced, apparently, though it looked as though the operations might have been left until a little late in the day. He had developed a most striking syncopated gait to compensate for his disability. There was a hint of Kenneth More playing Douglas Bader in *Reach for the Sky*, but Sir Nigel invested his movements with such manic energy that it seemed for all the world as though a biped were trying to return to its quadruped status, heaving its way backwards through evolution.

Now he was horizontal on a chaise longue, smoking an untipped cigarette. The blue smoke rose vertically from his mouth. A few sheets of typescript lay on his chest.

'Sit down, Tallnow.'

'Tallow, sir.' I sat on the one chair provided before him, positioned at ninety degrees to the line of his flattened body. He did not look up.

'What do you think of the moon, Tallnow?'

'The moon, sir? In what respect?' Not long before we had all been sitting in the television room watching Neil Armstrong kicking up moondust. It had been a great step for mankind, but merely a soft-shoe shuffle, short of gravity, for a man. Could this be what he was on about?

'You must have some view of the moon, surely. You study literature, after all.'

'History, sir.'

'And what does moon rhyme with?'

'Spoon?' I said hesitantly. He raised himself up on one elbow and gave me a stern look. His blue eyes were unnervingly precise beneath what was left of his grey hair. His head seemed too big for his body, but perhaps he'd been shrivelling.

'It might be a little more apt to remember the first syllable of lunacy, surely? Do you want a cigarette?' Before I had a chance to answer he continued, as he lit up once more: 'Well, you can't have one, even if you do. I'm an old man.' The smoke steamed out of his nostrils with sudden force as he laid his head back so that he was gazing at the ceiling. 'For me it doesn't matter. But for someone of your age it's ridiculous. Might as well offer you a gun and six bullets. It'd be cheaper, even if you weren't a very good shot. Having any problems here, Tallnow?'

'No, sir.'

'Enjoying it?'

'Not really.'

'Good. It's not meant to be a picnic after all. Off you go then.'

As I left, his voice called, 'Come!' and another forlorn figure outside the door stepped inside for his shilling's worth of elder's wisdom. The next day I sat in the bay window of my tutor's room overlooking the old quad.

'Had your interview with Sir Nigel yesterday, didn't you?'

'Yes,' I said, 'he called me Tallnow.'

'Surprised he got so close. What did you talk about?'

'He talked about the moon.'

'The moon?'

'Don't ask me why,' I said, 'it was all a bit strange.'

My tutor ran his finger along the spines of a ragged line of books.

'Sir Nigel is as mad as a hatter and always has been. Completely bloody barking. It's not age, by the way, in case you wondered – he was exactly the same when he was younger, even when he was sawbones-in-chief down the road. Don't think I'd have much fancied seeing him bearing down on me with sharpened blades. Anyway, don't blame me, Sean. I nominated Vera Lynn.'

The truth is that I didn't play much part in the social life of Oxford. The first symptoms of my migraine had started to manifest themselves intermittently as an extreme aversion to noise, though the embryo eyes of that grub within me were then no more than tiny freckles. Beige, were they? I didn't understand them then; I'd try from time to time to drown them, but it didn't work. And I was continually asking the students around me, however politely, to turn down their stereos. The bells of Carfax and Big Tom could sometimes have me wailing. Once, I had to leave a film by Jean-Luc Godard, in which late capitalism was represented by speeding French cars burning up the world's resources on their way to a fatal accident, only because of its clamorous soundtrack. Anything much louder than the turning of pages often had me wincing. The sound of day-to-day events, even on the unspectacular streets of Oxford, could sometimes force me back into my room. So the noise of Dan's arrival one evening was momentarily deafening, particularly since I'd no idea he was coming.

My room was one of the old ones. The electric-bar fire set into the wall was rusty, the curtains had long before lost anything but a fading memory of their colour, the carpet was threadbare and the wardrobe would hardly have qualified as one of my grandfather's binners. Daniel looked around him and clicked his tongue.

'So you call this Oxford, eh? Well, my mother wouldn't put up with it, I'll tell you that much. No, if this is what you get with an ancient university, then Jacqueline Pagett would want to know why she'd not been delivered a new one.'

Half an hour later, Dan was rolling a joint on a book of Elizabethan street maps I'd taken from the library; he appeared to do it with considerable expertise.

'Music, Sean, let us have music.'

In the corner cupboard I kept my record player. It was a dubious acquisition. Only half the size of a long-playing record – you had to perch the disc carefully on its tiny rubber turntable – it was made of blue plastic and ran on batteries. It couldn't really compete with the stereos in the rooms around me and it seldom saw the light of day. Dan looked at it, then he looked at me, shook his head slowly and smiled. I gave him the choice of my records: Louis Armstrong, Bessie Smith, Robert Johnson and Django Reinhardt. He chose Satchmo. And the hilarity and merriment in those early recordings soon transferred themselves through the smoke into our minds.

By the time we left college for the restaurant, our two mouths were shaped into the same permanent smile.

'Discovered owt of any use down 'ere yet then, young Tallow?' Dan said, in his Yorkshire mill-owner's voice.

'They've renamed me Tallnow. What did you have in mind?'

'Well, Mother would like a dust-free grave and, let me see, a dog that doesn't shit. Aye, that'd be grand, if you could invent a dog that doesn't shit.'

'I think that's next term.'

'Non-faecal canine manufacture, that's where the serious money's to be made. You've got to look forward, young Sean, not back all the time. When you're my age you can start peering over the chip on your shoulder.'

As we went into the courtyard of the restaurant, I pointed to Number 3 Cornmarket.

'That's where Shakespeare stayed when he travelled up to Stratford from London.'

'And what did he get up to, on those long Elizabethan evenings?'

'Depends who you believe.'

'Give me a chance to believe someone, at least.'

'It used to be a tavern, owned by a man called John Davenant. Had an extremely beautiful wife called Jennet. One of her boys was William Davenant the poet, who in later life, and after a drop or two, had a way of hinting that his gift hadn't suddenly sprouted from nowhere.'

'He was suggesting that the Bard had rogered his old mum in the attic and got her with child, is that the idea?'

'That's the idea.'

'Do you believe that?'

'I don't know. I'm not even sure I know who the Bard is. Not necessarily who we think.'

'You're making great progress down here with these historical studies, I can see that. Mind you, Mother always said to watch it with theatrical types. Insalubrious, she calls them. With a fruiterer at least you know where you stand. Do you think that might have been Eve's line when she handed Adam the apple? What have you actually been doing, Sean? Really doing?'

In normal circumstances I would probably have been a little more costive and circumspect. I had, after all, seen him in action many times, but I suppose the joint had loosened my tongue and so I started to speak. I spoke of my increasing conviction that the accrediting of all the works of Shakespeare to the man who came from Stratford was almost certainly wrong. I explained that I'd gradually come to see how *King Lear* was effectively a coded treatise on the subject of alchemy. Whoever this writer had been, he was someone immersed in the secret arts. Such a man couldn't have left off from his studies; none of them ever had. Look at John Dee, I said, still pursuing the arcana through poverty and old age. Look at Ralegh and the Earl of Northumberland – even in the Tower of London they went relentlessly about their strange business, fathoming the secrets of nature.

'So now take a look at Shakespeare,' I said, as Dan poured wine into my glass. 'The figure who retires to Stratford at the end of his life spends all his time counting tithes and proceeding in petty financial squabbles. Not an alembic in sight. Not a treatise on astrology or astronomy. Nothing. No books of any sort in his will, in fact. And that's not the man who wrote some of these plays. It can't be.'

'But now wasn't this one of Crawley's numbers?'

'He expressed doubts, that's all.'

'And does any of it matter anyway?'

'It matters to me.'

'What happened four hundred years ago?'

'There's not much point studying history otherwise, is there, Dan?'

Then I told him about Becky Southgate putting me right that evening, with her immaculate enunciation and the superior smile that kept crossing her bony, twitching face. He shook his head once more as he looked at me.

'Alchemy and tiresome women, and who wrote *King bloody Lear*. Trying to catch up with what happened four hundred years ago. First principle of cybernetics, Sean: the control system must be at least one step ahead of the motion it controls. But thought never catches up with history, if you ask me, not Crawley's and not yours; only money ever does that. Money's the fastest thing. If you want to know what's going on around you, check where the money's going, where it's piling in and where it's getting out. That's true of the past as well as the present. The rest is all talk. Suit Oxford very nicely, I should think. It obviously suits you.' Then he switched off, fell silent, pondered. I wondered where he'd gone as we sipped our coffee, until he looked up finally and smiled; a low-wattage, antiseptic, doctor-at-your-bedside smile.

'Sean,' he said, 'there's something I've got to tell you about Sally.'

(It starts with a blade going through the front of your forehead, a wide blade that seems to sever one half of your brain from the other. The throbbing begins in response to this blade's entry and the throbbing is you, the whole of your living mind, the flesh of thought itself. Then, almost simultaneously, your mouth dries, like a chamois left out all day in the sun. Soon it is parched suede and you are breathing the fetid air of a drought, cracked clay now grown solid where the lake once stood. Then nausea, a general state of emergency across the system, not located in the stomach merely, but a pervasive sensation of sickness through throat and chest and down to the bowels, already loose and quirky. Within ten minutes, total disablement; now you can no longer focus on anything without the severest punishment delivered from some part of your nervous system. Flat out on a bed, eyes clamped shut, curtains drawn, desperately attempting not to move by even the merest fraction, since that will send a scythe of lacerating pain through your head and double the surge of nausea from below. Sleep is an impossibility, hard even to imagine now, the country of lost content.

Perhaps that's how it felt for the maggot when our barbed hook severed its eyes. By then, the migraines still only hit me twice a month.)

That Christmas we sat before our drinks in the Yarnspinners, the three of us, Dan, Sally and me. I was surprised how quickly I had come to accept the idea. It's true that for a while I had woken again each morning and thought of Daniel Pagett, this time wanting not to be him, not that at all, but simply to hurt him very badly. But I had no means to hurt him, or anyone else for that matter. I seemed to lack the facility. I say this now without self-reproach. What is the point, after all, of lamenting who you are? You can't reverse things. Even to contemplate such a manoeuvre is a sin against time, for it spits in the face of all that's given. My indoctrination in the catechism has left me with an abiding conviction of the truth of the doctrine of Original Sin: we are all of us flawed, mangled, damaged, and no amount of therapy or solicitude will ever redeem us from being that way. The seeds take root and grow, and we are thus and thus. One of us is Sean Tallow and the other Dan Pagett. And Sally, my Sally, was now with Daniel. She also looked at me and smiled, but it was a sad smile. Who could blame her, after all, for choosing my companion? If I'd been a woman, I'd have chosen him. He didn't have any trouble looking in mirrors. He'd been designed to look in mirrors. He could have chosen one as his home. And they made a handsome couple, there was no doubt of that. Dan said it was one of those things. He said he hadn't planned it. The soft doors opened and he went in. She was wearing the same cashmere sweater my fingers had alighted on during our first night out. Perhaps I should have fought after all. But which one of us, if so? Daniel, Sally or myself? Which part of the river should I have chosen to push against?

As we stood before the urinal at the end of the evening he turned to me and grinned.

'What am I supposed to do, Sean? It's my animal magnetism, I suppose. Has exactly the same effect on the cat at home.'

9

Man makes his true maps in stone, only later recording them on paper. Thus Ralegh, according to Hariot.

One day in a pub close to Folly Bridge I met Roy Cairn. Roy had about him a carefree luminosity. His long brown hair fell down in a great swathe over his face whenever he laughed, which was often. The wind-tanned skin of his face creased in good-humoured lines that fanned out in all directions. He was not part of the university, but a sculptor from the Isle of Lewis. He had found some unexpected work, since the grotesque heads of emperors forming a broken ring in front of the Sheldonian Theatre had become so badly weathered that the authorities had decided to replace them. I regretted this. However eroded they were, however unintelligible their features, I felt they had gained a kind of authenticity simply from being there so long. Roy didn't regret it though, since it provided him with much-needed money.

His rented studio was a large dilapidated workshop down by the canal. I started to go there in the evening and by the uneven illumination that his lamps afforded I would watch him hack and chisel great blocks of sandstone. As the weeks went by, features slowly started to emerge. Flinty dust filled the air, riddling the beams of light. By the end of the evening there was always a desert dryness in your throat. I was fascinated at the way the shapes grew visible, defining themselves slowly in the half-darkness.

His accent was strange; more conspicuous than mine. He explained that he had spoken only Gaelic until he went to school, but after that he was not permitted to speak it at all – he would be beaten if he did. He invited me to the ceremony that saw the new heads fixed in place. They were novelties now, perched up on their plinths with their perfect features. They looked new, desolately new. They no longer reminded me of Ozymandias. The local morris dancers jigged and jingled to summon spirits of fecundity.

I had started explaining to Roy my obsession about how, whoever wrote the words ascribed to William Shakespeare, he must have been a man obsessed with alchemy as well as crime.

'Alchemy?' he echoed as he hammered away. 'I hadn't realised it was so important back then.'

'To the Elizabethans it was the equivalent of nuclear physics or the double helix today. It was the key to the riddle of life and its riches. Lord Burghley actually wrote to Edward Kelley while he was in Prague asking for some of his powder – what we'd call the philosopher's stone. He said the queen desperately needed the gold so that she could strengthen the English fleet, given the threat from Spain.

'So whether it was Ralegh sailing up the Orinoco or Ralegh in the Tower, conducting alchemical experiments with the Wizard Earl, he was after the same result both times. Searching for the brightest thing, for something so luminous, even though it was hidden away at the heart of matter, that, should it ever get to be uncovered, it would have made the earth itself shine.'

'Make the sun blink, you mean.'

'That's it, yes. Make the sun blink. Just once. As our nuclear explosions made the earth shake, if only an inch or two, on its axis.'

Then one evening I arrived at the studio to find it all locked up. It was the same the following day and the one after. I left a note for Roy, but I never heard from him again. He'd left in a hurry. He probably owed somebody money.

10

I had returned once more to the practice of my religion, which in truth I have never abandoned, despite long periods of neglect. It is, like the north of England itself, home – even when you stop going there for a while, even if you were never to go back there again. You still can't forget the austerities of its peaks and mineshafts. Or its lakelands of mercy, its unexpected rivers veining the stony ground. Somehow I had made my way to the Dominican house. I found both its atmosphere and its priests congenial.

I started to read deeply about the history of the order, and in my devotion to the eminent Dominican thinkers I soon grew attached to the apophatic theology of Father Victor White. His inverse manoeuvre of the soul described how all that could ever be said of God was what He wasn't; that no positive assertions about the deity could be made at all. The sole thing we might achieve here in this sublunar realm was a self-conscious nescience, a negative theology. All any of us could know with certainty was what we didn't know. This beguiled me, even though it stood in some ways as a rebuke to my own historical studies. I wanted to know more about what I couldn't know. I felt properly baffled. My incomprehension had its own part to play, since the blanks inside my head and soul had evidently been ordained. All I wanted to do was to fill them in, but without committing the capital sin against time.

'What exactly *is* intellectual ascesis?' I asked my confessor in his room in Blackfriars one day. Father Geoffrey was an enormous man, who looked affably mountainous in his white preacher's habit. He laid his head back against his chair and spoke.

'Simply the stripping away of the inessential from the world of thought, so as to enable the true perception of reality. Even the *sanctum sanctorum* can become so crammed with sacred furniture that one becomes blind to the original purpose of the space. What dear Victor White was talking about was how we must empty our lives so we may discover the fullness of which they are capable, since this particular *plenum* needs all the space in the world for its expansion; it cannot co-exist with the clutter of our usual preoccupations. You must be emptied to be filled; he who loses his life shall find it.

'As for negative theology, St Thomas really summed it up, you know, centuries ago: *Hoc est ultimum cognitionis humanae de Deo; quod sciat se Deum nescire*: here is the ultimate in the human knowledge of God; merely to know that we do not know Him.'

I went to mass each day. I took the communion bread on my tongue. I blazed with a brief sensation of holy nothingness. Transubstantial. The white disc melted slowly in the dark moist cave of my mouth. And I even began to derive a curious comfort from catachetics. After all, why *did* God make me? It's a reasonable question.

11

'I sometimes think,' my tutor said one day, 'that you might have been better off studying another subject. Something more explicitly scientific, perhaps something more exactly *provable*. You show such a scepticism in regard to factuality.'

'No,' I said, 'I revere factuality. My teacher Mr Crawley always said so. He thought I came close to mixing it up with religion. It's just I can never really believe I've found it.'

The two essays I had written which had impressed my tutor the most were neither, strictly speaking, historical, something that bothered and amused him in equal proportions. The first had been a short history of secret writing, a subject my entanglement with the Elizabethans had obliged me to look into, and the second an account of how the *The Tempest* and *The Alchemist*, written within a year of each other, took diametrically opposed views of alchemy and alchemists, the one crediting the activity with virtue, a noble and austere virtue, the other with nothing but vice, a seamy jamboree of chicanery. It was the distance between the saintly John Dee and his iniquitous scryer, Edward Kelley, the distance between praying and being preyed upon. My tutor had found it an intriguing study of the subjective position in history.

'Let me put the matter another way,' he started, puffing away busily as he lit his pipe. 'Given that factuality in the study of history can never be more than a tissue of probabilities, an interleaving of varying accounts which can nevertheless be collated in such a manner that one finally arrives at a certain point in the past and says, "It appears to have been thus," I still wonder if you might not have settled more easily into one of those fields which can truly end their expositions with a flourish of QEDs.

'I've often thought, by the way, that Wittgenstein would have been happier had he stayed with aeronautics. I daresay the rest of us would have been the poorer for his choice – though, who knows how much aerial flight might have benefited – but he himself had a mind of such steely precision, combined with such a craving not merely to know but to know with certainty, that perhaps a life among men of a similar disposition, all practical minds engaged on practical tasks, might have spared him much torment.

'It's as though you're always searching for another body of evidence underneath the body of evidence. This missing body, what is it, Sean, that you think could conceal it so effectively?'

'Transparency,' I said without hesitation. 'That's the best way to be invisible.' That was the way my mother's life had vanished, while her body remained visible. That's the way I'd found her, so they told me, since the memory had gone entirely into that labyrinth within.

In the summer vacations I found a job in a dehydration plant a few miles south of my grandparents' home. Fresh vegetables were driven in at one end and dried out to shrivelled seeds on hot metal beds, before being doused in a shroud of chemicals, then bagged up and hidden in the warehouse for nine or ten years. I was working on Chemical Control and realised in the middle of a shift that the sodium sulphide valve had jammed. The legal limit of this poisonous preservative per batch was 0.2 per cent. The batches now registered 2.5 per cent. I went hurtling down the lines between the hot-beds and shouted at the shift manager to close them down. He stood staring at me in silence as I mapped out the extent of the catastrophe.

'This shift is about to win a record bonus,' he said smiling, 'but perhaps you'd care to go round and explain to each one of these fellows why they're no longer going to get it.' There were some big lads raking those beds and I didn't find the idea at all attractive, so I wandered off quietly back to my gauges and kept my mouth shut. He was in fact a *trainee* manager: white wattle lightweight panama hat, lightly freckled milky skin and a softly spoken southern voice. He had stared with incredulity one day when he saw the book I was reading as I sat waiting for my chemicals to mix: *Alchemy and the Elizabethans*. The riddle assigned to me for the duration of my life was, I suppose, already being inscribed. Hieroglyphs were forming on the inside of my skull, whether writing over the ones already there or merely joining them.

Some time later I heard our man explaining to a young worker (female, as it happens, and pretty) about his intermediate factory training, and how he'd soon be heading back to college in Hertfordshire, and how management was essentially all about responsibility, responsibility was the main thing really and, surprised as much as he was at my own sudden temerity, I leaned across in my baggy overalls and my peaked white cap and said, 'I suppose you'll be out there in eight years' time explaining to people why they're all getting poisoned from eating Miller's Peas, will you? You'll tell them all about the stuck valve and the bonus and the rest of it, given your great sense of responsibility.'

Next day he put me on spraying duties. The colouring powders they used (to make the soups in those slick little bags still look like food when water gets added after so many years) would cake up on their pallets, technicolour scenes of lunar squalor, and in the hot weather wasps would gorge on them. More wasps than I ever knew existed. Cloudfuls like locusts in a film about the Midwest, where the man stands helplessly waving at the end of a field as the skies above him darken and buzz. And I stood there in my beehive suit and visor squirting poison at them, until they turned and went for me. One of them got through. I left at the end of the week. I couldn't stop thinking about those hidden poisons in the warehouse, silently about their business, rearranging the atoms with a hidden grin, day after day, year after year.

12

I once compiled a list of all the things I didn't do at Oxford: punt, row for my college, attend a May Ball, eat strawberries and cream on the banks of the Isis, wear a boater, get a First, act in a Jacobean drama. What precisely did I do, I find myself asking now, apart from studying that curious mixture of darkness and light which is the bridge between Elizabeth's England and that of King James? Well, I managed to come across my first mention of the School of Night, so the seed of crime was already being planted. There was something about the phrase that enticed me. It produced a thrill, almost one of recognition. What was it? What did it mean? What had once been studied so intently in the dark? This might sound ridiculous, but I knew, even then, that I was being given my life's assignment. I'd known it would come, known ever since I was little that a puzzle awaited my solution and that solving it was what I was for. We'll have to come back to this: I can't explain everything now. I learnt later all the terms that can be employed to describe this condition of mine, but they're all misguided, because none of them can accept one indispensable premise: that what I'm saying happens to be true.

The literal source of my lifetime riddle, whose tail is now at last uncurling as I turn the pages of the books on the table before me, is this: a single reference, a quote from *Love's Labour's Lost*, found originally in Thomas Bridewell's book about Walter Ralegh's circle. I quoted it to my tutor the next day, as a paradigm of historical knowledge, or rather as a paradigm of its absence, whenever you most need it. The School of Night.

'Your subject, Sean, I can see that,' he said, as he unfolded another map. Not his, obviously. So I started looking into the matter more closely. So closely, in fact, that I was soon doing little else.

There has only ever been one known use of the phrase, in Shakespeare's play, and the truth is that when history summons whoever Shakespeare was to answer for himself, which is to say to explain whatever heresy of hopelessness or expectation he has been seen to exemplify lately, by whoever his newest band of enemies are, his ghost will doubtless plead the text's unworthiness and point to four centuries of exegesis, a squabbling line of editors and scholars whose snaking succession only goes to show that there simply isn't evidence enough to hang a cat. Because between whatever Shakespeare wrote and the words ascribed to him today falls a mighty shadow.

All the same, my starting point was *Love's Labour's Lost* – since I could have no other. Upstairs in the Bodleian I worked away at the sources. The quarto text dates from 1598, though some say it is no more than a prompter's or actor's copy, corrupt beyond reconstitution. However this may be, the quarto is all we've got, since that is the primary evidence, even though, like the legendary directions on the road to Dublin, it might have been better not to start from here.

It was, we are told, 'imprinted at London by W.W. for Cutbert Burby'. W.W., I soon discovered, stands for William White, who had set up in business by himself in 1597, which did not give him long to practise before posterity landed him with his mighty task. Sadly, the evidence strongly suggests that he had never been much of a printer in the first place. Ballads and other ephemeral matter, read briefly or even sung in the tavern and then swiftly binned, seem to have been his stock-in-trade. With those, it is safe to assume, the rubric and typography were seldom of the first importance.

The text he bequeathed us is so incompetent, so riddled with errors both intellectual and mechanical, that the kindest supposition is that William White's print shop was still being built at the time this job arrived. The compositor responsible gives the impression of being semi-literate and partially blind, or perhaps merely permanently drunk. He doesn't appear to know how to use his own type-cases. He has often inserted the wrong letters in his stick, and even when he has the right ones the letters end up loose in the chase and fall out once the press has started rattling, and if the movement of the press didn't dislodge them, then the dabbing of the ink-balls did, pushing the unsecured type out of the formes and on to the floor. Shakespeare's words were coming astray even as they were being set; his text was falling apart at the exact moment of its translation to the printed page. The later the pull, the greater the debasement.

So in a text in which wrong becomes woug, and Ione Love, it is hardly surprising that any crux will provide endless possibilities for dispute. And so it has proved. The crucial lines for me were these:

> *O paradox, Blacke is the badge of Hell,*
> *The hue of dungions, and the Schoole of night.*

Creative emendations have not been slow in coming and school has been changed in one edition after another: to suit, scowl, stole, soil, to almost anything in fact except what it says, the School of Night. But, for the purposes of my study, I had to assume that in this one instance the compositor, despite himself, had it right; that School of Night was precisely what Shakespeare intended, even though there was simply no way of proving it. Short, that is, of the momentous discovery of an unknown and undiscovered text.

The School of Night. So the reality of this glittering cohort of human daring and folly, which was said to surround Walter Ralegh, hung by a single thread, thin and bright as gossamer: one half of a disputed line in Shakespeare's play *Love's Labour's Lost*. They were a group of men who had renounced the company of women so that they could give their lives over entirely to study. Other phrases had been used to describe them, including Robert Parsons' 'school of atheism', but the School of Night was what intrigued me. It conjured the danger, the secrecy, the notion of a truth so bright it must be shrouded in darkness. These were men with very dangerous ideas. Some of them spent most of their lives in prison. Some of them died at the hands of the State. They were careful that the words they shared with one another were never made public, and they never have been. The contents of the notebooks before me now have not been understood by a single human being between Hariot's day and mine. And I have just made out another entry:

> *When we knew that Kit Marlowe was to return to Star Chamber for questioning, we spoke of the possibility of him disappearing; living elsewhere and otherwise; continuing his important work in secrecy.*

I can still remember my tutor's monologue as he descanted on the long and often troubled marriage between evidence and belief, how history is always and everywhere whatever is forever gone before us, so that what we are left with is never history itself but merely its study, the pursuit of that which has already disappeared over the horizon. I could never understand why he seemed so cheerful about it and occasionally wondered if perhaps he might have been right about my choice of subject after all. But if a man can't travel into the past for certainty, then where is he supposed to go? At first I panicked when I realised that there were no documents to confirm there even *was* a School of Night, a group of dark and fearless intelligences, exploring with scepticism everything previously deemed unapproachable in any mode other than venerable credulity. Then I accepted the riddle as a gift. By now all my certainties about Shakespeare had disintegrated, except for one: that whoever wrote the works of William Shakespeare, it wasn't the man from Stratford called William Shakespeare. In regard to the authorship question I was at sea, and not always above the waves. It was almost enough to make you turn away from the past altogether and put your faith in the present instead. Which is perhaps why, when Dominique Grayson invited me into her college bed, I accepted the offer with barely a backward glance towards Sally and the feelings I'd once had for her, now squandered in the recklessness of passion. Her passion for my friend Daniel. Daniel Pagett. Dear dead Dan.

13

In my last term I gave my talk to the Historical Society on the history of Renaissance alchemy. Charlie Leggatt was there, drunk but characteristically articulate.

'They were searching for a world of slaves and gold. They just thought alchemy was a cheap way of getting there, that's all.'

'Ralegh never wanted slaves,' I said. 'He never treated anyone like slaves.'

'He treated the Irish like slaves. Butchered them in their hundreds. Never even expressed a moment's regret. You might at least make an effort to solidarise with your own co-religionists from darker times, Sean.' Charlie always did have the last word in any dispute.

By then Dominique and I were already preparing to leave for London. I had my job at the BBC and Dominique her place at the Tavistock, where she would train to be a therapist. She had arranged for us to live in part of a house in Swiss Cottage, owned by one of her father's friends. The students from my college year were about to disperse into a gallimaufry of vocations and employments: communications, commerce, education, industry, advertising, banking. Many went into the City, some I suppose into permanent exile and a few on to the dole. There was a rumour going the rounds that Henry Willoughby, whose face seemed to be carved out of lard, his delicate nose like the tip of a fin emerging from it, had joined MI5. Later still I heard he'd gone to Belfast. Intelligence work. Undercover.

But I nearly forgot. There was one other thing I never did when I was at Oxford and that's find out what it would have been like in the company of Daniel Pagett, because Dan never actually arrived.

Dominique was small. Her black hair fell in natural ringlets across her cheeks and forehead. The effect of such an abundance of dark curls against her sun-mottled skin, and her delicately hooked nose, reminded me of a painting I'd once seen. Maybe of a madonna, but a madonna who was a street girl or a peasant. Just possibly, it might have been a courtesan, but it was almost certainly fifteenth-century Italian, though Dominique, as she soon informed me, was twentieth-century Anglo-French.

She was so light that with one hand round her shoulders and the other in the small of her back I could lift her momentarily off the bed, before we both fell again upon one another. Her jackknifed legs had the delicacy of a grasshopper's when they ankled my thighs. On our second night together, I lavished my tongue on her breasts until they glistened with moisture in the dark.

'Don't drown me,' she said laughing and I fell away then, all desire abolished. I lay on my back and explained about my mother. She listened in attentive silence, then mounted me.

Her tongue caressed and queried what had suddenly turned into a whole world of flesh.

'You can drown me, Dominique,' I whispered. 'I don't mind drowning.' A salt tide surges into the fresh, mingles until slack water. In my memory now our bodies are fish-white under the night's surface where soft doors had opened. I had entered the soft doors at last and no part of me felt the same any more. Inside her, in the dark, the curse of self-loathing had finally been lifted. Was that possible? Until the morning light, anyway. But then I already preferred the darkness.

She was fascinated by my early years, and made me tell the story of them over and over again. I couldn't help feeling that notes were being made, stealthily, in the gaps between our words. I had the curious feeling, even then, that I might be providing evidence against myself.

Tiny as she was, she was the most self-possessed woman I had ever met, and unlike so many people who start to study psychology, she appeared to be in no need of immediate psychiatric care herself. Her intonations were cultured enough but with none of the stridency of Becky Southgate, so I felt unthreatened by them; felt in fact the contrary. Whenever Dominique spoke, in a voice that was lower than her frame would have led you to suspect, I felt hushed into her confidence, convinced by her authority and happy to accept it. She had taken control of my anxiety. I seldom disagreed with her about anything. I think she might have liked that. You could get on very well with Dominique as long as you didn't disagree with her.

14

And here's the reason Dan never turned up at Oxford: Daniel Pagett Senior, out journeying between two Pagett's General Stores, one day dropped down dead. I asked Dan how.

'Exploded, I think. He just blew up.'

Dan's eyes looked as though wasps had recently made nests in them.

'So what are you going to do?'

'Mother says I'll have to help her sort out the business. Postpone Oxford for another year.'

'You'll never come,' I said, thinking briefly of Indigo from Paris, Jaguars, detached millstone-grit houses.

'I'll never come,' Dan said wearily. And he didn't.

By the time Dominique and I drove up north to attend Dan and Sally's wedding, he had already been acting head of Pagett's for two years. I say Dominique and I drove; Dominique drove – it's a competence I've never wished to acquire. My work has obliged me to move more slowly over the revolving surface.

Dan had asked me to be his best man.

'How do you feel about that?' Dominique said as we sped up the motorway. I shrugged. 'But he stole her from you.'

'She was a pretty willing theft. Anyway, if he hadn't, I wouldn't be here with you.'

'Being driven.'

Dan had said we could stay at the house if necessary, but suggested a small hotel down the road might be better, all things considered. Within half an hour of our arrival, he asked me to join him on his last, prenuptial trip to the distribution centre.

'Maybe Dominique would like to come,' I said uneasily.

'It's only a two-seater,' Dan said, already making for the door.

'I won't be long,' I told her. Her face in return told me nothing. I became confidential. 'Maybe Dan needs to talk about a few things before the ceremony.'

The two-seater was a Morgan. British racing green. I remarked upon it.

'Traded up from the Anglia, I see. I should think this one performs even more creditably in the rallies.'

'I'll take you for a drive over the moors. We'll go the long way round.'

'Not too long, Dan. I don't want to leave Dominique by herself.'

'She's not by herself,' he said, already throttling away enthusiastically. 'She's with Mother.'

And so he drove me, with his customary *brio*, across the moors. It was a sunny day and the hood was down and after a few minutes I started to enjoy it too. After all, my memories criss-crossed those moors with the frequency of drystone walling.

'What's the distribution centre, Dan? Don't remember hearing anything about that before.'

'No. Dad was setting it all up when he died, so I've carried on. If you want to control the profits in this game, you've got to bring transport into it. Otherwise there's too many people ripping you off, dictating who gets what and when, not to mention the question of condition on arrival. Perishability, remember. So now, instead of having other people collecting and delivering to us, we're collecting and delivering to them.'

'Sounds interesting.' My voice probably lacked conviction.

'You don't find it interesting in the slightest, Sean, so don't lie about it, to be polite. You're with Dan, remember, your old mucker. Just because you went to Oxford and I didn't is no reason to patronise me. I don't find it all that interesting either, as a matter of fact.'

The moorland sped by until we came to a large ugly building at the edge of town. A metal sign said Pagett Distribution.

'Open up for me, will you, Sean?' I climbed out of the car and pushed the enormous, ramshackle iron gate so that Dan could drive his gleaming new motor off the pock-marked and dilapidated road outside. Then he unfastened the locks and led me into his fruiterer's cathedral. I stopped and looked about me at the central area, filled with lorries. All around its edges, on two floors, were rooms with metal and mesh doors, where an endless variety of fruit and vegetables were kept. The air was sharp with a citrus bite.

'It's very impressive, Dan.'

'Only the beginning. What are you doing at the BBC?'

'Editing news.'

'Why not make some instead?' We looked at each other for a moment. We were back in the playground.

'Anyway, come and look at what riches are mine,' Dan said as we began to move from one room to another, with him opening boxes and checking thermometers, and me following after. 'Oranges and apples. Kumquats, tangerines, avocados, bananas, grapes, damsons and plums. Eat anything you like, Sean. Eat until the juice runs down your neck. Olives, dates, raspberries, melons. Coconuts and hazelnuts and peanuts and Brazil nuts. And just to show that I don't share my mother's prejudices, pawpaw and mango, brimful to their skins with African sunshine. Vegetables now. Potatoes and cabbages, broccoli, sprouts, runner beans, string beans, haricot beans, broad beans, rhubarb. Jerusalem artichokes. Onions and shallots, red peppers, tomatoes. Mushrooms and, believe it or not, ladies' fingers. You are not eating, Sean. When you've been in the trade as long as I have now, you notice these things. Will you not taste my wares?'

'Not hungry.'

'No. It always has that effect on me too. Anyway, everything seems to be in order. One or two things already turning putrid, of course, but that's the fruit business for you. Let's go have a drink somewhere.'

'Dan, I don't want to leave Dominique . . .'

'Oh, love a fucking duck, Sean, this is the day before my wedding. You're my best man. This appears to be the nearest I'm coming to a stag night. Surely I'm at least entitled to a pint?'

83

At the pub he startled me by suddenly saying, 'Come in with me.'

'What?'

'Come into the business with me. I'll make you a director.' The suggestion seemed so ridiculous I started laughing. He reached across and took hold of my left ear. It was a gesture he had often made over the years and I'd always wished he wouldn't. He held it tightly, as my head turned round towards him; I was aware once again that if his mood were to darken suddenly, I might emerge from the manoeuvre looking less symmetric than when I'd entered.

'I can't see myself as a fruiterer, Dan, that's all.' The squeeze on my ear had tightened.

'Do you think I do, Sean? Do you seriously think I intend to devote my life to flogging perishable goods like my pink-faced old daddy before me? It's a beginning, that's all. Things will get interesting soon enough. Now do you want to come in with me?'

'But I've already got my job at the BBC.' He relinquished my ear and turned away in evident disgust.

'You could actually do something, Sean, instead of just talking about what other people do.'

'I am doing something.'

'What?'

'Studying the School of Night.'

'Wouldn't be something that happened four hundred years ago, by any chance?'

'Yes.'

'Going to move the world, is it then, Sean?'

'An inch or two.'

'Why did you ever bother getting born in the twentieth century?'

When we finally arrived back at the house, some hours after we'd left, Dominique barely looked up at me. I knew the dead expression on her face. It didn't often appear there, but when it did, it spelt trouble. Dan stared at her with interest for a moment, then went into the kitchen. I walked over and sat on the arm of her chair. I put my hand on her head. Fondled a dark ringlet. She didn't move.

'Did you talk?'

'She talked.'

'What about?'

'Immigration. And someone called Mother Shipton, who I gather predicted, some centuries ago now, how all these darkies would one day land upon our green and pleasant shores. Half-caste children. Prostitution, drugs . . .'

'Where she lived isn't very far from here,' I said quickly. 'If you wanted, on the way back, we could drive . . .' She removed my hand from her head and spoke with great deliberation.

'Leave me alone with the black widow one more time, Sean Tallow, and I'm off back to London by myself, wedding or no wedding.'

The following morning, after Dominique had driven me up to the house, I stood outside in the garden alone with Dan. We were both wearing our morning suits and buttonholes, both holding our top hats in our hands. Dan turned to me and said, 'What am I doing, Sean? Can you tell me what it is I'm doing this morning?'

'You're marrying Sally,' I said, 'the assistant librarian from the seventh floor.' But he just stared at me as though he couldn't understand the words, as though some letters on a misted glass were already disappearing.

Then came the ceremony, with its life-turning questions and answers. When the time for communion came, I went up to the rail and took it. And as I returned to my pew and knelt to pray, I felt Dominique's incredulous eyes upon me.

'You really do still believe in all that mumbo-jumbo, don't you?' she said afterwards. I didn't get the impression Dominique was enjoying this wedding much.

'Hocus-pocus would be better.'

'Why?'

'It was a Jacobean trickster's parody of the words of consecration in Latin. *Hoc est corpus.* Became the classic instance of all forms of chicanery. *Hocus pocus, tontus talontus, vade celeriter jubeo.* How to pull the wool over your eyes. The sheer non-sense of transubstantiation. The cant of smoke-sellers and sorcerers.'

'What a lot of pointless things you know, Sean. And they all seem to go back centuries. One day you must join us all in the present; employ that intellect of yours on learning something useful.'

'Suss out the transference, you mean? Abreaction; subli-mation. Get down to the nitty-gritty of existence, so I too might heal the sick and make the halt and the lame walk once more? Then we could solve each other's psyches and balance up our respective souls' equations. To each his own hocus-pocus, that's what I say, Dominique. At least I reserve all my credulity for my religion.' She let go of my hand and I realised that I'd grown a little crosser with her analytic manner over the previous year than I'd realised.

At the reception I told the story of how Dan and I had first met, but it somehow didn't come across as amusingly as I'd intended, particularly the sequence on the bus. I had meant it to be droll, but instead it sounded savage. Dan's mother, presumably as a simultaneous gesture towards her dead spouse and her nuptial son, was wearing a curious two-piece outfit, funereal blue-black alternating with bridal white. My eye was drawn continually to its magpie sheen. She emitted a sob at the 'I will's' but I couldn't help noticing, having perhaps taken too close a look, that her face powder and eyeliner were entirely unirrigated by anything resembling a tear. Bone dry.

Before we left I asked Dan where he and Sally were planning on living.

'At home,' he said. 'It's big enough.'

'With your mother?' My tone probably registered spontaneous incredulity. He stared at me in silence for the second time that day.

'Yes,' he said finally. 'With my mother. It was one of the conditions.'

'Conditions, Dan?'

'You don't have any conditions in your life, do you, Sean?'

'No.'

'Then why exactly were you so concerned about the state of mind of little Lady Muck in there, when I drove you back from the pub yesterday?'

That night in our hotel Dominique and I soaked the bedsheets with our sweat, as I thought continually of Sally and her soft doors. Forbidden entry now to everyone but Dan. Dominique's thighs were shorter and thinner, her breasts smaller. And the way she sighed had an intonation scented elsewhere and otherwise. Don't get me wrong: I was in love with Dominique all right, for all the irritation I felt at her attempts to decode me. I was grateful to be still permitted entry, whenever I was. It had simply never occurred to me, despite the lyricism of all those songs and poems, that my body could be so sweetly sheathed and cradled, that my risen flesh could find such a moist warm home. But I knew, all the same, as I pushed and murmured, that as of today, Sally, my Sally, was now Sally Pagett. Six months later, almost to the day, her first child was born.

Part Two

None of the spirits of the ayre or the fire have so much predominance in the night as the spirits of the earth and the water; for they, feeding on foggie-brained melancholly, engender thereof many uncouth terrible monsters.

THOMAS NASHE, *The Terrors of the Night*

1

Dawn won't be too long arriving, and I will be able to see those waves which now I can only hear. Men in tall black hats will come, bringing back the earthly remains of Daniel Pagett to his door and thence to the place where the furnace is being prepared. Sun will flare briefly out on the sea. Fire and water. I try not to think of the way Dan is already rotting inside. The housefly larvae we once hooked through the eyes are happy to live saprophagously, making themselves at home within the decomposing body. That, I suppose, would be their domicile of choice, with or without eyes. They never survive the flames, though. There are no phoenix maggots, unless you regard their re-emergence from the pupa in the form of bluebottles as a resurrection. And so that a buzzing darkness in the head shall not descend on me this day, occluding the solemnities to come, I do now pray: spare me, you powers above, that insect turmoil in the brain.

I have spent so much of my life staring down from high windows. From where we lived in Swiss Cottage you could see the Finchley Road; its endless river of cars didn't stop flowing, not even in darkness. It is an oddity of any capital city that the vehicles thronging its streets never seem to be going anywhere, but are merely one part of its fretful life, always there, always impatient to be elsewhere, endlessly halting and starting in a bluster of exhaust fumes. Don't ask me why I would once stand for so long staring intently at the congestion below, as though some fateful long-hidden clue might be found in the traffic's angry tangle. When my migraines came, the lights and horns would turn apocalyptically bright and loud, every single one of them angled at a point two inches above my right eye. My own vortex of pain, I realised one night, is precisely where Ingram Frizer pushed the blade into Christopher Marlowe's head. And that was the day the lights started going out inside the School of Night. This was the beginning of my understanding.

Dominique had grown used to it all by then. I sometimes think she may have looked upon my migraines as one of my more endearing traits. But she was convinced, ungainsayably convinced, that they had a psychological origin, and as her reading of Freud, Jung and Klein deepened, so did her probing into the recesses of my psyche. There were times when the migraines made less of a drilling sound up there than she did. I've only now worked out fully what the origins of those agonies were, and their purpose, but I'd at least received the first hints. Dominique thought she knew, though. It was a subject of some importance to her. Whatever chance I'd had of gaining a First at Oxford, you see, had been lost because of the aegrotats that had to be issued in place of half my papers – I was simply too sick and raddled to attend. Though my tutor thought I might have forfeited my chance anyway, by my relentless obsession with the thirty years of English history between 1590 and 1620.

I really should have spent more time studying benefit of clergy, land reform and the Whig ascendancy. When I left he had shaken my hand and said, 'Only one thing for it now, Sean. Spend the rest of your life studying the School of Night.' The best advice I've ever been given.

I was happy enough for Dominique to explore the labyrinthine passages inside me, but what started to grate after a while was the rising level of her certainty. She had made me recount my early experiences so often and in such detail that she now knew the facts as well as I did.

Occasionally I would say something and she would contradict me.

'No, Sean, you didn't do that until the following year.'

I would think for a moment and realise she was right. This mastery on her part of my formative details began to unnerve me. I felt as though my experiences were being extracted one by one, like teeth.

'I wonder if it might not be significant, Sean, that your migraines began at Oxford? The mind was extruding a barrier of pain; your unconscious created a membrane between yourself and a reality you found intolerable. It was a way of blocking out the whole of a world which made you so angry.'

'But it blocked out the whole of a world that didn't make me angry as well. Why do you always assume it all came from inside anyway?'

'What?'

'That's not the way it feels.'

'How does it feel?'

'That it's something trying to get in. The corkscrew's being turned from the outside.'

She had still not decided at that stage whether to lean towards Freud or Jung. I didn't know too much about either, but felt implicated in the decision, despite my severe doubts about this particular technique of soul-surgery, since I had unwittingly become her central case study. She would startle me sometimes with insights I found hard to ignore. One day I asked her to give me a clue as to how the method worked. She put a book by Freud in my hands and the first thing in it was his study of the Wolf Man.

I knew a little, inevitably, of the Viennese assault upon the coherence of the personality, its manifest coherence anyway, this exploration of a hiatus, a dereliction somewhere between desire and urbanity – our modern wasteland, ruled by gangs with surrealist names, Id and Superego, whose strategies are unpredictable, at times even lethal. It would be hard to make your way across any part of the contemporary world without at some point taking a look at Freud's psychic map. Where once a legend read, 'Here Be Monsters', now it reads, 'Here Commences the Unconscious'. And so I started working my way through his 'clinical account' of the history of the Wolf Man. Dominique sat across the room at the little round table, writing up her notes.

The Wolf Man, it seemed, was a very wealthy young fellow from southern Russia. His 'neurosis' or his incapacitation made him entirely dependent on the assistance of others, like the private doctor and valet who travelled with him. Freud came to link that present incapacity with a sisterly seduction and a witnessing of parental sexual intercourse at the age of one-and-a-half, later transmuted into a four-year-old's dream. After years of treatment with Freud, a cure was effected, though some years later the Russian returned with a different problem. I read it through once in silence, then went back to the beginning of the text and started again, this time with a pencil in my hand.

'Can Freud really mean this?' I said to Dominique, who looked up brightly, her face glassy and composed. 'I've read this passage three times now, and it has only one logical implication, which seems to be that a one-and-a-half-year-old child wanted to be anally penetrated by his father. *Wanted to be.*'

'Unconscious desire, or the Id if you prefer, doesn't acknowledge any civilised rules of existence, whatever the age of the host.'

'But presumably the age of unconscious desire must be related to the age of the host? I can't be a one-year-old with a fifty-year-old unconscious, can I?'

'The unconscious doesn't recognise chronology either, only desire. That's its only rule, the one law that governs it. Whatever it wants it takes, unless prevented.'

'And if it's prevented?'

'Then it throws things about inside the psychic household. Breaks things up. Its protest against the repression imposed upon it is illness and neurosis. That's what it does when it complains at being denied its freedom of expression. That's my job now, pursuing those signs.' She looked at me severely, signifying, I suppose, that I was one of her signalmen. I read on. Freud found nothing very remarkable in any of these goings-on. According to him, they were no more and no less than the normal movements of 'infantile sexuality'. The primal scene he identified as lying behind the dream of wolves in a tree, which gave the case study its name, came about because the child had been asleep in his cot, in his parents' bedroom, but woke up, possibly as a result of a rising fever, at five o'clock in the afternoon. It was a hot summer's day, said Freud, and the boy's parents had therefore retired, *déshabillés*, for an afternoon siesta. The boy then wakes and sees an act of coitus 'a tergo', which was repeated two more times. His mother's genitals were clearly visible to him, as well as his father's memorable organ. Freud said that all this was somewhat banal. It didn't strike me as banal, nor did it strike me as even glancingly believable. I began to experience something very close to anger – an emotion I then very rarely felt (or, according to Dominique, very rarely felt I was feeling). If my study of history had taught me anything it was to be fastidious in identifying sources and querying their reliability. I pointed this out to her, with considerably more vehemence than usual. She became intrigued at my tone. She was watching me attentively. I had the unpleasant feeling she was making notes again. The child, I said, was a mere one-and-a-half years old at the time of the supposed experience, though the material was then recapitulated in a four-year-old's mind. I hadn't been aware that a child of one-and-a-half could even count, so the preternaturally endowed voyeur here observing the thrice-repeated acts of sexual athleticism surely couldn't have been the infant, spotting first female then male genitalia, even noting (another act of remarkable precocity) the deviation from the missionary position.

'This isn't history, Dominique, though it's claiming that status for itself.'

'It's not history,' she said.

'Then what?'

'People forget he was trying to make a map in the dark.'

'A map of what?'

'The darkness still inside our heads.'

'A map in the dark of the darkness. I reckon he's adding to it, myself. I don't believe the Wolf Man was ever cured of anything by Freud. All we've got here is an accumulation of interpretation, most of it whimsical, over the given data. If this had been an essay Freud had been writing for my old tutor on the Holy Roman Empire, so much recklessness and unwarranted assertion would have forced him to take it away and start all over again.'

'There can be no *a priori* assumptions here,' she said quietly. '*A prioris* belong to logic and morals. The unconscious doesn't recognise them. But I'm intrigued by your anger. It's the same anger that produces the migraine, but you hardly ever express it verbally.'

I spent the rest of the day leafing through Dominique's other books. I hadn't realised that the psychoanalyst now had a whole iconography to himself. There was an etching by Max Pollack from 1914, with Freud gazing out over his desk, pen in hand, eyes distracted with a nimbus of luminosity. The shadowy figures foregrounded on his table were the primitive gods, but in silhouette only. Freud's vision obviously projected above and beyond them – he had passed through the stage of needing to make images to confront the dark and the light. There were photographs: the diagnostician of the uncanny in Berggasse 19 in Vienna, surrounded by emblems of the psychic past of man. Here the Roman and Greek gods and goddesses were mingled in perplexed proximity with Egyptian falcon-headed deities and Etruscan warriors. The only unifying factor seemed to be the transcendentally analytic mind of Freud, the founder of psychoanalysis, the first redeemer into significance of these markings in the cave of man's dark history.

There were even a few stills from John Huston's film *Freud*. Montgomery Clift trembled with intelligence and insight as the dark backward and abysm of time opened itself to him alone, then the lame and the halt started to walk again.

By the evening I'd calmed down, though I hadn't changed my views. We sat on the sofa. Some music, nondescript but passable, was seeping from the radio. Symmetric violins and cellos.

'But how do we even know there is an unconscious?' I said. 'What is it?' My hand had slipped inside her blouse. I was stroking and squeezing her flesh. I did this so often that I seldom noticed it was happening.

'A signature detectable in the manoeuvres of conscious-ness,' she said, 'a passage in the psyche you only know exists because of the distorted evidence it leaves elsewhere.' I unfastened another button. 'A symptomatic reading, if it's intelligent and persistent enough, might just divine it. You always reach for a breast when you're confused, Sean. Why do you mock Freud for trying to make a map in the dark when you spend most of your waking hours pursuing some chimera called the School of Night?'

'It's not a chimera.'

'You're always looking outside yourself for something you think is hidden in the dark. Why not look inside instead? There's no shortage of darkness there.'

'Wait a minute. I just want to get something straight,' I said. 'You say that the unconscious recognises no law except its own desire. That is what you're saying, isn't it?'

'Yes. But the desire is normally repressed and that makes us ill.'

'If desire had to choose a career for itself, wouldn't it be crime? The realm where no inhibitions apply? So if that's the logic, then we're all either criminals or ill.'

'Or both,' she said, as I coaxed the last button from its hole.

2

Daniel arrived one evening unannounced, as we were ladling spaghetti from a large white bowl. He handed me a bottle and sat down at the table, without waiting for an invitation.

'I'm famous,' he said and threw a copy of the *Telegraph and Argus* at me. 'Court Section.' I read the article. It seemed that one of Dan's lorries had been used for highly illegal purposes.

'The boy was a brilliant mechanic,' Dan said, helping himself to some pasta. 'The best I've ever had, so I let him keep the vehicles over the weekend. I knew he was probably up to something, but I didn't really mind. He was so reliable with his maintenance work that if he wanted to do a bit of moonlighting to make a little extra, that was all right with me. He always clocked the speedo, so I didn't know how far he was driving. But I'd no idea he'd been doing anything like this.'

I started reading the article to find out precisely what he had been doing. The writer began by describing a world unknown, he said, to most respectable inhabitants of Britain. A world in which vehicles would set off to Essex or Wales or Liverpool, collect their legal freight then bring it back up north, waiting till nightfall to start making other journeys, not to ports with customs officials hovering about clutching clipboards and tipping their peaked caps, but to empty lanes and disused airfields, to vacant lots by derelict factories or the edges of out-of-season caravan sites. And there, with no pro forma invoices or shipping manifests, men of few words in something of a hurry would unload cargoes from one vehicle and stack them smartly into another. Then they would drive off in different directions. It was still the transport business apparently, but this was its nocturnal side, manned by anonymous legions.

Dan's boy Simon had such an affinity with vehicles that he could hear the sound of a sick motor and tell you straight off what was causing its moans and squeals, why the great beast was hurting as it howled its way through the gears. He had also become involved in the shipment of furs. This had been going on for some time, and would have continued for longer except for a dispute that had arisen between himself and his partner, who had appropriated from Simon some of the furs which had so recently been appropriated from others elsewhere. Simon, Dan explained, was a big boy. Having realised after a while that the proceeds of the night were not being fairly divided between the two furriers, he had gone round to see his partner, taking with him the baseball bat he had acquired during a brief enthusiasm for American sports.

It had been argued in his defence in court that his temper might not have become as frayed as it did, had he not arrived in time to see his partner's girlfriend, who had not long before been his own girlfriend, trying on a pile of furs one by one. She was apparently wearing very little else. Hardly pausing to express his displeasure, Simon had brought the bat down with such force on his partner's right hand as it rested

on the table that five different bones had smashed simultaneously. And as his colleague howled with the pain of it,
pulling his hand instinctively into his belly, he had shouted
'You've broken my hand, you mad bastard', which had only
made Simon crosser.

'You've still got another hand though, haven't you?' he
had said, then the bat had whistled through the air once again
until it found his partner's knee. His left knee. One smashed
right hand; one broken left knee. Simon obviously liked to
leave a job looking symmetric. Even then, the matter would
not have come to the attention of the police had it not been
for the girlfriend. She had become hysterical and had
remained hysterical for some time, all the while ever more
determined to see Simon behind bars. During the investigation the whole story had come out, including the use of
Dan's lorries. Dan refilled his glass from the bottle.

'Remember what our old headmaster used to say, Sean,
just before he belted us: that the use of violence is always and
everywhere an admission of failure.' Dan was staring at
Dominique and smiling. She never took her eyes off him,
but she wasn't smiling.

'Now what moral would you draw from this episode?' he
asked her and she shrugged. The more I had told her of Dan
in our informal analysis, the more she had seemed to
disapprove of him, particularly his relationship with me.

'Sean?' he said, and I thought for a moment.

'Take care in picking your mechanics?' I said. Dan
snorted.

'What an unimaginative fellow. You must work for the
BBC. No, the lesson to be drawn is simple. People only buy
fruit during the hours of daylight. But transportation is

needed twenty-four hours a day. Even when darkness descends, the work continues.'

That night in bed Dominique rolled over towards me and said, 'Do you ever think of someone else when you're making love to me?'

'Yes,' I replied truthfully.

'Does she have a name?'

'Sally Pagett.'

Who had given birth two weeks before to her second son.

3

Years went by like this. Dominique finally qualified as an analyst and began her practice in the spare room where I had once sat and stared down at the traffic. And I edited news for the BBC, seeming to hear from time to time Dan's sour query: 'Why not make some instead?' The truth is I had no great wish to, not that sort anyway. I was not seeking my own promotion and it soon enough became apparent that no one else was either. Simply being in the BBC had seemed a sufficient achievement when I left Oxford. I still remembered my grandparents' faces when I told them where I was soon to be employed. They had smiled, both of them, small smiles of wonder, that one of their own should have passed at last through the looking-glass: I was about to join those on the other side of the radio, the invisible ones who spoke while lesser folk listened.

In fact, my relatively humble position on the news desk left me free to pursue my real interests, solving the riddle life had given me. This necessitated studies that were complex, involved, possibly arcane. Not merely the prevalence of alchemy amongst the Elizabethans, but the nature of Giordano Bruno's mission to England and the possibility of a

Shakespeare cryptogram. (I'd like to point something out here: I have no natural inclination towards the mystical. In fact, I've always steered well clear of the hullabaloo at midnight every solstice. Most Roman Catholics probably agree with Cardinal Newman about mysticism, that the phenomenon, like the word, invariably starts in mist and ends in schism. I wanted precise answers to precise questions, but between each question and answer lay centuries of darkness. The light really has been a long time arriving.)

So I had simply taken my old tutor's advice and decided to dedicate my life to pursuing the School of Night. I knew in some way that I was uniquely suited to the task, and London is a good place to study such things since in its streets you can still trace the topography of those times. The School of Night now had me enrolled. But in the grandiloquent building at the bottom of Kingsway what I was actually paid to do was merely reduce to digestible form the mighty transactions of human misery going on at any one moment; to provide a chronicle and abstract of the time. I made my précis of the groaning of creation out there, becoming very adept at it. I was complimented. From time to time I even complimented myself.

I also made a curious discovery: when I was on the late shift my migraines were greatly reduced and sometimes I didn't have any at all. So the streets of London by night became my world. Unlike most of my colleagues at the BBC's World Service, who worked nights unwillingly and intermittently, I started to do it all the time, by special arrangement. It paid more and my migraines were lessened, but those were only two of the reasons; there were others, perhaps as many as there were streets to walk. Making my urban pilgrimage from dusk to dawn, I often counted them.

I read once, in the work of one of those nineteenth-century writers who spent a lifetime meditating on metropolis, that all cities become one uninterrupted conurbation under cover of darkness. This I know to be untrue because as I made my forays and excursions, stepping through London's nocturnal murk, the labyrinthine maze threading about Lincoln's Inn Fields and the Strand, I found myself thinking so often of somewhere else. Somewhere else and someone else. Unlike the people whose shifts I proxied, I didn't feel I had too much left to hold me to daylight. Night had come to provide the perfect cover beneath which the mesh of my thought occasionally netted its prey.

It takes twenty-six minutes if you walk hard. That is to get from Durham House Street to the Tower; from the site where Walter Ralegh's elegant home once stood to the place of imprisonment where so much of his life was spent. En route you pass the spot where Essex House issued its perilous invitations, its owner another grandee destined for the Tower and the block. And then there are the wharves and churches, the tiny alleys leading to the river or dying suddenly amongst the precincts of the latest office block, hygienic fortresses of glass and polished granite behind which lurks the riddling sphinx called finance. I even walked once right through the underpass, as a few early-morning lorries honked and blared at me in incredulity, so I could fathom the monoxide thunder down there, the underground roar of London's myriad-headed beast. And I have stood on hundreds of occasions in varying degrees of shadow and light at the edge of the Pool of London, listening for the whispering cargoes arriving and departing in their stately clippers. Elephant ivories. Bananas. Then up the hill and down King William Street, like the crowd of lost souls in *The Waste Land*, ghosted by the bells of St Mary Woolnoth.

But mostly I would make my solitary way between Durham House Street, sheltering the unlovely backs of public buildings which aren't much lovelier from the front, and Tower Bridge, Traitor's Gate, the turrets and the flagpoles; the great emblem of incarceration and judicial execution so universally regarded that it now peeps decorously from a million souvenir cups and printed silken pennants. Such pretty mementoes for so much bloody terror, torture and death.

So I would walk, in the evening dusk, in the morning twilight. After a brief spell of infatuation with Jung, when the alchemical diagrams and symbols that I spent so much time gazing at came to fascinate her briefly too, Dominique had opted for Freud. For his hard-man rigour, his pitiless investigative probe. That and, I suppose, my night shifts meant we spoke to each other less and less often. In bed we sometimes collided, but seldom caressed. Our lovemaking, in any case, had by then largely degenerated into sex. We'd grown apart, in both body and mind.

We had only taken one holiday together during the previous two years, going to Rome. Even this had soon become a source of division. We walked the streets each day, often silent, riddled with our own preoccupations, but frequently hand in hand. So many temples and churches and columns and crypts. Here they wrote their history in stone. As the evening darkened, there was still a Piranesi grandeur about it all. Then one day, without even noticing where we were, we had stepped inside the church of Santa Maria della Vittoria, and there before us in its gloomy corner was Bernini's St Teresa, swooning in ecstasy at the wounds she was sharing with her redeemer; a smiling angel had arrived with the arrow of divine attention, lifting the saint's gown, the more expertly to pierce her heart. And the look on her face bespoke an ecstasy not merely spiritual but entirely physical too. Dominique snorted.

'It's not difficult to see what that's all about.'

'No, it isn't,' I said quietly, more moved by the statue than I would have expected to be from the many photographs of it I had seen in books of baroque art and wishing suddenly that I was alone. 'It's about the oneness of the saints with Christ's suffering. They used to call it transverberation. You could say it represents a sort of sacred transference.' Dominique's snort now amplified itself into a guffaw and the sound of her mockery echoed through the church's shadowy hollows. And as we walked the streets the divisions between us, divisions we had never before spelt out with such precision, started to be defined. Freudians, however loving they may actually be, have no real place for love in their schema, as far as I can see. Everything, logically, must be reduced to appetite, to the friction of unfulfilment and the brief relapse into comfort which any climaxing relief affords. All else heads off on its labyrinthine route either towards repression or sublimation. For that is the good doctor's teaching. And as Dominique enumerated the tenets of the doctrine to me once again, I realised how utterly repellent I found it. It wasn't true; that wasn't what we were. We were made of something more than mere mechanistic drives. But I knew that I risked sounding grand in trying to express the fact.

'The desire at the core of us, of my soul and yours too, is a yearning to be reunited with divinity,' I said as we passed the Pantheon.

'These are foggy words, Sean. Projection . . .'

'No,' I said, interrupting her, which I did not often do. 'No. At least I allow you to believe something, even if I disagree with it. Don't tell me that every time I speak it's no more than a ghost dance of projections. We're not just a jumble of repressions, not just a set of animal appetites. There's something sacred in here,' – I tapped my head – 'a little splinter of divinity. Some spark we keep catching sight of. Otherwise there'd be no poetry, no music, no painting and no sculptures of St Teresa or anyone else. That's why, when we make love, it's not just a physical release. It's more than that. Or used to be.'

'What is it then, Sean?' Her tone was gentle and solicitous but unconvinced. Perhaps even uninterested.

'It's hard to express.'

'Try anyway.'

'I think we're trying to get back into the *sanctum sanctorum*. That's why we push so hard. Because it's one of the routes we've been given to link ourselves back to all that's sacred.' Then I was embarrassed at the things I was saying on that foreign street, even though I believed them all and we both fell uneasily silent.

That night in our hotel I saw with utter clarity that we must either move forward in our relationship or accept that it was ending. I realised how much I didn't want to lose her and after we had made love I asked her to marry me. I lay on my back and waited for Dominique's response. It finally came.

'I'll marry you, Sean, but only if you'll agree to do analysis. Do it properly, I mean. The real thing, not some watered-down psychotherapy. No, wait a minute. Listen to me. You'd be amazed at what you'd discover about yourself, you know. There is a dark area inside you that's waiting for someone to map it. Something happened in that darkness a long time ago, I know it did, and you've buried it inside. But it won't stay inside. It comes out as migraine and all your other strategies of self-sabotage. You're happy with your menial job at the BBC really because something inside you doesn't actually want you to succeed. That's the School of Night you should be studying, not what happened four hundred years ago, but something more recent. This belief of yours that the migraines are something trying to get in and that you've somehow been marked out by life to solve this Elizabethan riddle – that's an incipient psychosis, Sean. It's the infantile will to control, that's all. It's the distorted expression of a reality you've never confronted. You make it occult inside you, then you pretend it's something occult outside. I couldn't believe it when you told me that you'd worked out what the migraines were; that it was the pain you felt when you resisted the information that was being offered. And it doesn't even fit in with your religion, does it? All this astrology and alchemy you go in for: I thought they didn't even do that stuff in the Vatican these days.'

'It's condemned.'

'Then why?'

I knew it was all over now and felt I had nothing left to lose. 'I suppose I think any tradition that continues long enough, even when the paradigm's completely mistaken, must have gathered about itself some truths, however out of the way they may seem.'

'So even Freudianism might qualify then?' She was yawning, pulling the sheets up to her chin, getting ready to sleep.

'Maybe. But not yet.'

'A century's not long enough?'

'Not this last one. And they never look any better, anyway.'

'Who don't?'

'The halt and the lame who come to your door. They never look any better to me, Dominique.'

'What are you talking about?'

'Your clients. I've seen some of those faces year in, year out. They look just as grim now as when they first arrived.'

'It can take a long time, untying a knot.'

'Maybe. But you'd expect them to look at least a bit more unknotted by this stage.'

'Are you saying I'm not a good analyst, Sean?'

'No. I'm sure you're one of the best. I'm just saying — what am I saying? I'm probably quoting my old history teacher, Mr Crawley, that's all: maybe the paradigm's mistaken. Maybe the process itself is misconceived. Maybe you're just looking in the wrong places for the wrong things.'

'Good night.'

And we were never to speak of such matters again.

So I suppose I wasn't really in much of a position to

complain when, back in London, I arrived home unexpectedly in the middle of the night (migraine, never take it for granted) and found her in bed with her colleague from the Tavistock, Dr Emmanuel, author of *Anxiety and Modern Life*. I'd had dinner with him and Dominique a number of times and had felt then that not one but two people were now taking mental notes regarding my repressions. They had discussed the twisted psyches of everyone they knew with a mutual glee only barely masquerading as professional detachment.

I had come up the steps and let myself into the room with hardly a sound – creatures of darkness learn to tread softly. And now, while he made his exit and they whispered to each other out on the stairs, words I couldn't make out, I found myself staring at the scarred wooden table in our kitchen. On it lay the remnants of the noodles they must have eaten the evening before, their congealed torsos tangled one over another in the ruins of that takeaway meal. Thirty minutes later, in bed exhausted with my eyes closed, those little yellow bodies were still making their slow progress across the room and into my mind. I suppose they entered finally as the migraine faded and sleep's door opened me up to the true, the universal darkness.

4

We had never gone to visit my father on the inside. The subject was simply avoided. Sometimes a letter would arrive and I knew by the sinister black markings on the envelope who it was from. I would sneak it out of the sideboard drawer once I was alone in the room. There it was again, the illiterate quiver of his handwriting, with the prison number stamped at the top. *And I only hoap young Sean iss grwoing up beter than hiss Dad.* My old man's spelling left as much to be desired as his thieving.

This might account for my own obsessively tidy hand, my tiny, regular characters and my horror of misspelling. A mistake on a page can stop me reading for a moment; two or three will make me throw the text away. An expanse of print sufficiently littered with errors makes me nauseous. This had intrigued Dominique. She thought it connected up in some occult manner with my migraines. Dominique. Anyway, let's say I am acutely aware of the patternings of script and orthography, which was why, the first time I ever set eyes on some of Hariot's papers, I was beguiled. A variant of the secretary hand, it is curiously linked and graced by unexpected devices, which seem almost to be characters in themselves, secret figures from a cabbalistic alphabet. Geometric shapes flourish in unexpected margins. Euclidean segments intervene between one hurried thought and the next. Planets and their dispositions break into the middle of a sentence. But only in these last two weeks have I realised that he also wrote in code. I am pleased that he did. It means that things I knew to be true might now be proven. Except, of course, that I can't tell anyone else about them without going to prison. There is a certain pleasure in the knowledge that prison was where Hariot wrote most of what lies on the table before me. It was also where my father was on the day I was born. Such hidden symmetries.

Coded writing. Secret societies. It seems at last that my eccentric studies are coming together. Anyone would think I had been meant to arrive here and sit in the darkness with my stolen books. You couldn't really have planned all this, could you, Dan?

Dominique had wanted me out sooner than I'd expected. I daresay it was difficult for her to continue romancing Dr Emmanuel at his place, with his wife and two children already *in situ*. I didn't argue; she would have known I wouldn't. She had, after all, made a study of what she called my providential superstition: my refusal to push against the river, my belief that what was given could not be rejected, that nothing was ever accidental. To think so is the capital sin against time. I once pointed out to her that she herself held a similar belief, however unacknowledged, since Freudians also reject the accident as too slipshod and unworthy a basis for explanation. They also are committed to the belief that every event, however apparently casual it may seem, is in truth freighted with lifelong significance, buried deep inside the wounds of time. Otherwise their diagnostic technique collapses.

She merely kept a weather eye on any rogue migraines, but she was evidently not minded to reconsider my removal from her life. I'd never had anything to do with the arrangements about where we lived. It was all done through friends of Dominique's family and I merely paid my portion of the monthly rent. So I went quietly. And there was only one place I could think of going: to Stefan Kreuz's flat.

I hadn't made many friends in London, in fact I suppose I had made one: Stefan, though I do wonder if friends is really the right word for what we were. I seem to remember once hearing someone define a friend as a person whom you'd not change, even if you could, since you've come to love their faults as much as their virtues, but Stefan and I didn't really know each other's faults. Not yet anyway. So, it was to him that I turned for accommodation.

He was one of the exotics who thronged the World Service. He seemed to be in his mid-fifties, though with a mane of silky white hair that could have made him look older. He had left his native Hungary in 1956 when the Russian tanks rolled in. In the years since he had acquired a ventriloquist's facility for speaking every European language with a pronounced, but engaging, accent. And he had become a translator of repute. He had produced the definitive Hungarian versions of Rilke's *Duino Elegies*, Apollinaire's *Alcools* and Shakespeare's *Sonnets*. He was deputy head of the Hungarian section. It was not a hard-and-fast rule, more an unwritten convention, that those whose first language was not English did not become head of any section. This had the curious result that many deputy heads were considerably more distinguished than their superiors and knew it. He had first come to my attention when he made a programme at Bush House called *Translating Shakespeare*.

Immediately after hearing it I had sought him out. We had sat downstairs in the bar, with the enormous aquarium full of luminous fish before us.

'Shakespeare is not translatable, as a matter of fact,' he had said, in answer to a query of mine.

'But you translated him.' Stefan considered this for a moment as I watched the fish describe invisible diagrams of great complexity.

'I think my translation was actually designed to point up his untranslatability.' Here he murmured some beautiful sounds in what I assumed was Hungarian.

'What's that?'

'"Therefore I lie with her, and she with me, And in our faults by lies we flattered be." From my translation of the *Sonnets*. That explains, rather beautifully I think, that no truth is translatable elsewhere – it can only flourish when connected with its own specific need. What I mean is, Shakespeare sounds out every register. It's unnerving enough even for the most attentive reader, but for a translator it's truly alarming. It's as though he can inhabit the language at any point without effort, as though the heavy gravitational pull that constitutes our very relation to speech and writing doesn't apply. It's eerie. I imagine this is what Wittgenstein meant when he insisted that Shakespeare wasn't a Dichter, though it's possible he'd only ever read the Schlegel-Tieck text.

'Of course it must have had something to do with English at that moment in its history – one new world achieved and another waiting at the door. Do you know what Yves Bonnefoy said in the afterword to his translation of *Hamlet*? That the English language is Aristotelian, all surface and practicality, while the French is Platonic, all depth and quintessential form.'

'Do you think that's true?' I asked, puzzled.

'No, but I think it's very French. They do love their binary oppositions. There's something spiritually amoeboid about a Frenchman: nothing ever seems to give him as much pleasure as splitting his little world in two.'

I soon realised that Stefan thrived on the company of younger people. He seemed to need the current of their energy about him. I think he fed upon it. Smoking his Gauloises, sipping his cognacs, or adapting the indigenous coffee to his requirements with the aid of the chicory beans he kept in one pocket and the tiny grinder he kept in the other, he would discourse fluently upon whatever subject he had alighted. I had spent many evenings at his enormous, book-filled, slightly dusty flat overlooking Museum Street, drinking into the early hours. Sometimes our talks went on so long that I would have had to walk back home.

'Sleep here,' he would say easily, if the weather was really bad. 'There is a spare room with a bed made up.' And so I had slept in it from time to time. Only for the night though. Now I was asking for something considerably more substantial in the way of hospitality.

'I was wondering if it might be possible for me to stay for a while.'

'A while,' Stefan repeated, his inflexion managing somehow to turn the words into a query, as he pondered the chronological elasticity of the phrase.

'I work most nights,' I said, trying to put my finger on some advantages of life in my company. 'Reading's normally the noisiest thing I do. I sometimes get migraines, you see. If I'm particularly happy, I've been known to sing. But I doubt there's much chance of that just at the moment.'

'What do you sing?'

'Old Bessie Smith songs.'

'The blues?'

'The blues.'

'But only when you're happy.'

'Yes. Otherwise I don't sing at all. These days mostly I don't sing at all.'

'Would you like a cognac?'

'Yes please.'

He came back from the kitchen with his mind made up. He handed me my drink.

'You may stay here for a while, as long as we both understand that it is for me to define precisely how long a while is. I'm sure that I shall often be glad of your company, Sean. There are, however, times when I shan't. And then, my friend – and I mean this in the nicest possible way – you must make yourself scarce. No arguments. No excuses. The notice given may be rather short.'

I shrugged in compliance.

'When I entertain a lady here you must contrive to be elsewhere. Whenever two people are in a state of intimacy, any others are, to my mind anyway, *de trop*, whatever the barbaric modern practices of multiple fornication. One must

know that the little cries and murmurs are for one's own ears.
No one else's.'

'How often . . . I mean . . .'

'Once a week. Occasionally twice. I am friendly with the
owner of a small hotel on Theobald's Road who will, I am
sure, be happy to come to an agreement with you in regard
to booking perhaps a full week in advance at a reasonable
rate, then permitting you to use up your allocation one night
at a time. Maggie is seldom completely full. There is usually a
vacancy. We will deduct whatever you spend there from the
total of your rent here.'

'How much rent would you want?'

Stefan waved his slender, manicured fingers in the air.
They rippled elegantly in an age-old gesture of indifference
from Mittel Europa.

'How much were you paying at your last place?'

I told him my half of the rent at the flat in Swiss Cottage.

'That would be fine. So when would you like to move
in?'

'Would this weekend be too soon?'

Stefan reached a hand into his inside pocket, took out a
diary and flipped the pages until he came to the appropriate
date, then looked at me distractedly.

'Fate has arranged a brief period of celibacy, as it so
happens. So we might as well be monkish together.'

5

It didn't take me long to discover that Stefan's open-handed manner disguised a soul as opaque as any I've ever met. Why was it that life kept presenting me with secrets I could not decode? I'm growing closer to a few of them, all the same. The books on this table before me are starting to yield up their riddles, if a little coyly. They're certainly in no hurry to be translated into the region of analysis and comprehension and in that regard I think I may know how they feel. Here's the last sentence I transcribed:

> *Sir Walter said today that no life ever ends: we merely move from one place to another. As he spoke, I tried not to think of the axe that will so shortly effect his removal from here. And I only wish he didn't have to go, for then our little school will surely be dispersed for ever.*

Dawn will be here before long, bringing its dew, greatest of all the alchemical solvents. And soon enough it will be time for Dan to make his last journey too.

Stefan and I would sometimes talk and at other times sit for hours in silence in our armchairs at opposite sides of the room. I was working my way through a collection of code books I had extracted from one of the murkier corners of the London Library. I wasn't even sure why I was doing it, but it's certainly turned out for the best. These notebooks would have been unintelligible to me otherwise. At night I tried to sleep and could think of nothing but Dominique. Odd the nights beyond number I'd lain beside her without reaching out a hand in her direction and now every muscle in my body ached for her presence. The memories I was enduring seemed more potent than the realities they recalled. Like the day at Thames Ditton with Dan and Sally. By that time Dan had long before sold the family business and gone into transport and freighting. Then, after a while, he was once more in the newspapers with his cut-price computer, the Pagio. *Pagio.* I had laughed out loud when I had seen the name. It was soon gleaming away in shop windows, all the same.

Dan collected us from the station at Thames Ditton in his convertible Bentley and as we drove up through the village he pointed out the little tower that had once been used for smoking eels.

The house was one of those Edwardian confections that you find alongside the Thames beyond Richmond. White-painted, fringed metal canopies adorned the whole of the ground floor. There was about half an acre of finely mown lawn running down to the water's edge. You expected long-haired girls to come out wearing embroidered frocks, ready for a gentle game of badminton. Instead Sally stepped through one of the French windows, flanked by her two sons. Could I really have forgotten how beautiful she was? A smile to make the sun blink. And it soon became apparent that her northern vowels hadn't budged an inch to accommodate her fancy new neighbours either, though by then my own chameleon speech had started to take its colour from those around me.

'Hello, Sean, and hello to you, Dominique. These are my boys, Freddie and Daniel. Daniel, as you'll soon see, is taking after his father. I always knew we were asking for trouble giving him that name.'

'Where is Signor Pagio, by the way?' I said. 'It was very nice of him to send his chauffeur down to collect us, but I'd like to see my old Neapolitan friend.' Dan looked at me with his well-practised, dangerous smile.

'Would *you* buy a computer called Pagett? Well, would you? We just needed something a few inches closer to an Olivetti, that's all.'

Half an hour later we were aboard Dan's Thames launch and heading downriver towards Teddington. The wine was poured, the sandwiches were passed around. And Sally was quizzing us about our life; I couldn't take my eyes off her. She seemed to glow with her own source of light. Suddenly Dan's sharp words turned our heads.

'Don't hit him,' he said. 'What are you hitting him for?'

'Because he annoyed me,' his little namesake replied from the prow.

'You annoy me sometimes, Daniel, but I don't hit you, do I?'

'Yes you do,' the little boy said defiantly.

Dan flinched. He turned away and looked over the water. He spoke more quietly.

'Well, I don't hit you often.'

'You don't come here often,' came the reply. Sally smiled evenly at us both.

'See what I mean?'

I started to wonder how often Dan did come there, and for what stretches of time Sally might be alone with her boys. He spoke of his trips to the United States, Canada, Germany, Spain.

We motored up and down the Thames, peering at bungalow-crowded aits, counting the swans and grebes, until on our final stretch down from Hampton Court, I found myself staring at the white wake of the boat, as so many traitors and kings had done before me on this same stretch of water. Finally Dan drove us back to the station. There were kisses, handshakes and promises, and then he was gone. Standing on the platform, waiting for our train, Dominique who had been silent for most of the afternoon, finally spoke.

'Done well for himself, your friend Dan, hasn't he?'

'Yes.'

'And he didn't even go to Oxford.'

'No. He's never been psychoanalysed either.'

Dan. Dear dead friend I'm here to bury.

When you wake at four o'clock in the morning with a poisonous sensation in your mouth it always tastes like the word futility on your tongue. And I suppose the end of love is as bad a taste as any, even if the love has been slowly dying for years. I am a Gemini. My planet is Mercury, presiding spirit of intellectuals and thieves. In the alchemical schema it is Mercurius, who facilitates the union between Sol and Luna in the chemical marriage. Mercurius is the *prima materia* and also the *ultima materia*. He is called upon to rain his precious fluids down on the work's body, blackened by flame, thus enabling, on the far side of putrefaction, a resurrection of matter and spirit which is no longer divided, no longer separated by corruption. Mercurius is effectively the universal material, being all things to all men. But just now I didn't feel like anything to anybody. All that was left for me to do was to work obsessively, press further and further on with my research on the School of Night. I'd already established that's what I was here for, but even so I was glad for a while each time my shifts resumed and it was time for me to go to work again. Keeping up with things.

Corruption in India, violence (black or white) in Africa. An occasional dictator deposed in all his peacock splendour, an eminent cleric caught, minus his cassock, between the legs of one of his parishioners. Memories of wars long gone, anticipations of worse ones to come. Occasionally a member of the royal family would marry a mere mortal and the nation would go berserk: the skies would weep confetti and the streets sprout bunting. Then back home again to my new life with Stefan.

6

Stefan didn't go out much since everyone he ever needed seemed to come to him, so I was surprised one day when he invited me to *The Watchman*'s summer party. He said he thought a little wander down the road might help to offset my prison pallor – and it was true that I only ever seemed to see the sun in the form of Sol gleaming through one of my alchemical illustrations.

In a Georgian house somewhere between Holborn and Clerkenwell stood the editorial offices of *The Watchman*. The name was meant to echo Coleridge's journal of the 1790s, providing the same edge of intellectualism, even a kind of urgent radical thought – well, that was the idea anyway. A glossy tabloid in appearance, it had become a fashionable weekly, with advertisements for shirt shops in Jermyn Street, jewellers in Bond Street, wine merchants in St James's. In grainy photographs supplied by expensive admen to expensive department stores, women in evening dress would smoke a cigar while staring straight at you. Savvy, sassy, streetwise and cool.

Its latest editor was Jim Chambers, whose smiling features, complete with permed grey hair, had for years gleamed from the masthead of his column in one of the broadsheet newspapers. He had made his name writing affable, boisterous and essentially lightweight pieces of reportage about the goings-on in Parliament. He could be amusing, though his routines had grown somewhat predictable over the years. His patented technique was displacement. At the end of the week in which Elvis Presley had made his last journey from one place to another, he started his column, 'Three days ago an appallingly bloated body issued its final gasp of life, while the notes of one famous song died on its rouged lips . . . but just before we say farewell for ever to the Trade Union Movement and its anthem, "The Red Flag" . . .' It would do if you were between stations and hadn't brought a book.

But transplanted to the editorial page of *The Watchman*, the essentially bantam size of Jim Chambers' intellect began to look like more of a liability. He tried to be serious to begin with, but the frolicsome after-dinner raillery that governed his soul would keep breaking through. After dropping one too many clangers, about the amusing properties of landmines or how AIDS was more of a lifestyle emblem than a lethal disease, he had suddenly changed his tune, embarrassed presumably by one or two distinguished words in his ear. Now for the last six months all had been *gravitas*, post-prandial no longer in jollity, but only in portentousness. Hygienically free from any taint of military service himself, he would compose sonorous paragraphs about bloodshed, the soldier's heart and the beloved homeland. His style, once seemingly a prose version of opera so light it blended imperceptibly into operetta, now struggled soulfully towards the Wagnerian. Editorial pages were littered with such words as slain, hazard, avenge, extreme jeopardy, misgovernance and danegeld. He had all of Kipling's prejudices without any of his talent or his bite.

'The thing to remember about Jim', Stefan said to me as we made our way towards the summer party that *The Watchman* was holding in its back garden, 'is that he is entirely Jim. It's impossible to think of him as James. You'll see when you meet him that his smile has been stapled on somewhere below the scalp. His democratic Jimness. Call me Jim. Not Jimmy, which might be just a little too demotic, but certainly, most certainly, not James. Good Lord no. Don't you stand on ceremony with me, sir. Jim's the name. Honest Jim. And how do I make a living? If you don't hit me, then I'll make you laugh. Except now he's trying to make us cry and for the first time I think I'm beginning to find the bugger genuinely funny.'

I was introduced to him as we went through. The smile remained constant, but the voice sounded unexpectedly disembodied and uncertain.

'There you are,' Stefan said as we walked away, 'like I told you: don't hit him and he'll make you laugh.'

'He didn't make me laugh,' I said. Stefan stopped and stared at me.

'Then go back and hit him. But no, on second thoughts, better not. He might take some of your stuff on the School of Night and Shakespeare.' We had been talking in the evenings about our shared interests.

Stefan went and got us both a gin and tonic.

'The famous *Watchman* gins,' he said thoughtfully. 'Might be slightly more gin than tonic. Sip, don't gargle.'

The magazine's fame and popularity were based on a certain maverick inclusiveness. It was simply impossible to know from one week to the next what might be in there. Ex-cabinet ministers slagging off their erstwhile colleagues. Mercenary majors explaining what had really happened in the latest African massacre. A millionaire supermarket owner would be given space to supply an *apologia pro vita sua*; a sacked television chief would expatiate on why he had not been dumbing down, or for that matter why he had and what a good thing it was too. Articulate eccentrics queued up with their stamped addressed envelopes and their grubby typescripts. If a village in Scotland suddenly discovered that it was in truth the thirteenth tribe of Israel, then *The Watchman* would be the place to announce the discovery.

And this was why we were here, since Stefan occasionally wrote a piece about the ups and downs of Hungarian politics which appeared in the journal's pages. There shuffled next to me a heavy man in what had once been a white suit. I would have thought him to be in his late fifties, though his face was oddly boyish, despite the ravages to which drink had subjected it. He still had a quiff that looked like a memento of the 1950s.

'Tom Silehurst,' Stefan said with a feint smile, 'meet Sean Tallow.' The head jerked forward in a hint of a bow and the greasy hair briefly fleeced his forehead. There was a bruise across his cheek, which was a few days old. He had collided, or fallen, or been belted. He started to talk and I found it very difficult to make out his words. He was not drunk; that word does not begin even to approach the condition. He was one of those who had become so inveterately sodden with alcohol, so drenched right through to the bone with the stuff, that he had developed a manner of speaking which I suspected remained constant whether he was taking a drink at the time or not. He seemed to be speaking of Turkey. I gathered through the bleared swerve of his vowels that he had recently made a trip to Bodrum. There had been a young man whom he had met; they had ridden on horseback together for days at a time. He had wanted the young man to return to England with him, but that had proved impossible. Another sadness in his life. The young man, it transpired, was married.

'You married?' The words blurred towards me from the corner of his mouth.

'Yes,' I lied instinctively.

'Always the way,' he said. 'Same with my friend Francis. Not gay, either of us. Queer. Always liked straight chaps. My father was an alcoholic, you know. Know what you're thinking. Not me. I'm a drunk. Different thing altogether.'

With the word Francis, I registered who I was talking to. He was one of the epic Soho boozers, part art critic, part historian. I had read that he retired for much of the year to his parents' house in Devon and laboured on his books, which came out with a frequency that certainly suggested industry. Then, once every few months, he took the train to London, became shouting drunk within an hour and attempted to revisit his old haunts, almost all of which, sad to say, had barred him many years before. Then after some gruesome homosexual episode which involved either the police or the hotel management, he would board the train back to Devon and the family home he had to himself now, and settle down once more at his typewriter. As we spoke, or as he attempted to speak and I attempted to understand, the minister presently in charge of trade and industry had been pressed by the crush to within a few feet of us. Unlike everyone else, the politician was in evening dress, his wife beside him bespangled in her gown, both of them seemingly gift-wrapped for the occasion. They held their glasses of wine at an angle that suggested they had no idea what they were for. Silehurst finally focused on the man's face and some message managed to clamber through the acres of debris that guarded his mind with such a comprehensive baffle. He lurched the few feet necessary to bring himself alongside the minister, only spilling a single wavelet of gin as he went. Then, in what was obviously intended as a whisper but managed to achieve a far greater volume than any of his confidentialities to me, he boomed, 'You know what the matter with this country is?' Minister and wife both winced, smilingly, and finally took a synchronised swig from their glasses. 'The fucking wankers who run it, that's what.' I noticed as I looked down that my drink had been replenished for at least the third time.

Then the confusion of the crowd leeched from the outside to the inside of my mind. Faces came and went before me: a man who wrote books of obscene verse; an expert on megaliths; a startlingly beautiful young woman who was apparently training to become a trapeze artist in Paris. There was a poet, whose best work over the years couldn't quite hide the fact that he was an obsequious toad. He had devoted an extraordinary amount of his life to cultivating minor members of the royal family. He appeared to decide whether or not he was crippled, depending on how far he was from the drinks table at any one time. And, finally, a female campanologist from Ealing.

Then Jim Chambers came over and pointed his smile at me.

'Stefan tells me you're doing some interesting work. On Shakespeare and . . . what was the other thing?'

'The School of Night,' I said.

'What exactly was that?'

'I'm not entirely sure myself. Still working on it.'

'Well, if you do manage to work it out, you could always try us with a piece.'

My glass kept being refilled and I kept emptying it. And at some time around eleven, as people were leaving, Stefan came over to me and said quietly, 'I know this is very short notice indeed, Sean, but I wonder if you would mind staying over at Theobald's Road tonight. It's just that I have met an old acquaintance and she is unfortunately without accommodation. Maggie will be happy to take you in. I just telephoned her.'

I watched him leave with the old acquaintance. She didn't look so old to me. Considerably younger than me, in fact. Stefan's final words before departing were these: 'I sincerely hope you didn't have too many of those bloody gins, my friend. I reckon there must be at least four measures to a glass.'

7

The next day, unshaven, my mind half-ruined from the *Watchman*'s gin, I went up as arranged to Swiss Cottage so that I could pick up the remainder of my things. Dominique had just taken a bath and was in her robe, her hair wrapped in a towel. We kissed, a little remotely, as people might when commiserating with one another over a shared bereavement. The way we'll probably be kissing later today at the funeral.

'Daniel came the other night,' she said offhandedly as I filled up one of my bags. I stopped what I was doing and turned to look at her.

'Daniel?'

'He was trying to find you. I told him you'd moved out. It was late when he came, so he stayed for a drink.'

'Couldn't he have phoned me at the newsroom?'

'I gave him the number, but he said no. Said it was your physical presence he craved. He's a great one for physical presence, your friend Daniel. Said to tell you Sally and the boys are well. They'd all like to see you some time. It's only a train ride to Thames Ditton, he said. He's working on something new in London at the moment, did you know that?'

I stared at her in silence.

'How's your head, Sean?'

'Not too bad. I'm not sure half a pint of gin helps much.'

'Things are still going in then, through the night?' I decided not to answer that.

'How's our friend Dr Emmanuel been?'

'I wouldn't know. I don't see him any more.'

'Then . . .' I hesitated.

'No, Sean, it's over. Had been for a good long while and you know that as well as I do. But like so many people, we didn't want to face the fact. We hadn't even made love for six months. I must have been desperate to start doing it with Emmanuel. The Tavi's Don Juan. If you ask me, you've been living alone since the beginning anyway. You still have your vocation, after all. I'd just been getting in the way of it, like a priest's doxy.'

I finally dropped the last book into my bag and walked over to the door. Dominique came and kissed me a little less remotely on the cheek and then spoke again.

'Maybe you should try getting angry. The only times I've ever seen you really angry were with Sigmund Freud and once over that mystical statue in Rome. Who was it again?'

'St Teresa.'

'The only thing the two of them have in common is that they're both dead.'

'Maybe I can only get angry with the dead.'

'Or maybe it's the dead you're angry with — it's not the same thing, you know. One of the most important functions of the parent is to be there to get angry with. You can't even remember your mother, or you say you can't, and your father finally wandered off and disappeared after one of this century's most unsuccessful criminal careers.'

'I didn't know either of them well enough to spend too much time grieving.'

'No, and that's why you're going to spend the rest of your life doing it through other means. You should be careful, you know, Sean. There *is* a lot of anger in there, actually. I know, because I located it from time to time. And if you leave it long enough, when it finally does come out you'll probably kill somebody. There and then. How's the School of Night these days?'

'Still in the dark.'

'Suit you then.' I noticed as I looked down at the flesh on her neck a small red welt. It looked more like a tooth mark than anything else.

On the way back on the Underground I remembered the one time I had taken Dominique to stay with my grandparents. She had been entirely natural with them, for which I had been grateful. On the day we left we had driven to the glen outside town, a glacial valley strewn with mighty boulders. It had been early spring and there had been an overnight frost. She'd found a tiny wild flower, the name of which neither of us knew, its heart a vivid yellow. It was bright from its icing and I could still see the wonder on her face as she gazed at it, brilliant in its unexpected diamond.

I lay in bed and thought of what Dominique had said. Anger. Deep inside me. Not towards her, though. Towards someone else then, but who? Sally? No, I certainly felt something about her, but it wasn't that. And it was surely not my old friend. I didn't feel capable of any truly negative feelings towards Dan any more. Dear dead Dan.

8

You start to notice certain figures, luminous in their small cubes of light, suspended over the city. I liked to think of them as my fellow students: nocturnal lepidoptera, night-imps and night-hags, the incubi and succubi who prey upon the body of the past. They too shunned daylight's kingdom as too bright and noisy for important recollections. Then home again to Stefan.

As a translator of the *Sonnets*, he was intrigued by my work on the School of Night. We were both in no doubt that they were riddled with clues, but neither of us was sure where the clues might be pointing. He peered over my shoulder at the sheets spread out all over the table, then, reclining on his ancient sofa with a cognac in his hand, he demanded that I explain the cat's cradle I was trying to disentangle. And so I started.

'I think Ralegh's in here somewhere,' I said.

'Ralegh?'

'Elizabeth's pet name for Ralegh was Water. Take the L out of Walter and you have Water, and it's surely appropriate enough, given his trade, though perhaps not quite as amusing as the good lady imagined. So, pushing it a little further,

Ralegh calls himself Ocean. And when he's in the Tower in 1592 he's writing "Ocean's Love to Cynthia", Cynthia, as you know, being his name for Elizabeth. Well, London back then was a leaky sort of place and I doubt many literary secrets were kept for very long. What I mean is, I should think quite a few people knew that Ralegh was petitioning, in the name of Ocean, to his queen from his imprisonment. Petitioning to be reinstated inside the court of her sulky little heart. It strikes me as only to be expected that sheets would have been copied and passed around. Maybe not round the taverns, but then whoever wrote the works assigned to Shakespeare was moving in circles higher than the tapsters by then. So Ocean had run dry. The king of the seas was locked in a tower.

'Of course, a fair number of scholars have assumed that some at least of Shakespeare's sonnets were written in the early 1590s. So take another look at Sonnet 64.' I picked up my sheet from the table and read:

> *When I have seene by times fell hand defaced*
> *The rich proud cost of outworne buried age,*
> *When sometime loftie towers I see downe rased,*
> *And brasse eternall slave to mortall rage.*
> *When I have seen the hungry Ocean gaine*
> *Advantage on the Kingdome of the shoare,*
> *And the firme soile win of the watry maine,*
> *Increasing store with losse, and losse with store.*
> *When I have seene such interchange of state,*
> *Or state itself confounded, to decay,*
> *Ruine hath taught me thus to ruminate*
> *That Time will come and take my love away.*
> > *This thought is as a death which cannot choose*
> > *But weepe to have, that which it feares to loose.*

'Ralegh, that man of towering pride, put in the tower and so down-razed. The advantage that he, as Ocean, had gained in the kingdom now reversed and all his treasure squandered, "Increasing store with losse, and losse with store". I think the writer of this was probably astounded by Ralegh's fall from grace. It was like watching God die. Look at the known facts. Even his judges later were to say, "You have lived like a Star, at which the World hath Gazed." Everyone knew how gloriously he shone, what a height he'd scaled. To end up in the Tower. The Tower represented two of the last four things: death and judgement. And it was the entry point for the other two: heaven and hell. People went in there and came out alive, to be sure; Elizabeth herself had done so as a princess. But while you were there you represented to the world the absence of liberty, the curtailment of movement, the presence nearby of the axe. It was a very public place: later, during his last imprisonment, they had to stop Ralegh walking up and down one of the galleries because of the cheers the sight of him elicited from sailors on the river. You were put in the Tower as an emblem to the age; but now and then the emblem came to represent something the authorities had not intended.

'This, our writer must have thought, was a definitive circumscription.'

'Our writer, Sean? You're referring to your national poet. What are you saying?' Stefan lit up one of his Gauloises and blew the smoke up towards the ceiling.

'I still think he's our national poet, as a matter of fact, but I don't think he's necessarily who he's been assumed to be.'

'Forgive my ignorance, but has anyone else ever linked up that sonnet to Ralegh's imprisonment?'

'Not that I know of.'

'Shakespeare was Southampton's man, not Ralegh's.'

'When you say Shakespeare you mean the man from Stratford.'

'Ah. You don't, obviously.'

'I'm sure of one thing. Whoever wrote that sonnet held Ralegh very close to his heart. I'm not at the stage where I can answer any questions, Stefan, I'm still asking them.

'Ralegh, remember, had come pretty much from nowhere – the court aristos thought the way he spoke ridiculous. They hated and despised him for the way he'd gone straight to the top. If even he could be imprisoned, then thought itself was now a prison. And the building mentioned most often in the Shakespeare works is the Tower. See how the word *ruminate* in the sonnet actually contains the word *ruin* inside it. "Time will come and take my love away." That doesn't sound like decay so much as arrest by the Guard, such being the law of mutability in the interchanges of the State. Ralegh's wife was imprisoned with him at the time. I think the Tower entered deep into this writer's mind then. With the fall of Ralegh nothing was secure in this sublunary realm. And then, one year later almost to the day, Christopher Marlowe was done to death by Ingram Frizer in Deptford.

'Marlowe and Shakespeare, Shakespeare and Marlowe. There's so much collaboration between these two that it's hard to disentangle Shakespeare's early work from Marlowe's hand. Their imaginations fed upon one another. In some ways Marlowe seems to have shown whoever Shakespeare was how it could be done and that's why he quotes the other poet's line as a token of remembrance in *As You Like It*, "Whoever loved that loved not at first sight?"'

'And Marlowe was close to Ralegh, a favourite of his, in fact,' Stefan said, 'and he was also, unless I'm mistaken, a leading member of the School of Night.'

'He was, and I've been coming to think he might well have written the sonnet I just quoted.'

'Do you think he wrote the rest of the works attributed to Shakespeare too?'

I took another drink of cognac before answering.

'I suppose that's where my thoughts would lead me, if it weren't for the one indisputable fact: Marlowe dies on 30 May 1593 and by then we can only be certain that whoever wrote Shakespeare has written *Henry VI, Richard III*, maybe *The Comedy of Errors*, *Venus and Adonis* and *The Rape of Lucrece* and some sonnets. All the rest is still to come.'

'Yes, that does seem to present something of a problem.'

We both fell silent for a moment, then Stefan went and took his Shakespeare down from the shelf.

'There is supposed to be an actual reference to Marlowe's death, isn't there, in *As You Like It*?'

'Yes, I said. It's at the beginning of Act Three, Scene Three.'

'I'm impressed,' he said, finding it there as he turned the pages, then he read it out:

When a man's verses cannot be understood . . . it strikes a man more dead than a great reckoning in a little room.

'Isn't that the quarrel over the bill?'

'That's right,' I said. 'The official cause of Marlowe's death was said to be an argument over the reckoning in a little room in Deptford; there's a whimsicality about those words that could be offensive, don't you think? But it always sounds to me more like a man whistling in the dark to cheer himself up. It has about it an air of bravado. I don't believe the tone here really tells us much, to be honest. I wonder if the writer could even admit to himself what he really thought about it, not until much later anyway, in *Macbeth*, when the three murderers are sent after Banquo and Fleance. And there were three in the room with Marlowe that day when he died, remember – all of them, it's become apparent since, employed on and off by the State to get up to no good, the third a piece of low-life dross. There's that strange speech made by Macbeth to the murderers, a speech that seems to stop the play dead for a moment and sounds to me like the playwright inadvertently talking to himself.' I turned over my notes until I had found the passage. 'The first murderer says "We are men, my Liege". And Macbeth replies,

> *Ay, in the catalogue ye go for men;*
> *As hounds, and greyhounds, mongrels, spaniels, curs,*
> *Shoughs, water-rugs, and demi-wolves, are clept*
> *All by the name of dogs . . .*

Something ominously personal about that, don't you think? There's an actual revulsion there. Incidentally, allowing for the vagaries of Elizabethan spelling and letter substitution, there's an anagram in amongst those nouns. They'll let you spell Ingram Frizer, Poley and Skeres – the three men in the room when Marlowe was killed. It's always been a slight oddity in the play that only two murderers go to see Macbeth, but by the time they kill Banquo there are three. But then the third doesn't much signify – he's just another piece of low-life dross.

'A few lines later comes a crux the editors still argue over to this day. It's still unresolved. Macbeth says, giving instructions for the murder:

> *I will advise you where to plant yourselves,*
> *Acquaint you with the perfect spy o'th'time . . .*

What could it mean? Well, I think it means Banquo. He was the perfect spy of the time, because he knew Macbeth's secrets, he had been with him when the weird sisters made their prophecies. In other words, he knew too much. Just as Marlowe did. So the State set its curs on both of them, three men in both cases who made a profession of selling themselves body and soul, and were only too happy to sell the lives of others too.

'It's an odd thing, but Shakespeare's works don't speak too badly of spies; it's a word that has an almost redemptive ring to it when it's used. Remember what Lear says to Cordelia: "And take upon's the mystery of things, As if we were God's spies." Not so, though, with the word intelligencer, which is nasty. Richard III is referred to as hell's black intelligencer. The real crookback schemer, of course, was Robert Cecil, who takes over from Francis Walsingham when he dies in 1590. What he takes over is the business of intelligence and projection. He decides in other words who is to be made to talk and who will be kept silent; who will be positioned at what precise position of peril in the spider's web. There are racks and prisons at his disposal and if necessary blades too, like the one that went through Kit Marlowe's head, just above the right eye, and found his brain. The man who wrote Shakespeare was still brooding on it over ten years later.

'Everybody seems to be speaking in code here. That doesn't necessarily make analysis any easier, does it?'

Stefan put his drink down on the table.

'Well, speaking as someone who has lived under a communist regime, let me tell you this much: the only intelligent response to a world that is entirely encrypted and encoded is suspicion. At its worst this leads to paranoia; at its best to a profound scepticism in regard to human motivation and witness.' By now I was hunting through my papers again.

'Here it is. This is a phrase from a letter by the pursuivant and torturer Richard Topcliffe, a phrase I sometimes think is the most terrifying in all Elizabethan literature. He speaks of how, in regard to some poor sod attached to the old religion, he had endeavoured to "decipher the gent to the full". I think it might explain why there's something close to hysteria in Hamlet's wish not to be inquisitorially known.' I turned the sheets on the table before me again until I found his passage: '"You would play upon me, you would seem to know my stops, you would pluck out the heart of my mystery, you would sound me from my lowest note to the top of my compass . . ." It was better not to be known, wasn't it? To be known could be very dangerous, so people encoded themselves, became mysterious ciphers to their own contemporaries, so as to ensure their survival.'

'But that's what those works are all about, Sean, I realised that much during my translation work. You've summed up the theme that runs through each of them, even the comedies. But you don't think the man from Stratford wrote them?'

'His life doesn't seem to correspond in any way to this man of secret studies, this dark obsessive with his terrifying revelations.'

'But do you seriously think you could ever prove that it wasn't him?'

'Not at the moment, no. Maybe never. I'd have to turn up another source, wouldn't I, to provide something in the way of triangulation. It's far from impossible, though. I don't doubt myself that there's enough in Shakespeare's work to read the age by, but what intrigues me about his life is that the facts lead nowhere. There's something disconcertingly banal about them. They don't tell you anything that helps you to interpret the plays. It's almost as though they're a provocation.'

Stefan had risen and now took another book down from the shelf. He turned the pages as he spoke.

'I suppose there is another way of looking at it though, isn't there?'

'What's that?' I said.

'That his life, or rather the inconsequentiality of what's known of his life, could be a standing rebuke to all those who worship the world of fact. To live entirely in facts is to be dwarf-brained and dwarf-spirited. Keats got it absolutely right, as so often. Here, I've found it: "That quality that forms a man of achievement, especially in literature, and which Shakespeare possessed so enormously – I mean *Negative Capability*, that is, when a man is capable of being in uncertainties, mysteries, doubts, without any irritable reaching after fact and reason . . ." In other words, if the mind is to expand into the space provided for it, what he called elsewhere the vale of soul-making, we must have faith. Now Shakespeare, whoever he was, knew that to place your faith in the wrong thing can lead to madness, but he knew just as surely that to refuse to place your faith in anything at all leads always to evil, to the howling pit. The zero of no belief at all is the black hole through which all that is good disappears. All Shakespeare's villains end up as nihilists, even the ones that didn't start out that way.' Stefan took another sip from his glass and looked distractedly towards the window. 'But I do know what you mean. There seems to be something unanswerably adrift between life and work that does make you wonder if another, hidden hand could have been involved. Could that solid and tiresome-looking burgher in the portraits really have undergone all the torment and passion that the words contain? This man who, when he's hoovered up sufficient profits from his businesses in London, heads back to Stratford to count his tithes. Dante's words do at least correspond to his life and his exile – not that you could have predicted them, but there's nothing in the life that actually contradicts them. But nothing in Shakespeare's life corresponds to what he created, as far as I can see. Nothing. So where does the School of Night come in?'

I shrugged.

'Maybe that's where I'll find the hidden hand, if there is one.'

Then the telephone rang. I could tell within seconds by Stefan's intimate tone that it was a woman. His responses seemed discreet, ambiguous, until he finally said, 'I'll look forward to seeing you later then.' He turned to me with his winning smile.

'Sean, I wonder if you would mind staying over at Theobald's Road again tonight . . .'

9

London, fluked in a dawn light, can reinvent itself; appear inexplicable and unexpected. Each street you walk down seems to have only just happened. In my search for historical paradigms I once read the work of Walter Benjamin and was fascinated by his notion that the past has an afterlife which is neither more nor less than our consciousness of it, and that unless we struggle to sustain this afterlife, in our ceaseless polemic with time, the past will die once more. More importantly I seized upon, or perhaps was impregnated with, his concept of the dialectical image, by the simple law of which the products of any given society contain within themselves both an aspect of the past and an aspect of the future, the former as a memory trace riddled cunningly into its technology, and the latter as an unconscious vision, whether dream or nightmare, or even sheer hallucination. Every commodity, every instrument, can be seen as a little moon containing a series of occulted faces, which are revealed only through darkness and revolution. Thus do the objects themselves dream what is to come, an impending world which has already started to engulf and obliterate them, though a few will survive, severed from all that once kept them alive, like fragments of bone in a reliquary.

I stood in front of the shop window in Covent Garden. I had just finished my night shift and was now almost alone in the early-morning mist, as the first glimmering of dawn life bestirred itself out on the streets. I stared at the items displayed: scientific instruments from hundreds of years before. Navigational, chronometric, astronomical, medical. Ancient clocks stood next to astrolabes of the same period. There were orreries, compasses, brass telescopes and quadrants, and suddenly I was back up north during one of my grandfather's ghostly visitations. It would happen now and then in the afternoons, following a trip to the pub at lunchtime, when he would retrieve objects otherwise destined for the municipal tip. These would vary in the extravagance of their unusability, depending on how many pints he'd had. I acquired at various times the following items: a black bicycle with crooked wheels; a long sheepskin coat, home to a myriad of tiny creatures; a miniature snooker table, its green nap already shiny with baldness; a pair of luminous rubber swimming caps with gold hearts impressed in formation across them; several reproductions of Victorian paintings showing wide-eyed animals about to be hunted to death; an upright Remington typewriter, none of the keys of which could be depressed without each prong jamming into all the others; and a vintage radio, still boasting its original fluffy valves. This last I kept in my room, but everything else departed the day after its arrival, with my grandmother's muttered curses accompanying the unwanted goods all the way back to the tip.

I never could think of the north without thinking of Dan

and now he was in the papers once more. It appeared that he had created a network of companies sufficiently complex to baffle even the City analysts, but it was a new age of surging trade with Europe and his various businesses had mostly thrived. He floated the company. Shares were bought eagerly and were soon worth several times their purchase price. You could turn to the financial pages and find his name there every day, the fluctuations of his quoted prices a matter for ceaseless speculation. My old friend Daniel was becoming seriously wealthy.

And now he was opening little cafés and restaurants here and there, all called Davenant's, so it seemed I might have had some small effect on his business dealings after all. Jennet would have been proud of me, whatever she might have done in the attic with the man they called Shakespeare. They were clean and elegant, these cafés, with décor the precise opposite of his mother's tastes: Scandinavian chairs, Italian coffee, well-made and well-packaged sandwiches, wine that was unpretentious, potable, acceptably priced. The word went about that once again Mr D. Pagett had got it right. There was one in Southampton Row, only a few minutes' walk from Stefan's flat, where I would go from time to time. It was odd, as I handed over my money, to think that it was destined for Dan's pocket. Davenant's was approvingly remarked upon by almost everyone, and presumably emboldened by his success Daniel had continued his expansion into the world of fashionable catering. I picked most of this up on my news trawls for the BBC. I hadn't actually seen him since that day in Thames Ditton with Dominique.

10

If I was working my shifts, then there was no problem. Stefan might ask me to leave a little earlier in the evening than usual. I even occasionally saw one of them coming in as I went out. They always looked my age or younger. It was when I wasn't working that it started to become tiresome. Whether it was merely the monthly cycles of his libido, or simply the good fortune fate intermittently brought his way, there were times when I had to spend two, even occasionally three, nights at Dalrymple House.

'Stefan *has* been busy entertaining this week, hasn't he?' Maggie would say to me. She knew things about him I didn't. She spent a lot of money on her hair and lavished her face with daily make-up. I couldn't help wondering if, some years before . . . But no, I wasn't going to start speculating on Stefan's love life. That way madness lay. It was hard enough keeping up with his contemporary lovers without trying to archive the historic ones. There was a portable television set in the corner of the tiny room where Maggie always put me. I only switched it on once, to see the features of Gus Markus, Australian commentator and wit. I stared at the screen for a moment and marvelled at the extent to which he had become the robotic mannikin of his own slickness. His permanent wry smile had hardened into a mask, a passport now for meeting celebrities. His little eyes gleamed with the brilliance of proof coins and I quickly switched the television off again. And left it off.

So I would go out more and more often; to the pubs round about, the sandwich bars, the pizza restaurants, even to Davenant's. I would read my books and make notes in their margins, sitting in a corner of the Plough or the Museum Tavern rather than go back to the solitary cell of Dalrymple House. Maggie had offered to make me dinner some time, but I didn't take up her invitation. Stefan had asked me never to return to the flat, after one of his evenings of entertainment, before ten in the morning, to allow for any delayed departures. When I arrived, there was always a trace of perfume in the air and it always seemed to be a different scent from the last one.

I had never done so much research, not even while living with Dominique, but I suppose it was really a relief, all the same, when Dan turned up on that Saturday evening. I had been standing looking at a map of the Elizabethan capital which Stefan had hung on his wall. I had only just noticed the date: 1593. A plague year. Back then you could have walked within the liberties of London and seen the ravaged bodies proliferating under hedges or in the cages where they were often fastened, sometimes three at a time. Plague years meant the closure of the theatres, so emblems shifted from stage to street and from thence to the graveyard: flowers of all sorts were scattered when maids went to their graves and rosemary was always worn to mark the passing of a bachelor. Maybe that's what, in her clairvoyant prevision, Ophelia meant: 'There's rosemary, that's for remembrance – pray you, love, remember.' Hamlet would die a bachelor like her brother, to whom the words were spoken. That particular plague was merely an epidemic of mendacity shrouding the State with its murderous untruths. There'd been plenty of others.

Stefan and I had been sitting in silence as I went to answer the door.

'Guess what I've bought, my friend?' Dan said, standing in a shaft of summer light from the window, with his jacket over his shoulder. I smiled at him.

'What?'

'The Pavilion on the King's Road. Go and get your coat and I'll drive you over.'

I explained to Stefan that I was going out for the evening.

'Good luck,' he said and smiled. 'See if you can find yourself a little female company for once.'

Dan now drove a Porsche 911 Targa. Its black roof had been removed and its white bodywork gleamed in the evening sun.

'Not too fast, Dan,' I said, fastening my seatbelt.

'In London? The chance would be a fine thing.' It felt fast enough all the same, the way he throttled and cornered. I think Dan imagined I was afraid of speed. It's not fear, in fact, but a kind of vertigo when things blur by, lose their precision in the surge of movement. I feel as though I'm the one who's disappearing. Probably why, for me, walking is the only form of locomotion compatible with keeping your wits about you.

'Had this long?' I asked as he swerved round Trafalgar Square and up on to the Mall.

'No. Not long. To be honest I've just about got its number. It's a real beast, this one, believe me. You have three litres of serious German engine crouching on the axle back there. As the acceleration increases, the rear weight hunkers down closer and closer to the road, which is fine unless you have to lift off suddenly while you're doing a bit of hard cornering. Then, mild understeer turns into pronounced oversteer before you can even blink.'

'And what does that mean?'

'It means you lose the car, that's what it means. The back's suddenly round the front of you. I know, because I took it out on a skid-pan a few weeks back and did it.'

'And is that likely to happen?'

'You've got to be going fast, Sean. *Fast*. You never have managed to get your brain round the speed of things, have you?'

'I suppose not.'

'But then, given the speed the BBC moves at, I don't suppose it matters too much anyway.'

And on we went. Buckingham Palace went by swiftly and soon we were humming down Eaton Square, then round and up along the King's Road. Two minutes later Dan pulled into the forecourt of his new possession.

The Pavilion was an enormous confection of white stucco, its façade contrived to provide the stone impersonation of a marquee. A large purple banner was now draped across the broad lintel, which read: *The New Pavilion. Opening Tonight*. I looked at Dan and he grinned.

'Fancy a drink, Sean?'

'Know anywhere round here that's decent?'

153

'This place isn't bad, I've heard.' And in we went.

Everything glittered and shone. Metallic chairs and tables winked at the chrome bar, which in turn reflected the gleaming fittings of the ceiling lights. Whatever wasn't painted white was painted a bright primary colour. The waiters and waitresses went about their tasks dressed in yellow uniforms, the men in jackets and the women in some form of zippered jumpsuit.

'Two restaurants, one burger joint and three separate bars.' Dan said as we arrived at one of them. 'What'll you have?'

'A gin and tonic,' I said without thinking.

'No you won't,' he said, 'you'll have a pint of this.' And he laid his hand on the tap of the draught beer we both used to drink in Yorkshire. Tetley's.

'Does it travel?' I asked.

'Better than you do, I should think.' As the pints were being pulled, Dan suddenly darted off and I watched him as he spoke to one of the young men in yellow jackets. The movement of his arms looked menacing. Then he was back again. He lifted his glass and chinked it against mine.

'So what do you think?'

'It's very impressive, Dan. Congratulations.'

'Only the beginning. In this particular field, anyway.'

'You keep saying that.'

'Give this character here whatever he wants,' he said to the barman, who nodded, 'he's an old friend of mine. My oldest friend, in fact, isn't that right, Sean?' Then he was off again, shouting instructions, shaking his head at something or other, disappearing downstairs. And I was left to sample his free drinks and look around me at all the dizzy sheen and glitter.

'Known Mr Pagett a long time then?' the barman asked, as

he spilt a stream of change into the till with a professional jangle.

'Yes,' I said. 'A long time.'

'How did you meet?'

'He beat up someone who'd annoyed me.'

Soon the place filled up. Invitations had evidently been scattered across London. People had been tempted to come and have a free glass of champagne. Most of them were dressed so elegantly that it was hard to believe they needed a free glass of anything. Food appeared on trays. Canapés and savoury chunks on sticks, tiny cubes of cheese, folded little whispers of meat. From time to time Dan appeared and nodded to me confidentially, as though we were the only ones who knew what was really going on. I turned round halfway through the evening and saw Dominique in the reflection of one of the full-length mirrors. I walked across to her. She was made up up for the occasion and wearing a black trouser suit I didn't remember seeing before. She kissed me lightly on the cheek.

'Impressive, isn't it? Your friend is doing well for himself.'

'And he didn't even go to Oxford.'

'Or do analysis.'

'Didn't expect to see you here, Dominique.'

'You always expect too much or too little, Sean.' Then Dan was beside us. He took me by the arm.

'Come, come now. This isn't the time for old faces,' he said, pulling me away and grinning. 'It's an opportunity for you to meet some new ones.' Ten seconds later I stood before a woman in a tight white dress who had the brightest orange hair I had ever seen.

'Kate Halloran, meet Sean Tallow. Sean's my oldest friend and a very distinguished author. Get him to tell you about his book *Oral Sex and Dental Hygiene*. I found it full of useful tips, myself, though you might as well skip the archbishop's introduction. Even you might learn a thing or two, my love. Kate, Sean, is a model.' Then he was gone. Kate looked at me and shrugged.

'Was he always like that?'

'No,' I said, 'he's definitely improving.'

So we found a table and sat down. A bottle of champagne was delivered with the compliments of the house. I told her, since she asked, how I knew Dan. From time to time I caught sight of Dominique, who moved in and out of his circle at the bar. She seemed to laugh a lot, a lot more than I remembered her laughing. What was so funny, all of a sudden, and why had no one told me the joke? Odd how lonely seeing her laugh like that made me feel, so I tried to focus entirely on my new companion, who seemed more than happy to be focused on, and some time around midnight I went to get her coat. Dan was in the foyer, with a gaggle of men about him in various states of inebriation. They were all spraying him with the congratulatory dottle of their bonhomie.

'Glad you've hit it off with Kate,' he said and gave me a knowing smile. 'I had a feeling you would. Was it the flaming hair attracted you?'

'You know me, Dan. I just like girls whose hearts are in the right place, that's all.'

'I never got as far as her heart, but I think you'll find all the other bits and pieces are more or less where you'd expect. Her exits and her entrances. You might find it a pleasant change, Sean, to be honest.' A few minutes later, Kate and I were in a taxi heading for Museum Street.

That night we made love repeatedly and, given her cries and gasps, I suppose noisily. Dan had been right, I did find it a pleasant change, so pleasant that only in the morning light did I start to consider Stefan. He had, after all, encouraged me to go and find a female companion. On the other hand, he had been very particular about maintaining the boundaries of amorous discretion. Or did that only apply to him?

When I finally emerged from the bedroom, he was already there in the kitchen, percolating coffee.

'Hello, Stefan,' I said. He smiled at me. Given the byzantine complexity of his facial semiology, one could never be sure, but it looked like a smile of congratulation.

'I brought a friend back last night.'

'Yes, I heard. Is she still here?' On cue, Kate padded in, having finally disentangled herself from the sheets. She was barefoot and barelegged.

'Kate Halloran, meet Stefan Kreuz,' I said, a little shyly. 'This is Stefan's flat, by the way.'

'Hello, Stefan,' Kate said, the words flowing slowly from her lips, still sticky with sleep, syrupy with solicitude. He took her hand and shook it very gently.

'And hello to you, my dear.'

Kate went away that day, but only so that she could bring some of her things back in the evening. Our days together turned into a week. Stefan said nothing. I kept observing him closely to catch any signs of disapproval, but I could see none. During the following week, Kate started preparing meals for all three of us. She had never discussed this with me, but Stefan seemed more than happy to join in with the preparations. She was a very good cook. I came back one day to find them both in the kitchen, cooking and chatting amiably, as Stefan guided her through the preparation of an authentic goulash. I edged back out quietly, leaving them to it, humming a Bessie Smith tune quietly to myself as I went.

She told me she had been born in Portsmouth. At the age of eighteen she had entered the photographic files of the Southsea Model Directory and soon found herself walking down some of the less attended catwalks of the Home Counties, simulating smiles, cavorting to the syncopations of desire. Soon she had come to London, hoping to be photographed for the tabloids. Two days later she was surprised to find herself in a draughty studio in Wandsworth, alone with a photographer who was unshaven and hung-over, his pale flesh ghostly in the morning light. He had spent three hours shooting her topless. A few of these pictures were subsequently published, not however on Page Three of her chosen red top, but instead in magazines with predictable names that always end up on the top shelf at the newsagents. Which was why, she explained, needing money as badly as she did by then, she had found herself working four nights a week at a nightclub off St James's Square, which advertised itself as 'an exotic oasis in the city for gentlemen'. The waitresses all served topless. No physical contact was permitted in the main bar, but there was a separate room below, dark and spiky with music and smoke, where plenty of touching took place to make sure all the bits and pieces were in the right places. And if a gentleman in pursuit of his urban exotica was prepared to pay £100 to the management, either by credit card or cash, he could start out into the night with the waitress of his choice, with whom he must then make his own *ad hoc* financial arrangements regarding hourly rates and services to be provided.

All this information was provided in sleepy conversations over the pillow, between our frenzied engagements. The teeth-clenched intensity of her thrown-back head was new to me. Dominique had never done more than moan quietly to herself, as though chasing whispers down the corridors of her repressions. Or could they have been mine?

Kate's flesh seemed powdered somehow, like her face, chalky-white with moondust. And she was usually fogged as though she had just emerged from sleep, or was about to make the long descent back into it. Somehow she seemed to spend half the day either dressing or undressing, though she could be snagged for hours at a time in a limbo of dishevelment somewhere between the two. The white flesh of her legs and sometimes, when she only wore one of my shirts and sat drinking coffee in the kitchen, that of her breasts, was easily visible as she loped about, curled, stretched, or leaned forward with an easy motion to reciprocate whatever gesture had just been offered.

I couldn't keep my hands off her and it took a few weeks before I started to register the discrepancy: Kate would go into her frenzied mode before I'd barely touched her. Her cries and contortions always arrived with the same regularity, continued at the same pace, died away with the same attenuated fall. I started to wonder if Kate's body could be telling me lies. I felt some strange and unwelcome memory stirring, of touching the flesh but knowing the spirit was elsewhere. Then one day, when she had gone for a walk down Oxford Street, I rifled through the bags in the corner where she kept most of her things, and found her portfolio from the Southsea Model Directory. When I saw the teeth-clenched intensity of her thrown-back head, with nothing more sensual than strobe lights caressing her breasts and thighs, I felt curiously hollow; felt as though I'd at last found the body of evidence under the body; caught out my own desire as somehow fraudulent, entrapped and entangled in a scheme that had preceded it.

I could no longer connect, not with any conviction, and asked myself whether she'd ever truly connected at all. Soon I couldn't bear to hear her moans. I had a feeling that she'd once recorded them, then simply memorised the performance. I didn't feel as though they had anything to do with me and I longed once again for Dominique's soft and self-beguiling murmurs, as she sank further down and I sank further in.

'It's been wonderful, Kate, really, but I just feel I need to be alone again for a while, that's all. I'm essentially the solitary type. But Dan probably told you that.' She looked at me and then shrugged. Exactly how we'd met.

'I'm going up north for a fortnight,' I said, 'and I've had a word with Stefan about you staying on by yourself here while I'm gone, so you can find somewhere else. He said that would be fine. I've settled the rent. I'll be back on the fifteenth. So, if you could find somewhere by then . . .'

'As long as you enjoyed it,' she said.

'Oh, I enjoyed it, believe me.'

And that weekend I took the train from King's Cross to Yorkshire.

11

On the way up I tried to register all the different counties, but half of them seemed to have melded one into another by the time the train finally pulled into the station. I caught sight of one of the old public buildings and was back twenty years before. I had gone to the local art gallery one weekend and stood next to a Henry Moore sculpture of a woman, the great gaping mountain of a woman, with outcrops for breasts and a vast void of a womb. I had placed my hand carefully on its rough-cast surface, just above the blind declivities of her eyes. A uniformed figure had beaked swiftly out of a corner.

'Hands off, if you don't mind.'

Fresh from my reading of a Thames & Hudson book, I turned and replied, keeping my hand in place, 'Henry Moore says that if people don't touch his sculptures, they'll die.'

'That's as maybe, son,' said the man in the uniform, 'but if you don't take your hand off that particular one, I'm going to cut it off.'

My grandmother had not been well. She was even shakier than usual on her legs. Her eyes had sunk a little deeper into her face, whose flesh was now ivory white, with dark hairline cracks across it. I asked her what the matter was, but she only gestured to the lower part of her torso.

'It's a funny thing about being uneducated,' she said later in a meditative tone as she sipped a glass of whisky, 'but you only ever find out the names of all the things inside you after they start packing in.'

'Stay young, lad,' my grandfather said, looking through the window at his roses. 'Stay young as long as you can, that's your best bet.'

By this time my grandfather had been retired for a while and spent most of his days, when it wasn't raining, playing bowls in the local park. I arranged to take them down to the Metropole that Saturday night, ferried there by the local taxi service, to sample the buffet meal at the carvery.

My grandmother couldn't grasp the concept of the carvery, no matter how often I explained.

'You can go back as many times as you like,' I said. 'There's no need to pile it up like that.'

But she kept piling, and when she'd eaten everything that was on the plate she edged across to me and asked in a whisper if I might sneak back and get her some more of the roast beef and potatoes.

'We don't have to sneak back,' I said. 'We've paid for the meal. You can have as much as you like.' She looked dubious.

'But won't you have to pay them again?'

'No,' I said, 'just the once. You can clear the table, if you're that hungry.' I thought as long as she had her appetite there probably wasn't too much to worry about.

'You get it for me anyway,' she said, just in case, offering me her plate. I went dutifully and piled once more. After I had placed it before her and sat down, she leaned across conspiratorially.

'You didn't have to pay them again, did you?' My grandfather stood up.

'I'll go get her another lager,' he said. 'She was always more logical with a bit of drink inside her.'

By day I walked the streets where I'd grown up, called into pubs where I'd drunk, even saw the occasional face I recognised. On a piece of wasteland near a wrecker's yard there were still the ravaged shells of motors long defunct. I remembered how I had once sat in them, heaving the steering wheel this way and that as I gunned along some imaginary highway. That was as close as I'd ever come to driving and, odd though it may seem, as close as I'd ever wanted to. I stood on St Enoch's Road and looked down the hill to where I'd once watched a Lister have sex with some local girl, while twenty feet above him one of his brothers threw stones at them both. There'd been white twitches of flesh under the chaos of her clothes. I remembered the excitement I'd felt, laced with dread.

My grandmother couldn't face any long trips out, so I made my own way by bus over the moors. I travelled to the glen and stood in the exact spot where Dominique had found her yellow-hearted flower. There were none now. I walked up through the mist to the top of the hill where the sheep emerged from the inkwash grey, still wrapped in their genesis wool. They stopped dead and stared, and I felt for a moment as if I were dissolving in their gaze, then somewhere below us a churchbell exploded. In bed at night I found myself thinking of Kate. Might I have been a little hasty there? A certain asynchrony between desire and its expression surely wasn't the gravest misdemeanour in the world. I wondered if I was really ready for the monk's life yet. I could still feel her tongue enticing me, the way they say amputated limbs carry on sending their messages to the brain long after they've entered the incinerator. I thought of Dominique, too, and even of Sally Pagett, but I didn't really want to think about her. I had to think really hard not to think about her. The trouble was that I couldn't think about her without also thinking of Dan. Dear dead Dan.

Then one afternoon at five o'clock I was back on the train again, heading for London. And on the way down I decided to retrieve Kate from wherever she'd landed and bring her back to Stefan's flat. He liked her, that much was obvious; they were at ease in one another's company. Maybe we could live as a family. An unorthodox one certainly, but then that was the only sort I'd ever known. And the next time Stefan had one of his women in, we could all be introduced; go off at the end of the evening to our separate bedrooms, with smiles of wine-bright anticipation on our faces. I felt a surge of warmth towards both of them.

It was after nine when I let myself into the flat and as I made my way through the living room I heard a sound I knew only too well. Kate was already past the initiatory moans and had moved on to the tiny yelps. I sat down slowly on the sofa and listened as the third movement, the *basso profondo* of labyrinthine passions at long last located and now gaspingly explored, began its progress. 'Stefan, Stefan,' she cried, calling out his name exactly as she'd once called out mine, though with what seemed to me, from the auditory gallery, a more unambiguous enthusiasm. Then she moved to the attenuation, the dying fall, and Stefan uttered some lyrical sounds in Hungarian, which I could have sworn were lines from his translation of Shakespeare's *Sonnets*.

Five minutes later he emerged, wearing nothing but an open bathrobe that flapped about his torso. He stopped in the middle of the floor.

'Sean, I didn't realise you were back.' I nodded, in acknowledgement of the fact that I was and that he evidently hadn't realised.

'Have a cognac.' I nodded weakly. I certainly needed something. He came back with the drinks and sat down next to me on the sofa.

'Kate,' he began, then faltered. The only time I had ever known his English give way.

'Has moved into your bed, Stefan,' I offered helpfully. 'Yes, I heard.' Stefan smiled at me, his ancient seducer's smile. His brown eyes were always warm, always amused and tolerant. I could see, I suppose, what they saw in him. He reached into the pocket of his robe and took out a Gauloise. Blue smoke soon enshrouded us both.

'I wonder if you'd mind very much,' he said and faltered again, then he stood up and walked across to his mantelpiece, where he stared down at the acorns and trilobites he'd collected over the years, 'mind going to stay in Dalrymple House instead of here. It's just, it could seem a bit crowded otherwise. That's the way it felt before . . .'

'You want me to move out?'

'If you wouldn't mind.'

'Would tomorrow be all right?'

'Tonight would be better. I mean, you could come back and get your things tomorrow. Just pick up what you need for the moment. I already notified Maggie. Your room is ready: she aired the sheets.'

So that night I stayed at Dalrymple House.

'I gather you're moving from there to here,' Maggie said, a little cautiously, as she gauged my mood.

'So it seems.'

'Stefan must be keen.'

'Must be.' She was an attractive woman, older than me but younger than Stefan, and she gave me a smile then, a smile that bespoke either the possibility of intimacy or the established fact of complicity. Both were equally unwelcome.

Next day I walked down to collect my things and stopped outside the British Museum. I decided to go inside and look at the one thing I always ended up looking at. This was the obsidian mirror into which Dr John Dee had so often gazed with Kelley, a black pool making visible the vast invisible agencies that surrounded them. The kindly female curator, Annette, had one day taken it from its case when no one else was about and let me hold it in my hands. I wasn't sure what exactly I was holding, or whether the images of any spirits had ever really moved across its surface. Dee said they had, though; he'd been in no doubt of it whatsoever. On alternate days came Modimi, in the shape of a pretty female child, and another feminine spirit named Galvah. Their speeches had needed to be decoded from Kelley's unreliable reports.

It was by way of a magical speculum, which over the years had come to be called the devil's looking-glass. Obsidian was sacred to the Aztec god Tezintlipoca, who would gaze into his own black scrying pool, there to observe the curious doings of humankind. Aztec priests preferred reflective surfaces for divination – smooth water, polished stone. The good doctor's interests, it struck me once more, had been very dangerous indeed, as dangerous as casting the queen's nativity, which he had in fact once done, landing himself in prison in the process. Aubrey records that he was reputed to have the power to raise tempests and he also claimed for himself the faculty of discovering hidden treasure. All he wanted was to be allowed to exercise his gift under the protection of the Royal Letters Patent, then he would set out into the world to discover mines of gold and silver 'for her Grace's only use'. But an ancient belief was still prevalent in those days: that treasure sunk under the earth was in the keeping of demons, and that their help must be solicited for its discovery. Stringent statutes were extant against such sorcery. You could die if you were caught at it.

Next to the obsidian mirror was the shewstone, a crystal ball, a polished glass zero pregnant with nothing, though seemingly patient with the possibility of everything. A translucent egg of mystical vacuity. Had Dee been the model for Prospero? How close was he to the School of Night? He certainly knew its most important members. How to fathom the past when we had so little notion what was going on in the present.

A few minutes later I let myself back into the flat. There seemed to be no one about. I assumed they were both probably recuperating from their nocturnal exertions in Stefan's bedroom, the door of which was closed. It only took ten minutes to pack my things, which were mostly books and a few clothes. As I came out into the living room, I walked across to the bookshelf and ran my hand across some of

Stefan's ancient volumes. I was saying goodbye, I suppose. I had a sad feeling that I'd not be back.

I smelt her before I saw her. Kate was behind me, wearing one of Stefan's shirts, a candy stripe with a button-down collar.

'Hope I'm not causing too much inconvenience round here amongst you boys.' She kissed me easily on the cheek, then went and poured herself a drink.

'Cognac?' she called from the kitchen.

'No thanks. A little early for me.'

She was sitting on the sofa, her legs crossed beneath her.

'Just out of interest, Kate, why did you stop working at the Oasis?'

'Daniel Pagett paid me to do some work for him instead.' As she said this, she turned and looked towards the window. The clouds had briefly scattered and sunlight was shafting through. I bid her the fondest farewell I could muster and went quickly down the stairs.

Stefan called at the hotel a few nights later.

'You are not angry with me, Sean?'

'Not at all, Stefan. The soft doors opened and you went in. Isn't that the way everything always gets started.'

A starred note from Hariot:

> *Women from that point on had no further place in our study. They were matter only for dreams and speculations.*

I was glad to get back to work. I resolved myself against any murmurs of resentment; it's not my way, after all, for that would be to commit the capital sin against time. Wishing things otherwise is merely another name for urging the years to go backwards, spitting in the face of what has been given, and I knew I'd never fathom my own particular riddle if I didn't accept what was given. Anyway, I had the night to myself once more – apart from the news, that is, but I was well enough used to living with that. The great thing to remember about the news is that it always happens to other people.

Part Three

So ere you find where light in darkness lies,
Your light grows dark by losing of your eyes.

WILLIAM SHAKESPEARE, Love's Labour's Lost

1

Dawn is arriving at last. Well almost. The new day is dithering on the horizon amongst a few final feints and eclipses. So I had best press on, or we'll never bring this history into the present.

I stayed at Dalrymple House. By now it's probably clear enough that I have something in common with inanimate objects: I tend to remain in the inertial state wherever I've landed. Newton's laws regarding the movement of bodies largely cover the movement of mine too, though it's taken long enough for one of them to be proven. I'm in a position finally to confirm that every action does indeed have an equal and opposite reaction, and I can only wonder that people don't find the fact more alarming.

I didn't have much space now, so I dispensed with almost all my books. I kept my Shakespeare and a couple of biographies of Hariot, Ralegh and Marlowe. And of course my notebooks. There were already ten of these substantial A4 volumes, filled from first page to last with my meticulous and tiny writing. From time to time I might pick up some catchpenny tract or inkhorn effusion on the Farringdon Road, something I knew would not be available elsewhere, but I got rid of them again after I'd taken whatever needed to be transcribed. I didn't want to be cluttered up, even with sacred furniture.

My régime from this point on became more rigid and mechanical. I worked my shifts with what everyone at the BBC agreed was exemplary efficiency. It seemed to be the one part of my life never afflicted with any form of chaos. It was my sheet anchor. If the weather permitted, then I would take my walks in the evening or the early morning, for my pilgrimage track had to be maintained. I would eat in pubs or the cheaper cafés, spending hours and sometimes even days, when work permitted, in the London Library or the British Museum. I suppose people take refuge in different activities, to fend off the demons and hobgoblins. There are many antidotes for the terrors of the night: a body to cling to, drunkenness or drugs, sunny expectations, since hope is such a great illuminator, a flame for the spider's hole. Of course the fly often gets torched along with the spider, but there we are. For me it had become my research, of which both reading and walking were now complementary parts. And I did start to wonder if the rules that had applied in my old Oxford college a hundred years before, the ones that precluded any man marrying if he wished to remain a don, might not have contained a little more wisdom than I'd once supposed, for the solitary life does bring to your attention data which a more sociable existence couldn't possibly supply. Thomas Hariot wouldn't have stayed up all night at Syon House studying the stars if he'd had a wife and children to fret about. Giotto was lucky enough with his spouse, but he still had to endure the mockery, as she caught him stumbling about, ashen-faced at dawn: 'Perspective again, is

it, Giotto?' I was grateful, to be perfectly frank, for my new
condition, with no Kates or Dominiques to entice or distract
me. Now, the solitude and the darkness between them were
revealing connections and constellations so bright that
sometimes I could hardly bear to look. The inside of my skull
would flash, brilliant with illumination. The migraines had
even started to return intermittently, probably to keep my
brain from burning up.

It doesn't take much to create a myth, I'd certainly learnt
that in the newsroom, if nothing else. All that's needed is for
a few people to speak compellingly and some others to stay
silent. And once a myth is launched on its career, no amount
of refutation will ever abolish it completely. Within a few
years it will have become tradition. So I worked hard on
Shakespeare's identity and began to feel at last the beginning
of a paradigm shift. The trick here is not to be bullied by
conventional wisdom, not to snort, as Dominique had
snorted at Bernini's Teresa, because of your assumption that
you already know all the facts. Suspicion of certainty is the
first requirement. Total solitude, and a life spent largely in
the dark, undoubtedly help. Intellectual ascesis, you see:
getting rid of the unwanted clutter. I wrote at my little table,
after first covering the mirror on the wall behind it with a
black sheet. Whenever I left the hotel, Maggie would come
into the room and remove that sheet, and whenever I came
back, I'd put it back again.

'Why, Sean?' I remembered Dominique asking me once,
'why do you hate looking in the mirror so much?' I
shrugged; didn't even mention that I was said to be the living
image of my dead mother. When I did stare into one of those
silvery pools, which was not often, I always saw her face

coming up out of the depths to meet me, and felt then something like panic. Felt a different sort of dark around me, one that no one had ever even attempted to map. Dominique was deep into Lacan by then.

'When you were young your gaze should have been met by your mother and father. They vanished from view. When you see your own face now what you're seeing is the void that no one affirmed, no one responded to.'

'I just don't like looking in mirrors, that's all,' I said. So I kept the mirror veiled. The tiny proportions of the hotel bedroom reminded me sometimes of the celibate spaces of the Dominicans at Blackfriars. I had tried to convince myself once that I might be able to live in one of them, but Brother Geoffrey had gently dissuaded me, realising long before I did that my psyche wasn't tailored to the task. You'd have to be far more sociable than I was to be a real monk. But it had begun to seem as though I'd have to get used to a life of celibacy, all the same.

Now the shift system had given me three days to myself, so I had taken the train to Mortlake and walked along the river, where I found the old church of St Mary's, and then mapped out from there where Dr Dee's house must have stood in relation to it, though not a trace of the house now remains. Robert Cotton had paid for the whole field round about to be dug up after the old man's death, convinced that documents beyond price must be hidden there. Elias Ashmole sent maggot-headed Aubrey himself on his own search. In its time Dee's library had been for some people by way of an omphalos, the very centre of a mystic world for those who would see the unseen and hear the unheard, those who needed intercourse with the spirits beyond this realm.

Queen Elizabeth had come down here to the legendary site of Bibliotheca Mortlacensis. The stacks of books and codices together probably formed the greatest collection England could boast at the time, much of it gathered up from the sacked libraries of the monasteries, particularly St Augustine's Abbey, but Dee's house was soon buried under the new Mortlake tapestry works and then his own books were scattered throughout the world.

When later that day I arrived at the London Library, I checked some dates in a Shakespeare biography. I was still troubled by that question: could the figure of Prospero actually have been based on John Dee? Was it biographically possible? Once again we seemed to be back with that recurring question: whom and what did Shakespeare actually know? Who and what *was* he? In 1605 the King's Men stopped over at Mortlake. Nobody can say exactly where the Warwickshire Shakespeare was, but he might have been with them. We know that Dee was back there by then in his house. A broken man, near the end of his life. A man of immense learning, all of which seems to have come to nothing. But still a most striking-looking fellow – we have this much on the authority of all who came across him: a long white beard, slender and tall, and the gravest of demeanours. So it's just possible that Shakespeare might have encountered him there. One thing was certain: the members of the School of Night all knew him well enough, and Hariot had been a lifetime companion.

I found myself thinking again of that imagination we've all heard so much about. Whoever the man was, no mind has ever been more susceptible to having impressions made upon it. Place before it this figure of legend, this living Merlin, this alchemist, astrologer, cabbalist. A man who appears to have spent his life labouring through the world's bookshelves, transforming the inside of his skull into a tiny microcosm of the universe of knowledge.

All the exotic ingredients of alchemy – all the metals and minerals and compounds – are in truth one, and that singularity is neither more nor less than the person of the alchemist himself. If the base metal is in need of purification then so, even more so, is he. Out of the corruption and confusion he must find a oneness in which nature and divinity are reconciled. Out of the unstillness of his own impurity must come the transforming power to achieve redemption. Curiously, the best scryers in a shewstone were said to be the tainted ones, since too pellucid a medium precluded any visible manifestations.

But Dee's unworldliness had already led to his ruin. Insofar as he trusted the powers of this world, those same powers had brought about his downfall. He had been cozened by bogus scryers, his library despoiled and looted, his scientific instruments vandalised. He was reduced to selling his own books; his daughter sold even more of them without telling him, there being no other way to get money. On hearing of it, the news was said to have sped his death.

It seemed to me almost impossible to imagine the writer we call Shakespeare not responding; impossible not to see him placing such a luminous and tragic figure in a play. And he knew only too well what had destroyed Dee: zeros. That cipher which had only recently entered the English language and English calculation. The O which by itself signified nothing except vacuity, but which, with any solid number before it and its own kind breeding a train of hollows behind, meant riches. The whole world could now be contained inside an O, as Shakespeare said it was inside the wooden one of the Globe.

This word had grown unexpectedly out of a Hindu void through an Arabic symbol, but now the zero of accountancy was becoming all-powerful. That might have been exactly what Hamlet meant when he cried, 'For O, for O, the hobby-horse is forgot.' It's almost certainly what the Fool meant when he said to Lear, 'Now thou art an O without a figure'. The cipher of nothing had permitted the pricing of everything. Double-entry book-keeping was not possible without the zero. Shakespeare was obsessed by it; by nought and its symbol, and the way it enabled contemporary humanity to calculate, control, consume, circle the whole of existence like a snake swallowing its own tail. The terrible decline of Lear begins when Cordelia utters that one word, 'Nothing'.

Dee was aware of it too, crystallomantic that he was. What, after all, was his crystal but an O whose very emptiness permitted it to become an *omnium gatherum*? He was aware too of the theological doctrine of *horror vacui*, which was soon secularised into the simpler notion that nature abhors a vacuum, but so many of his topographies and herbals, his anatomies, glossaries and alchemical treatises, could never have come into his hands had it not been for the despoliation of the mighty monastery libraries. There was a dreadful O to ponder there. The beginning of the great private collections was based on the vastation of the great public ones. Bare ruined choirs where late the sweet birds sang. Aubrey recounts the memories of old men who saw fragments of illuminated manuscripts being blown around the edges of country towns like dirty leaves, rammed into roofs as insulation, piled up in the jakes. Vellum sheets that had cost devoted monks years of their lives and half their eyesight.

For all his intellectual riches Dee could not get his hands on the financial variety. His queen decided to place the noughts behind other chosen figures and Dr Dee died in want. I had walked for a few hours after my trip to Mortlake. In the light rain that had started to fall a power station hissed with potency from the other bank. A supermarket trolley lay on the river bed, with an ancient one-eyed doll trapped inside it, bobbing about in the current.

The next day I was at the Bank of England. This was where they had buried Thomas Hariot. Well, in fact they had buried him in a little church called Christopher le Stocks, which had gradually vanished, its site incorporated into the cathedral of finance on Threadneedle Street. At the very heart of this mausoleum of money there is a tiny garden, a sanctuary of peace and silence surrounded on all sides by the noise and speed of the ledger that encircles the world. And Hariot's body lay here. At least I'd read that it did, but after persistent questioning of one of the officials I discovered that the remains of many of the interred had been removed in the nineteenth century and no one knew which ones. Again it seemed that the body of evidence had led me to a place where the body itself was missing.

Hariot, I'd come to feel, was the silent figure who could tell us the most about those days, if only one could get him to talk; to explain who and what really constituted the School of Night. He could also resolve the matter of Shakespeare's identity, I knew that. I couldn't prove it, but I knew it. How many things that we really know can we prove? The School of Night had finally taught me to read. Because no text was too sacred for their savage inquisition, they set themselves to gaze anew upon the world and its beliefs. Traditions were mere confusions in which superstitious men unnecessarily enmeshed themselves and reverence was no more and no less than fear of true knowledge. Marlowe was reported to have said, 'Moses was no more than a juggler; Hariot can do more than he.' So the light of the mind, given its liberty, could burn away the darkness and the dross. How seldom, though, these men appeared to be telling us, was it given its liberty.

Hariot was in effect the inventor of modern algebra, devising the signs of inequality. He was also the first man in England to see the planets of Jupiter, through a telescope of his own creation, one reputed to be as fine as Galileo's own. When he died many years later at Syon House, where he had lived courtesy of the Earl of Northumberland, the alchemical Wizard Earl, his papers contained important observations and conclusions regarding mechanics, hydrostatics, specific gravity, magnetism, harmony, solid geometry and infinite series. Many years before he had sailed with Ralegh to Virginia and written an account of the place which still remains exemplary for its clarity and economy four hundred years later. I had searched for the little house which Northumberland had built for him in Syon's grounds one day, only to discover that it had vanished entirely. Not a trace remained. Another disappearance.

Why exactly had the Shakespeare text dubbed this gifted crew the School of Night? The name itself might have come from their devotion to astronomy, since if you wish to observe stars you'll need to stay awake through the hours of darkness. Perhaps it was this that led one of their group, George Chapman, to write his poem 'The Shadow of Night', in which he praises the world of darkness and exalts melancholy over celebration: 'Come to this house of mourning, serve the Night.' Chapman spent some of his time in prison too. He knew all about melancholy; he felt that joy imprisoned the mind in unwanted earthly confusions.

It was said of them, though unreliably, that when they met together, this troublesome cabal, they delighted to point out that God was an anagram of dog. Marlowe offered sneeringly to rewrite the gospels, but this time in decent Greek. Of the group, the two most famous members were killed – Walter Ralegh publicly and straightforwardly with an axe on Tower Hill after many years of imprisonment; Christopher Marlowe by subterfuge in murky circumstances, put to death, it would seem, by men who were at times agents of the State. Two, Thomas Nashe and George Chapman, spent time in prison for writings deemed subversive and both died in great poverty.

Ralegh himself was called the Witch, perhaps for his bewitching effect upon the queen, though he did live in the heart of witching England; Cerne Abbas has a potent reputation to this day. The Giant there, cut into the chalk of the hillside, represents a protest on behalf of paganism at the Christian banishment of the old gods of darkness and fecundity.

By the end Ralegh was renamed the white eagle, ravaged by fever, a spectacular failure, his son dead under his command, heading home at last without the promised gold, to final imprisonment and death. For the School of Night by this stage there was only one final examination to come. And always at the centre of it all was the elusive Hariot, thought by some like the Jesuit Robert Parsons to be the intellectual hub about which this dark wheel spun; the mysterious figure they all looked to so they could find out what they were meant to believe. There wasn't too much going on in the intellectual world, either in England or anywhere else, that Hariot didn't know about. Whatever your question about that age, Hariot could surely answer it.

On the third day I went down by train to Deptford, and walked from there to the churchyard of St Nicholas. This is where they said they'd buried Marlowe, assuming it was Marlowe, assuming they'd ever buried anyone. The church-yard is guarded by two white skulls on gateposts, which have a singularly unredemptive look about them. I walked up and down amongst the gravestones, but there is only a sign on the wall saying that the brilliant young Kit was buried 'nearby', and I thought I heard Dan's voice in my head again, from all those years before in Yorkshire, where he had walked between the graves, having already lost patience with this graveyard-stalking business of mine: 'Anybody would think you're expecting them to get out of there, Sean,' he had called to me one day. 'Do you really think they're going to sit up and start talking to you?'

Marlowe, the shoemaker's son from Canterbury, had worn the black gown of the scholar, prefiguring the one he would soon enough wear as a priest – or so his parents had fondly thought. There were startling parallels with Shake-speare. Both born in the same year, both fathers workers in leather, since Shakespeare's was a whittawer, softening his hides and skins with alum and salt before readying them for glovemaking. Both with a raging appetite for technical words and phrases, from soldiering, sailing, the court, theology, the law, to the extent that Shakespeare was actually mocked as a 'buckram gentleman' or noverint, one employed as a legal copyist. Marlowe had also received the classical education which would have enabled him to learn that mass of allusions people sometimes puzzle over in the Shakespeare text.

And as I walked up to Deptford Strand, where they said that Marlowe had been murdered at Eleanor Bull's house for lonely sailors, I found myself thinking of Marlowe's Faustus, who flies through the air, transports fruits from one hemisphere to the other at speeds thought preposterous at the time, just as Puck does later; who studies the true nature of the movements of heavenly bodies, as Prospero had done. All of these were Hariot's preoccupations too, and perhaps all had arisen out of Hariot's dangerous tutorials, given to the School of Night in the dead of night. And I started for the first time to see a possible solution to my problematic study, but I could barely bring myself to ponder it. Surely it was ridiculous? Ridiculous to most, certainly, but not necessarily to me. I had, you see, separated myself by now into a strong-minded isolation. I was no longer dependent on the opinions of others; I seldom even shared the daylight with them. I stood at the water's edge and stared at the cormorants perched on a rotting wooden structure, stretching out their black, gothic wings to dry in the chilling breezes.

There didn't seem to be any Eleanor Bull establishments offering their welcomes to lonely sailors these days, so I took a boat back to Westminster and there stood once more by the water's edge. Could I really presume to move such a mighty paradigm so far? I looked down into the lapping waves and detritus to see a single red rose shifting about forlornly in the swell. I couldn't help wondering whose it had been.

2

Over the years I had developed a nose for the status of news. Why not make some? Dan had asked me so many years before. Well, I still couldn't make any, but I could sift it instinctively. I knew what should go in and what could be left out; I could even leaven the grave transactions of global catastrophe with the odd tiny anecdote whose wryness might leak an invisible smile across the airwaves. One had to balance massacres in distant places with economic summits, destruction of the rainforests with shifts in interest rates, skirmishes in Westminster with the pursuit of ancient war criminals, those improbable old geezers who stumbled out of their semis in Eastbourne blinking into the congregated flashlights of the press, only to mutter in thick, dark accents about mistaken identity. The raped child, the nuclear emission, would be hushed with a brief look at the football results and a prediction as to pole-position in the forthcoming Formula One event. I also learnt the strange superstitions of the newsroom, for example never to assume that Christmas Day would be a quiet one, despite the brandy and the paper hats, for that was when Sadat had chosen to fly to Israel and offer his hand in peace; it was also the day when

they took the wretched Ceauşescu and his equally wretched
wife out into a frozen yard and shot them both dead. The
spirit of good will affects different people in different ways. I
fear my view of life might also have become gradually darker
as the years passed, though I can hardly blame that on the
newsroom or the BBC. Optimism is nothing but a blindfold
where the truth's concerned. From time to time I remembered what Dominique had once said to me: that my study
of the School of Night was no more and no less than an
attempt to prove to myself the truth of my Catholicism. All
my psychological default settings, according to her, were
Catholic. Original sin on the one hand, redemptive grace on
the other; the one pervasive and inescapable, the other
seeming elusive at times, even to the point of absenteeism.
'Do they know they've got a tormented medieval monk
gathering the news?' she asked me one day, while she was
drying her hair, coiling the long dark ringlets around heated
tongs. 'They wouldn't care,' I said. 'They've had a lot worse
than that in there.' Dominique's flourish of black ringlets I
had at first thought entirely natural, but I'd come gradually to
realise how much work she had to put into their maintenance. Her Medusa coils, she called them: no myth is ever
lost on a Freudian. You looked upon those black snakes at
your peril. The analytic stare that came back was enough to
turn any man's heart to stone.

My grandfather had worked for the council all his life and
I suppose I'd assumed I'd do the same at the BBC. Perhaps
I'd even come to think that capitalism was something that
went on elsewhere, involving other people, the manipulable
masses, something I merely noted and summarised for the
desk. Without thinking about it much, I felt I'd joined a

collegiate institution where people, as long as they were competent, had jobs until they retired. It was the one part of my life I didn't need to consider. Which is why it probably came as such a shock when Andrew, the newsroom manager, invited me into his office one day, having arranged for my union representative to sit there beside me, and then told me I was to be made redundant in three months' time. I stared at his big sad face and tired eyes. He was a kind man who wrote desolate plays about contemporary Britain, which were very seldom performed. Everybody liked him.

'But there's never been a single complaint about my work since I came here, Andrew. Not once in all those years.' His face creased into an even deeper frown.

'It's nothing to do with the quality of your work,' he said. 'There's this process of rationalisation going on, that's all.' He gestured exhaustedly towards the computer in the corner of his room. Its green screen seemed to glow at me with muted venom. It seemed that Dan had been wrong: the BBC was speeding up after all. 'There'll be a lump-sum payment, of course, but I'm afraid you're too young for a pension. Denis here has all the details. Maybe you'd like to go off and discuss it with him. We can meet again tomorrow. I'm sorry, I really am. But you know as well as I do what's been going on in this place over the last few years, Sean. Now it's all about management consultants and cost-to-reward ratios. And I suppose someone who's never even met you and never will has decided you're more of a cost than a reward. And that's all there is to it. You know as much as I do.'

I suppose I did know – I just hadn't thought they were going to apply this costing regime to me. I didn't think I was significant enough to need to be rationalised away. I went down to the bar in the basement and watched the luminous fish swerving this way and that in their fluent internment as I sipped my gin. I'd never really learnt how to do anything else except précis the news, so what was I supposed to move on to now? At least I'd have the better part of six months to think about it from the payment I was going to receive, according to the union representative. A little reading time then. This probably cheered me more than it should have done. I never have been able to think very far ahead, worried such anticipations might constitute another capital sin against time. Something else had been given, that was all, so I couldn't get entangled in worries about money and invest-ments, could I? I'd always been sure enough of that. If I didn't save all my energies for the solution of my riddle, then it wouldn't get solved. In which case, I might just as well climb into the fish tank and drown.

3

I made two trips up north over those next six months. The first was when one of those parts inside her, which my grandmother had only recently found the name for, ceased functioning completely one night and she died. And the second was when my grandfather went to join her.

Black millstone grit had now become brown and grey, in the intervening, smokeless years. It no longer corresponded to my chiaroscuro recollections. Methodist chapels had metamorphosed into curry houses, with bright welcoming signs draped across them. And the old mills stood to lonely attention, like mausoleums after the grave-robbers' visit. Everything had been stripped out, even the lead and the floor brackets. Looms had been hefted long ago, munched back to dross in a scrap-iron maw. Some of the mills and warehouses had been converted into apartments, Victorian solidity now colonised by modernist hygiene, with formations of gleaming new German cars parked outside and CCTV cameras controlling the entrances. I stumbled about amongst the wreckage of the old buildings, though don't ask me what I was looking for. Beckoning to the ghosts of long-gone bronchial wheezers. The perennial crippled pitmen. Emphysema. Silicosis. I stared at the little Pakistani children, their enormous eyes mournful inside the northern rain.

And as I walked the streets of my childhood I came back, again and again, moth-like to the lethal flame. There *was* a way of explaining the astonishing intellectual adventurousness of the works that had come to be known by the name of Shakespeare, also of approaching their utter desolation. Nothing, after all, has ever been written which is more desolate than the major tragedies. What could have happened to any life so annihilating as to confront this intelligence with such a ceaseless pageant of horror? Here was a man who had known murder and subterfuge, who knew the dreadfulness, the hourly torture of exile. He had endured as much as any person who'd ever lived. I had become feverish about it all by now.

After I'd arranged my grandfather's funeral, I put a notice in the *Telegraph and Argus*. It seemed ridiculous that I should have only come to take his hand again, only kissed him once more on the cheek, only shed my shy tears of love all over his lined old face, after he was dead. I should have done that while the blood in his body was still warm, shouldn't I, so that he could have taken me in his arms too? But maybe he would have been as incapable of it as I was. Now I'll never know.

The funeral was a week later. I stared at the raw newness of my grandmother's headstone, only just settling in. Now the upturned clay in the ditch next to hers was waiting to close its mouth on her husband too. I made a large effort not to cry, though I felt the salt urgency of tears beginning behind my eyes. Strange and ridiculous, only to realise how much you love people when you're watching them sink slowly into the ground. Then I looked up and saw Dan on the other side of the grave. I'd not noticed him in church, but then I suppose I hadn't been looking. He was turned out immaculately in black and was easily the most elegant figure amongst us. He bowed slowly and I nodded and smiled, if a little grimly, my eyes constantly moist with the possibility of tears. There were flecks of grey in his hair I'd never seen before. His head had the mottled texture of a thrush. My friend Dan.

Once we had thrown our clods of earth on top of the coffin, the little throng started to disperse raggedly and Dan was at my side.

'You should have told me, Sean. I only found out about all this from a clipping my mother sent me from the paper. You should have told me, you know.'

'I'm sorry,' I said, 'I suppose I should.'

'I loved that old man.'

'Not as much as I did.'

'I didn't even know you'd lost your job at the BBC. Where are you living?'

'In a hotel on Theobald's Road, but I can't afford it much longer.' This last was said with a weariness I could no longer disguise and didn't wish to. 'I'm going to have to find somewhere else to live.'

'I've got somewhere for you to live, Sean.' Then he put his arms around me and I finally let the tears come scalding out.

4

The Pavilion had an attic storey high above the King's Road and Dan had converted it into a penthouse apartment. When I finally stepped in there, I halted and whistled quietly in admiration.

'You should have been an interior designer, Dan, you'd have made a fortune.'

'I have made a fortune, Sean. Told you I would. Even once invited you to come and do it with me, remember? But you wished to devote your life to broadcasting, or something of that nature. Touching the way they finally decided to reward you for all your conscientious hard work.'

'It doesn't matter since I've really been devoting my life to the School of Night, Dan. Remember?'

'That's all right then. Cracked it, have you?'

'Nearly.'

I was walking around and running my hand along the smooth surfaces. It was as though his mother's expensive bad taste had inoculated him entirely against any hint of it himself. There was a perfectly proportioned co-ordination between the minimal furniture, the polished floorboards, the understated rugs. Everything was enticingly light and airy. A few pastel colours here and there offset the brilliant whiteness. The only curiosity was a large low bed backed up against the wall in the living room.

'People spend a lot of time in bed,' Dan said meditatively. 'It's always struck me as odd to want to hide yourself away in a tiny little room for a third of your life. I like to be in the centre of things when I'm lying down. So will the accommodation be to sir's liking?'

'Yes, but what am I supposed to do to earn it?'

'Earn it may be putting it a bit strong. But there is something you can do for me while you're here, as a matter of fact. Something you could only ask of an old friend. Don't you have more luggage than that?'

'No,' I said. 'This is a bit more than I normally carry.' Along with the bags containing my clothes, notebooks and my few remaining texts, I had the book of photographs of my mother I had taken from my grandparents' house and my grandfather's ancient snooker cue. Don't ask me why I'd taken that; I don't even play snooker, but somehow I couldn't leave it there. The rest I had arranged to be collected. The men had given me thirty pounds, then stripped the place of every saleable item, even pulling the encrusted cooker out of the wall.

'You don't have any clothes that are maybe a little more formal, do you?'

'No.'

'Is it really possible to live so entirely the life of the mind?'

'Yes.'

'You know, Sean, given your singular incompetence in the normal procedures of life, I do sometimes wonder if you shouldn't have joined that religious order you used to knock around with at Oxford. Who were they again?'

'Dominicans.'

'There was a rumour going about that you'd signed up. Then you could have made a feature of your unworldliness.'

'A feature, Dan?'

'That's how estate agents refer to awkward and immovable facts. If your west wall falls down the night before you go on the market, they say, "One of the original features is a lovely open prospect of the sunset." With you we could say, "A total absence of material preoccupations is one of our candidate's more endearing features in these pursey times." But as things stand I can't help thinking it's something of a liability. Anyway, the first thing we'll do is pop down the road and get you some new togs. Don't worry: it's all on the account. I'll put it down to company expenses. Did you really used to make money dressed like that?'

'Not much.'

'Life at the BBC, eh? The monk's parlour.'

'Not any more.'

Thus did I acquire the first dark suit I'd had since the one I'd worn at Oxford for my examinations. Some shirts. A few ties. Then, looking down at my shoes, Dan had taken me a few doors along and bought me some new black ones. When we got back he suggested I change into it all, which I did. Staring into the full-length mirror, if only for the briefest moment, I hardly recognised myself.

'Right,' Dan said, as he came back in, 'you'll do. Do you want a drink?' I nodded. He picked up one of the telephones on the low table by the bed and ordered two gin and tonics.

'This one's the internal phone,' he said. 'That one's the outside line.'

'What is it you want me to do, Dan, that's worth installing me in here and kitting me out in all this clobber?' Dan went and stood by the window, looking across the rooftops of Chelsea.

'I'd like you to be the one person in this building who's here on my behalf rather than his own, that's all. I don't suppose you know much about the catering business, do you, Sean?' He didn't even wait for my reply. 'The thing to remember is that cash is constantly moving. Out of pockets on to tables. Out of pockets on to bars. From tables and bars into tills. And out of pockets into pockets. What I'd like is for most of the money that comes out of pockets in this place to end up in my pocket. I'd like to put the amount I specify in the pockets of my employees, rather than having them specify how much they'll put there themselves. *Comprendo?*'

At this point there was a knock on the door and after Dan had shouted, 'Come in', a man in his mid-twenties entered, well groomed, blond and bearded. When he asked where to put the drinks it was evident he was American.

'Jess, this is Sean Tallow. You'll be seeing a lot of him. He'll be staying here in my absence.' Jess bowed slightly and said he was pleased to meet me. If there was anything he could do, I was to let him know. Then he left us.

'So what do you make of Jess?' Dan said, handing me my drink.

'He seemed pleasant enough.'

'That's because he is pleasant enough. Why do you think he's working here?' I shrugged.

'The start of a career? Work experience? Between two other jobs?'

'Get something clear in your mind, Sean, or you'll be no use to me at all. He's working here because that's the best money he can get. He doesn't have a valid work permit for a whole year, but I don't care about that. The labour here is largely cash and no questions asked. He wants to make enough money in twelve months to get himself through college back in the States. He'd do just about anything to acquire it. If I were to toss him down on that bed over there and roger the boy, he probably wouldn't complain too much as long as I gave him a large enough pile of readies afterwards. He doesn't get paid all that much, to be honest, and if he were to see a nice pile of money downstairs and feel confident no one would notice if he took it, then he'd take it. And I don't blame him because I would too, if I were in his shoes. And that applies to just about everyone in this building. None of them's doing it for love, believe me, and I don't trust a single one of them. But I trust you. Which is why you'll be my ears and eyes while I'm gone. All you have to do is be here and look and listen. And the fact that they know you're here, my old friend from the north, looking and listening, will make it a lot less likely that they'll put themselves in the way of temptation. Places like this go bust because they're left in the hands of a manager, who starts helping himself, or not paying attention, or cutting deals with the suppliers. All you have to do, Sean, is be here every day and keep watching what's happening. You'll soon get the picture, believe me. Someone spends hours on the phone to her boyfriend instead of serving the customers. Someone has a funny habit of disappearing every hour and when he comes back his mood has noticeably improved. Can't just be the one Silk Cut then, can it? Always keep a close eye on the very friendly ones, the ones who smile even in the morning. They're usually nicking something. And if you catch anyone at it, you phone this man.' Dan took a card from his pocket and handed it to me.

'He'd be round within the hour. I'm not expecting you to do the hiring and firing. You're not a natural manager, are you? I'm not really sure what you are. You should probably have got your First and become a don instead of just staying in bed with a headache. Anyway, I can re-dress you but I can't reinvent you completely, not at this stage in the game. So you're my spy, Sean. That's what you can do for me. Congratulations on your new appointment. Now let's go downstairs and have a walk around.'

We stepped briskly from one room to the next, from restaurants to bars, Dan making brief introductions as we went. His yellow-clad minions all nodded to me respectfully and smiled. Inside the main entrance stood a woman in a brilliant green trouser suit, her hennaed hair twisted into twiglets, and gilded at the end with tiny scraps of foil. Both Dan and I stared at her for a moment in silence before he spoke.

'Yes, Cinderella, you *will* go to the ball.' Her male companion, a little shorter than she was, dressed in a Hawaiian shirt and a jacket that looked two sizes too large, heard this and turned, with an expression as menacing as he could manage, towards Dan. Evidently defending the good lady's honour.

'What did you just say?' Dan smiled at him confidentially, man to man. He lowered his voice.

'Perhaps you could inform your wife, for future occasions you understand, that in the Royal Borough of Kensington and Chelsea it is still a criminal offence to impersonate a Christmas tree. The management will, however, see fit to overlook the matter on this occasion.' Then we were off once more on our tour of inspection.

'It won't be the same when you're gone, will it, Dan?'

'What won't?'

'Words of welcome in the atrium. Must pull them in, I should think.'

'It certainly hasn't been keeping them away. There's no need to fawn on humanity, Sean. They don't really like it anyway. If I learnt one thing from Shakespeare myself, it was that even the kings hold courtiers in contempt. Rosencrantz and Guildenstern couldn't stand the sight of themselves, as I remember, which is presumably why fate had split them into two, as some sort of amoeboid punishment. Then they couldn't see anything but the mirror image of what they most loathed.' We walked in and out of rooms. The king and his newly appointed intelligencer.

'Don't get too autobiographical, Sean,' he said to me as we were walking upstairs. 'After all, nobody knows whether you have any experience in this business or not. They don't know about your hidden years at the BBC and you don't have to tell them, do you? All they know is you're my man. And that's all they need to know. Keep a certain distance, all right? And if you want to unzip a banana, do it discreetly.' The curious protocol of early Dan, the fruiterer. After our drinks we went outside into the courtyard.

'Give me the details on your driving licence and I'll put

you on the insurance policy. You might as well have the Porsche while I'm away.'

'I can't drive, Dan.' He turned to look at me, then started shaking his head.

'Everyone can drive, Sean. Even my fucking mother can drive. Not that she does, but she can.'

'Well, I can't.'

'The life of the mind, eh? Get it cleaned once a week, then. I can't stand seeing performance cars collecting dust. The place is usually open to between three and four in the morning. Most of the funny business would happen after midnight, if my experience is anything to go by. That's when folks in the city loosen up. And that's more or less when you get up, from what Dominique tells me.'

'A bit earlier.'

'But you're a night owl.'

'Yes.'

'Stay awake then. Now, money. Come back up with me to the flat.' So up we went once more. On the way Dan shouted at one of the young men in yellow suits, 'Get this mess cleared up, David. And quick.' Then we were back in the apartment. Inside the drawer of a desk was a large black metal box. Dan took a key from his pocket and opened it. There were a lot of notes, both large and small denominations.

'Once a week the man whose name is on that card is going to come here and give you some cash. Count it. Then put it in that box. Take what you need out of the box. You've already got board and lodging round here, so you shouldn't need more than five hundred a week. And there'll always be more than that there.'

'Where does it come from, Dan?' He looked at me for a moment as though the years between Mark Scully and the present had never occurred. 'In for a penny, in for a pound, I suppose,' he said. 'Right. This is a cash business and a little bit of the cash comes here, that's all. We don't bother notifying the VAT man or the Inland Revenue.'

'A sort of slush fund?'

'There you are, Sean, you're getting the idea already. If you'd come in with me all those years ago, instead of joining the BBC, you'd probably even have a driving licence by now. So, that's our little pile to keep you in the manner to which, I'm sure, you'll very soon become accustomed. Don't advertise it and don't lose that key. And on the sheet of paper in the bottom of the tin you write down the amount Freddy brings in each week so I can check it all out when I get back.'

I said what was on my mind. 'Is this completely legal?'

Dan sighed and laid a hand on my shoulder.

'One thing always amazes me about you intellectuals: you spend the whole of your life studying information, but you still never get to the facts. And the fact of having money is always a bigger fact than where it comes from. It really doesn't matter whether it's precisely legal or not, does it? As long as only a few of us ever know. We can keep a secret, can't we, old friends like us? After all, you're not going to be much use to me as a spy otherwise. I already pay more than enough tax to keep Yorkshire in social services for the next half-century. I'm not stealing anything; I had to work for it all, you know.'

'Where are you going, Dan?'

'To America. By boat. My new partner's boat. Always fancied sailing the Atlantic.'

'What are you going to do there?'

'I'm going to buy, well, we're going to buy, a company called Arborfield.'

'What's that?'

'Deals in timber. Lots and lots of timber. North American at the beginning and now South American too. One of the world's most popular commodities. We really can't do without it.' He tapped my head gently. 'We'll be needing some to do the repairs on you up there one of these days. Always a good idea to buy a big pile of what people can't do without, Sean. And I don't even intend to sell this place to do it.'

'Is that because it's cheap?'

'No, it's going to be extremely expensive. But the Americans are smarter than we are about how convincing money can be when you just let it get on and do its own talking. It seems to make more and more of itself as it goes along. The line of zeros gets longer and longer. High-yield bonds, my friend, are going to change the way we run the world. You'll see.

'Come to St Katherine's Dock next Saturday. We're having a little party on the boat before we set sail in the early hours. Who'd have thought it? My dear old friend Sean Tallow on the payroll at last.'

That Saturday night I took the tube to London Bridge. I walked around the harbour until I found the *Zeta*, the forty-five-foot ketch where Dan was holding his party. A little crew was standing on the deck with drinks in their hands, talking and laughing. All the navigation lights were on, giving the boat the twinkling air of a window display. Dan was at the prow, clutching one of the stays. He beckoned me on board and told me to help myself to a drink from the buffet table in the cabin. Then he introduced me to some elegant men and women, and finally to his partner, Gerry, an American with golden hair and a heavy tan, who looked about fifty. And he looked rich. His skin and his teeth and his hair all spoke eloquently of the virtues of money. Sunshine, vitamins and money.

'You're the guy holding the fort for Dan here while he makes some on the other side of the Atlantic.'

I nodded. 'I'm his spy.'

'All good businessmen need one.'

'And what do you do, Gerry, when you're not captaining boats?'

'I'm an arbitrageur,' he said. Then with a wry smile: 'Do you know what that means?'

'The only thing I know is that it involves large amounts of money.'

'That'll probably do.'

Later that night I headed back to Chelsea and my new apartment at the top of the Pavilion, and Dan headed west across the ocean to the New World. I thought of his last words to me: 'And call in on Sally from time to time. She gets lonely, too, you know.'

5

In Zimbabwe people are buried with straws coming out of their mouths. When the first maggots emerge into the air, then the spirit is known to be escaping at last. So maggots aren't always bad news. The early alchemists were fascinated by how the lion, that golden king of the sun, could be transformed in days into a seething lake of gentles. This gave them hope regarding the transmutation of metals. They did not concern themselves with such things as flies and eggs, only with the ultimate universality of matter and how different forms could be imposed upon it, depending on the disposition of the planets and the commanding spirit.

I believe in the universality of matter too – always have; believe that if you could follow the stars back to their noisy births, or trace with minute enough attention and exactitude all the myriad subatomic particle dances, the shifting microscopic spiderweb that constitutes the universe, you would find stuff of a unitary splendour, thriving in a nest of time. In the matter of the text of life, I am not a disintegrator: atomism is merely a phase humanity had to go through, a pupa from which it is at last emerging.

So I would have to say that ultimately Daniel Pagett and I

were shaped out of the same material. Only the form differed. Now, of course, his earthly form has been lifted from him. His matter is free once more to transmute into anything. Or anyone. And his spirit is as free as Puck to girdle the globe. Remember, Sean, he had said to me as he drove me along the Embankment in that Porsche before leaving for America, if we could travel at the same speed as money, we'd be everywhere and nowhere at the same time. Money's the same as a shark; it can only stay alive by keeping moving. As he said this, I remembered being back with my grandfather in Blackpool three decades before. As we had entered the aquarium under the Tower, I had looked up at him and asked, 'Are there any sharks here, Grandad?'

'Only those buggers who just took our money at the door, lad.'

Daniel had made it plain once again, over those last few days we were together, that he was disappointed in me; sad that I had simply resigned myself to the world of thought, though he probably overestimated the amount of it there really was at the BBC at any one time. He reckoned thought was the husk left over when the real thinking ended. And the history of thinking was the history of money, according to him. If you had a comprehensive chronicle of every monetary transaction in the world since the beginning of time, then you would know pretty much what everyone had ever wanted or disliked, what they had loved and hated, what they had been prepared to go to war about and on what terms they had finally made peace; even what poetry had been worth reading. Coins changed hands, sooner or later, wherever anything of significance occurred. Where money was, according to Dan, was where the real action took place, and that was where the important thinking was always done, the thinking that kept you alive. I was trying to come up with exceptions to this rule of his, which married thinking and money quite so monogamously, and I mentioned Bletchley Park, briefly remembering a newspaper article I had recently read. At this Dan had grown excited. Bletchley Park, he reminded me, as we cornered hard through a roundabout, was not in the middle of the country so much as in the middle of the war. That was its true location. Otherwise, it could never have attracted so much money. The brains arrived along with the investment. Universities, he said with some vehemence, housed the residue of talk, after history was already settled: the edges and grass verges where you went when nothing much else was moving down the highway. Greensward in an age of tarmac. Did he really say that? I can't think why I'd have made it up. And did he only say such things because he had never managed to get to Oxford? Could there still have been an edge of bitterness from all those years before, when millstone-grit mansions and Indigo from Paris had replaced the last stage of his education? I didn't know, but there was certainly poison in his bite from time to time: 'Tell me the last university that made anything happen, Sean. Whenever anyone wants to make things happen they leave the university, don't they? They have to go somewhere else to really do anything. Whether it's Downing Street or Silicon Valley.'

Myself, I simply sank ever deeper in thought as I sat on the leather seat beside him, trying to work out what I was doing there anyway. But I knew really. I wasn't about to start sinning against time, not at this late stage. I was being provided with the wherewithal for my studies to continue, for the Sphinx's life-threatening riddle finally to be answered. It was one more of life's gifts; they simply came in different wrappings. And now here I was in his penthouse apartment. Tomorrow I would put on the suit he had bought me, and the shirt and tie, go downstairs with an authoritative air and wander about mysteriously, giving the impression that I was in some way important.

Which was precisely what I did.

I don't know if anyone has ever pointed out that different clothes change the way you walk. As I've said before, I seldom buy new clothes, but dressed as neatly as I now found myself after my refurbishment, I found that my gait became more brisk as I stepped from restaurant to bar, from bar to restaurant. I lost my apologetic air as I sat down at one of the tables to order my meal, courtesy of the house. Instead I looked at my watch and then askance at whoever was meant to be serving me, if I judged its arrival to be too tardy, even by minutes. I grew to recognise the regulars, even learning some of their names. One of them I already knew, rendering Dan's introduction superfluous when he showed me round that first evening.

'Come over here and meet the thinnest man you'll ever see,' he had said, indicating the back of a tall drinker standing at the cocktail bar. 'He's a civil servant during the day. Comes here in the evenings to get both the civil and the servant bit out of his system. He lives in a lovely little flat round the corner on Markham Square. Always looking to pick a quarrel, which he usually does very successfully. If he were twenty years younger I'd probably have to bar him. Can be very entertaining, though, if you're in the mood.'

'Why's he so thin? Has he got a disease?'

'No, he's a cerebrotonic ectomorph.'

'How do you know?'

'Because he told me. Not enough spare flesh on him to feed a mosquito.' And then, as Dan tapped him on the shoulder, Charlie Leggatt turned to face me. The goatee beard had gone; the spectacles were now square instead of round. Otherwise he hadn't changed much.

In drink, which was where he invariably already was by the time he arrived at the Pavilion, Charles Leggatt would these days sink swiftly to bright-eyed venom, and when I came down this particular evening to find him at the bar, he had evidently dipped beneath the surface of his civil service persona a good hour or so before. Now he was sharking about at periscope depth, moving in stealthily on any buoyant targets in his range. He was addressing a young man, who was still staring at his copy of the *Financial Times*.

'When I began my career in the civil service, the City was thought on the whole to be a place of probity. If you could swallow the basic premise of the capitalist enterprise, then that was thought to be the most reasonable contraption for keeping it going. There was the occasional scandal, to be sure, but one looked to most of its personnel as men of honour. Now if I were to learn someone works in the City, I'd be disinclined to leave him alone in the room with my budgerigar, let alone my daughter.'

'You don't have a daughter, Charles,' the man said, without looking up from his paper. 'And you don't have a budgerigar either. Your presence is inimical to most forms of organic life. You told me, remember? Now, if I buy you a

drink will you go and pick on someone else for a while?'
Charlie spotted me as I approached.

'Ah, Sean. The prospect of some civilised company.
Makes a bit of a change round here these days.' So we sat
down at one of the tables with our drinks.

'To think that those years at Oxford should have finally
landed us both here, with you as a functionary of Mr Pagett,
no less.'

'And you as a civil servant, Charlie. I shouldn't think
anyone would have predicted that future for you.'

'No. A fellow must look to his pension though.'

'Are you still a revolutionary, out of interest? You shaved
off your Trotsky beard, I see. Did your dialectics go with it?'

'I reckon I've worked out where we went wrong back
there,' he said meditatively. 'I reckon I've cracked it. We had
to get to one side or the other of the endless and voracious
maw of capitalism, but we went the wrong way. I mean, if
profits are all that life is about, then it has no horizon, does it?
And where there's no horizon, there's no light. And we are
obliged at least to *try* and see. We can't live in the dark all the
time, can we, Sean?'

'I do my best.' I was touched that Charlie was still
searching for the mystic cipher, the riddle at the heart of the
system. He seemed to be brooding now about his old beliefs.

'Accumulate, accumulate. According to Marx, that was
Moses and the prophets,' he said, and I thought briefly of
how invisible money had become; no more and no less than
the space needed to fill the inside of the figure zero. But he
was already off again. 'We pretended to choose Demos when
the truth is that we were all really leaning towards Aristos.

Don't get me wrong. I'm not talking about fascism, which is, frankly, even more vulgar than capitalism. But we didn't *really* fancy Marx anything like as much as we did Byron, deep in our hearts. Freedom fighter, lush, lord, fornicator *and* poet. That's one in the eye for the nation of shopkeepers. *Kapital* never had quite the same swing to it as *Don Juan*, if you ask me. Or even if you don't.' Charles threw back his head and recited:

> *'I say – the future is a serious matter –*
> *And so – for God's sake – hock and soda-water!'*

Jess appeared thirty seconds later, carrying a glass, which he placed before Charlie.

'Spritzer, sir.'

'He's smart, that boy. He'll go a long way, if you ask me.' He fell silent for a moment. 'That's the reason we chose Trotsky, you know.'

'Is it?' I asked. It all seemed a long way back and had never much concerned me in the first place.

'Trotsky is the Byron of revolutionary movements, though I suppose Che Guevara has been bringing up the rear lately. Lenin was the bureaucrat, labouring away in his office, filling in forms in triplicate, adding soviets to electricity. And Stalin was the butcher, the big brute in the abattoir we'd rather have nothing to do with. But Trotsky is blessed with a substantial intellect, cosmopolitanism and total and utter failure – he's therefore irresistible. He even had the good taste to get assassinated. And no Trot anywhere in the world has ever really believed they'd come to power. Power, after all, is vulgarity incarnate. But to be in beleaguered opposition, that's Missolonghi. That's to be lordly in your disdain for everything this tawdry world might offer.'

'And these days you get your kicks as a civil servant. What do you think Byron would have had to say about that?'

I suppose I'd pretty much settled in by the end of the week. I was lying on the bed when Jenny arrived with my drink. She placed it carefully on the table by my side, then hesitated.

'Is there anything else I can do for you?' She was attractive. She was small, but her tight yellow jumpsuit made what Dan would doubtless have called a feature of her figure. I could smell her perfume. She pushed her long blonde hair back over one shoulder, and said, 'Mr Pagett told me that, if you wanted the same range of services he did, then I should provide them.'

'No,' I said quietly and picked up my drink. 'That's very kind of both you and Mr Pagett, but it won't be necessary, thank you.' She left then as she had entered, zipped.

6

During the next few weeks I acquainted myself with all the odd corners of the place, the times of deliveries of food and drink, and I tried to memorise everyone's names. I grew so used to silently checking everything and everyone that I even went through Daniel's dresser. There were some nice clothes and one drawer overflowing with invitations, letters, scribbled notes, all dumped in there. One card was scratchily inscribed with handwriting I easily recognised: *Thanks for that. For all of it. I never knew it could be that good. Love, Dominique.* I couldn't work out the date from the smudged postmark, but maybe I didn't really want to know. And there was a photograph of Sally, an early one, just as I remembered her on our first date. I put it in my inside pocket. At the end of the following week there was a phone call from Dan.

'A friend of mine's arriving this evening. Known, for the moment anyway, as Dave Lambert. Take him where he wants to go. Use taxis. Stay with him. He's been having a little surgery and now he needs to visit some casinos. He knows his way around. Be polite. I owe him one. Just remind him to be discreet, will you? On the subject of which, do give my love to Jenny.' And then he hung up.

So I showered and dressed and went downstairs. I visited
each bar in turn, staring with my newly practised expression
of inquisitorial scepticism into the faces of the staff. They had
all started to look guilty. Or at least I thought they had.
Charlie Leggatt was already in the first-floor bar, hungry for
something to get his teeth into.

'That's right, keep an eye on the buggers,' he said merrily,
easily on his fifth or sixth drink. 'His eminence Mr Pagett
always did, and I do rather take his point. Some of your staff
here are lovely – even the chaps are lovely, if it comes to
that, but I don't doubt they're not past a bit of thieving,
given the opportunity. If twenty years in Whitehall has
taught me anything, it is that the urge to acquire pelf, to
defraud, embezzle and purloin, is one of the most universal
human instincts, second only to breathing, eating and
sleeping. And the other thing, of course. I've noted from the
newspapers that several old Etonians this very year . . .'

'Shut the fuck up, Charles,' I said quietly. His voice was
loud. Both staff and customers were staring over in our
direction.

'I beg your pardon, sir?'

'I said, shut the fuck up.'

'I find that remark very offensive, Mr Tallow. I'm inclined
to take my custom elsewhere.'

'So, take it.' And with that, I went to check that the tables
had been laid properly in the restaurant.

At eight o'clock Dave Lambert arrived. I was down in the
bar, sipping meditatively on a gin and tonic. He would, I
suppose, have looked like any other American businessman,
except for the one noticeable detail: his face was entirely
covered in white bandages, leaving only a slit through which

he could see, and another through which he could breathe, speak and eat. His hair sprouted from the top in small curly squibs. Jet black. One of the yellow-clad barmen led him over to me.

'Mr Lambert, this is Sean Tallow.'

'Hello, Sean,' Dave said in a low voice, holding out his hand. 'You're a friend of Dan's and that means you're a friend of mine too.'

'Let me get you a drink,' I said.

'I'll take water. Carbonated with ice. Need to keep my mind clear for the night ahead.'

Half an hour later we made our way in a taxi towards the Cromwell Road.

'Only a little place,' Dave explained, 'but I'd like to get my hand in again, before the bandages come off.'

The taxi was pulling up outside the L.A. Limits and we climbed out. I paid the cab and we stepped into the big luxurious interior of the casino. Dave went into action. Blackjack. For an hour he played for ten-pound stakes, as I watched from the side. He was starting to do well. The pile of chips in front of him was growing. Then he asked for the stakes to be raised from ten to a hundred and was immediately hushed across to another table, where he now played alone. I whispered urgently as we made our way from one patch of green baize to the next, 'Dan said to remind you to be discreet,' but Dave only patted my arm. He was happy.

One hour later a gentleman in an evening suit appeared and asked if we could accompany him into the next room for a moment. He was a small, neat man, with grey hair and an air of great authority.

'I'm not sure I know your name, sir.'

'Lambert,' Dave said, evidently accustomed to this routine.

'We'll cash in your chips for you, Mr Lambert, and I hope you've had a pleasant time, but the management would appreciate it if you didn't return. You seemed to be monitoring the cards very well, if our observations are anything to go by. I can't help thinking you may be in the wrong place. This is merely somewhere Joe Punter comes out for a decent evening, sir. We're not really set up for professionals. Had some sort of accident, by the way, have you? In which case, I'm sure we'd all like to wish you a very speedy recovery.'

So there we were back on the pavement, around midnight. I managed to spot a cab.

'Do you have a hotel, Dave?' I said as we climbed in, but he ignored me.

'Take us to Dexter's,' he told the driver, his earlier affable mood now vanished entirely. The taxi started off.

'Dave, do you think it's a good idea . . .'

'Just can it,' he said, so I did and stared through the window as the blur of the London night went by. When we stopped at the traffic lights where Knightsbridge turns into Hyde Park Corner I found myself looking at a couple on the pavement, the girl in tears and the boy with both his hands on her shoulders, talking and talking as she stared down at the ground and wept.

We entered the club in Mayfair with no trouble, though Dave's bandages provoked a few glances. I sat down near the blackjack table where he elected to play. The female staff in their tight clothes pointed their breasts in one direction or another. It was sex for someone else, not you, that was for sure. Dave played for hours, until after dawn in fact, and I was wondering how long it would take before we were ejected from there too, but as it turned out we had no cause to worry. Dexter's was happy enough to have Dave Lambert patronise their premises that night, whatever the level of his professional expertise, for the simple reason that Dave kept on losing. Seriously losing. By my count the end of the session left him down the better part of forty thousand pounds. When we came out and climbed into our taxi, he said, 'Is there somewhere you could take me, where I could have a stroll? This hasn't been a very good night, Sean, and I won't be sleeping for a while yet.'

I told the taxi driver to take us to Battersea Park, and there we walked up and down until Dave's nerves eased up a little. We walked for two hours or more, until I was dropping on my feet.

'Did Dan tell you anything of this?' he said, pointing to the bandages that covered his face.

'No.'

'Had to change the scenery above my neck. I'm a professional gambler, Sean, but you probably worked that one out.'

'Dan only said you'd had a little surgery.'

'Do you know what a card counter is?'

I shook my head. And then he started speaking with an unexpected fluency, almost lyricism, as we walked back and forth at the edge of the river, by the Peace Pagoda. Up and down we went as he talked, by way, I suppose, of exorcism for his losses, and I just tried to keep myself moving. He'd been barred from all the big casinos, apparently, both in

London and the States. The card counter, he informed me, had a precise and capacious enough memory to note every card that had already slicked out on the baize out of the packs that were shuffled on a blackjack table. This nudged the odds fractionally away from the house. Not enormously, but sufficiently that the house didn't like it. 'Really don't like it, Sean.' In fact they so disliked it that they would soon make it plain how much they would prefer you not to come back, once they'd noticed who you were and what you were about. Hence his surgical identity switch. Dave talked on as we walked. The card counter, he explained, must suppress every hunch or glitch of spontaneity, in order to lessen the lethal machinery of the odds. His memory of the occurrence of all the preceding cards, together with the unremitting application of basic strategy, was the only route to success. His job was to become an automaton, severing any link between memory and imagination. No playing on hunches. He could only beat the system by making himself equally systematic. Tonight, though, he had failed. Tonight it was as though he had been entirely human. A quirk apparently. A statistical oddity. You certainly couldn't have blamed his spontaneity because there hadn't been any. But by now I was feeling entirely human too.

'I'm going to have to get some sleep, Dave. Really am. Sorry.'

'Sure. I'm sorry too. Sorry to have kept you up. I was sharp earlier.'

'It doesn't matter. Any friend of Dan's.'

We sauntered at last towards Chelsea Bridge and a little boy who was walking along with his mother stopped in front of us, staring up at my companion with his bandages blanking out his face and said, with the nib-like precision of a child's voice, 'Mummy, is that man dead?'

When I finally got back to the apartment I switched on the television without the sound and lay on the bed. Open University. Some film about whales. They sleep upright, it seems, just under the surface of the water, shifting about gently like grey megaliths that gravity has stopped holding in place. It looked as though Stonehenge had started dreaming. And as I sank into sleep myself I reflected that the only thing I could be sure I knew about Dave Lambert was that his name wasn't actually Dave Lambert.

7

Mirrors. I've spent a lifetime avoiding them, but now I was trapped inside them since Dan had spanned them along each wall in every bar. Looking into them one evening, I noticed as though for the first time the whiteness of my skin. So many faces around me looked golden and tanned against it, and I looked as though I'd never seen sunlight in my life, never encountered a vitamin, never been slapped about by the wind. The nocturnal existence. On one of the Open University programmes I'd watched in the early hours, I'd seen images of creatures which live underground all the time, losing their pigmentation and finally going blind.

I had never even thought about it before, but standing naked and glancing in the mirror at dawn the next day I registered the fact that I did indeed look like the victim of some deadly modern plague, or just an old-fashioned example of pitman's pallor. So when I was next walking through South Kensington a few days later and saw the sign saying Sol, I went over and read it carefully. Below the piece of paper that read *Staff Wanted: Enquire Within*, were these words: *Acquire an authentic suntan swiftly and safely*. So I walked down the steps and into the upholstered cellar that was the suntan parlour.

A slightly obese man with no tan at all extolled the virtues of tanning to me. He spoke of vitamin enhancement and the lowering of blood pressure, but I cut him short and told him I just wanted to be golden instead of white.

'Do you tan easily?'

'I don't know. I've never done it.'

'You obviously have extremely fair skin, so you'd best put this cream on.' He held up a tube to show me. 'You're starting from zero, so a course will almost certainly be necessary. A two-week course. Would you like to pay in advance for that?' I nodded.

'That'll be a hundred and fifty pounds.' I looked at him in disbelief and he shrugged. 'It's still cheaper than going to Ibiza. And nobody will vomit over you down here.'

So for the next two weeks I walked each day from the King's Road to South Kensington and lay underground, sandwiched between the glass slices of the tanning machines, as the glowing tubes burnt their way through the lotion to my skin.

I now had the texture of the sun all over my body, but I still hardly ever stepped outside while it was actually shining, except for my trip each week to the London Library, where I seemed to be making my way through some of the darker swathes of books. The static electricity that accrued about certain shelves seemed to give off a particularly potent charge these days.

I was now once more plugged into the right city, and my hours were largely the hours of darkness. There is a topography of the mind that corresponds precisely to the mapping of metropolis. I'd come to feel the circuitry in both had hidden, unexpected parallels. And now I was back on my chosen streets again. I read as much with my shoes as with my eyes. I'd made a note of Paracelsus's remark: 'He who wishes to explore Nature must tread her books with his feet.' And what was true of old fields was even truer of modern roads.

I suppose it must have been about this time that the School of Night stopped being confined in my thoughts to the sixteenth century. That eerie constellation had already sunk into my mind, its shape ceaselessly dissolving and reforming, one moment a tower, the next a scatter of shivering reflections on the Thames. History always flows through the courses of rivers, so Ralegh had written in his *History of the World*. I started to see them everywhere: behind the closing door of every School of Day, a School of Night. Just another name for any place where the darkest suspicions might truly prosper. I listened intently to the rumours given off in the bars of the Pavilion.

If Shakespeare really had based his Ferdinando in *Love's Labour's Lost* upon that actual Ferdinando, Lord Strange, his early patron, then it was a cruel enough joke. For soon after coming into his full title as fourth Earl of Derby, Ferdinando had died in circumstances as sinister as his name (something else that issued from the left hand of God). Died horribly and inexplicably. It seems that he had been approached by a papist conspirator in a bid to have him connive at the crown, since his mother was descended from Henry VII and since the outcome of Elizabeth's reign was still a long way from certain. Derby denounced the traitor, who was promptly executed. But soon after he himself died, some said by poison, some by witchcraft, for his portrait was found with a spike of his own hair stuck through the image of his heart. Perhaps the Catholic conspirators had taken their revenge for his betrayal. Or perhaps it was down to William Cecil, Lord Burghley, whose own intelligencers were then seeping across England like an invisible contagion. Whether he was killed by the State or the State's enemies, his pain was presumably undiminished. The poison in his gut had him writhing like a snake.

And now I would see a School of Night behind the weary smiles of the married couples down in the bar, as one's boredom started to overtake the other's love, or in the unmarried as I saw them returning through the dark to solitary rooms and silence and the growing whispers of mortality. Just a flicker in the eyes, no more, but enough to start me thinking. I even read one day about the School of Night concerning Hitler, for whom there was no School of Day at all. They spoke of golden showers in the bedroom, or even the possibility that he needed to have his flesh pastured by faecal matter. That would have fitted with the nihilist's true worship of the wrong end of creation. But out of what black hole came his hatred of the Jews? A Jewish whore was conjured, who transmitted the spirochaete to his blood, leaving Hitler merely to translate that syphilis into politics. Alternatively, a Jewish trader had cheated him and the crater thus shaped inside by that anonymous schlepper's pelf could only get filled up again after the entirety of Jacob's nation had been buried in it. An eclipse of malignancy. I read that Eichmann said he could laugh his way into the grave knowing how he'd helped turn five million human beings to ash. Perhaps the most self-enclosed circle of darkness anywhere on this earth was that described by Primo Levi, in the story of the man who had uttered the word why, in regard to some outrage in the death camps. The guard had answered, 'Hier is kein warum.' Here there is no why.

Then back to Ralegh in the Tower. Everybody in the England of that time had to dream continually of an ending in the Tower, for the Tower was the reverse of the jewelled crown, and the closer a body came to the highest in the land the greater that body's chances of confinement. The Tower was the enthronement of despair, the place where all preferment foundered. So what did Ralegh do there? Wrote a history of the world, acres of verse; conducted scientific experiments with Hariot regarding matters terrestrial and celestial, grew herbs for medicines, cast horoscopes, meditated ceaselessly upon his death, for his death was the one companion that could never leave his side in that place. Studied alchemy, with the Wizard Earl for company. He even had his portrait painted with his son Wat, the son who was later to die on an expedition commanded by his father, to Orinoco in search of gold to quell the king's displeasure, a seam of ore bright enough to make the sun blink, however briefly. He had been released to redeem himself and had failed. Ralegh was thus to find himself in old age with nothing at all to gainsay the darkness. Thus did time and providence reverse themselves. Then back with him to the Tower, the true home of the School of Night, the museum of all dreams of rebellion, where the law kept the tightest of holds upon all those who might conceivably escape it.

I had long before become an ochlophobist. A detester of crowds. Not merely nocturnal but noctivagant, a night-walker, a prowler, a nomad of the midnight streets, attempting to abolish the distinction between the light that comes from outside and the sort that shines within. And I was even sitting once more at a high window looking down at the world and its traffic. The Thames was only a few minutes away. The only river I could actually see was the moving, smoking, metallic river of motors. And when I moved amongst the crowds in the bars below I was now invisible.

Transparency, I'd always known, was the only effective way to vanish, and nobody ever noticed me these days except for those whose attention I needed. I had learnt the first crucial trick of my new trade.

My walks in the dark had acquired different locations. I seemed sometimes to hear the acres of grass breathing in the park across the river. Battersea Power Station loomed out of the dark, a torn and gaping ruin still waiting for capital's promise to fulfil itself. There was the church where Turner had sat in the window sketching, until he retired to the other side of the river and refused to be known as anything but Captain Booth. Then the house on Cheyne Walk, where Dante Gabriel Rossetti kept his jabbering menagerie of exotic animals, armadillos, kangaroos, wombats and raccoons, shrieking and defecating in the night and making poor mad Swinburne even madder than he was already. And just down from there the statue of Thomas More, slowly silting from the exhaust fumes of the ceaseless cars flowing up the Embankment. That was where the barge had come for him, to take him away for arraignment at Westminster and imprisonment. He had told William Roper then that the field was won, and had seemed almost glad to go. To the Tower, of course. Where else?

8

One of them kept smiling, never stopped smiling, and I remembered Dan's words that those were always the ones to watch. I kept an eye on him day after day. Discreetly. But with extreme suspicion. One night I caught him at it. I had been standing at the bar listening to the conversation of the couple sitting at the table behind me.

'It doesn't matter what you do at the end, John. That's not how it's transmitted anyway. The doctor told me yesterday.'

I never took my eyes from his hands and this time I saw the twenty-pound note make its way back out of the till and furtively into the side pocket of his yellow jacket, and I was there behind him in seconds. I pulled the note back out of his pocket and held it in front of his face.

'I think it's time you left,' I said. 'Go and get changed and clear off. I don't want to see your face here again.' And he fled without another word. There was a hush to the place that night. Charlie Leggatt held up his glass towards me in a theatrical toast.

'Ladies and gentlemen, Pagett's silent zany has finally come to life.'

I felt curiously exhilarated. I went back up to the

apartment early. There was only one bookshelf there, which Dan had stacked with lavishly illustrated volumes I had barely looked at. I took one down. It was a photographic record of some bordello in New Orleans at the end of the 1890s. I was looking for sex, but I kept seeing death instead, perfumed and proffered bodies communing only with the dead. I thought briefly of Jenny. Then I opened up Dan's drawer and took out the card I'd seen so many times before, the one he had left there, the one with the word Oasis printed on it, along with an address. I took a handful of money from the metal box and set off to find the place. That wasn't difficult: the taxi driver seemed to know it well.

It must have been there that Kate Halloran had learnt to powder her body. They all did it, to make the flesh smell fragrant and to render it dazzling white under the spotlights. So many naked breasts moving about you in the darkness. Everything else they wore was black, so the only visible thing that moved in the murk was naked flesh, and I felt as though some potent electric memory had been triggered inside me. There was a thrill of recognition, but I couldn't have told you of what. Darkness and mirrors. I soon started going every week in search of white bodies in the dark.

In the early hours of the morning, or the early hours of the evening, I would walk along the river. Up and down the towpaths relentlessly, obsessively. Why? It occurred to me at dawn one day as the city was growling crossly into life. I was on a pilgrimage again, wasn't I? I was re-enacting the Corpus Christi processions of my boyhood when, dressed in white and holding our crosses and icons aloft, we had walked the streets of my northern town, harking back to the days when hundreds of thousands of feet stepped solemnly from sacred well to burial shrine; from holy grave to reliquary. Our reflections in dusty shop windows, our hymns laid on the air, assaulted the dark streets, seeming to open a lethal crack in their blackened, millstone-grit façades. All pilgrimages make the clock hands turn more slowly, at least for the contours of their duration, beckoning heaven into a renewed scrutiny of the earth and a renewed communion with it. The pilgrim marks out sacred circuits; his itinerary inscribes a slow but potent current. His journey is a prayer, a topographic emblem only entirely visible in any case from above.

Canterbury had become the greatest medieval centre. Canterbury, in whose ecclesiastical shadow Marlowe had been raised until he was ready to shine in his own darker fashion. Here had been the shrine of St Thomas à Becket, slain by hands and swords eager to assuage the king's wrath, and now remaining as a potent indictment of the whited sepulchre of earthly power. You can almost hear the sigh of relief, even perhaps a belch of satisfaction, as Henry VIII smashes to bits those monuments worn smooth from the urgent caresses of millions of penitent fingers. But there had also been plenty of pilgrimage tracks and circuits through the streets of London itself, before the Reformation sealed them off with State hygiene, just as the invisible portcullises of security checks and CCTVs have now started their enclosure of the modern City. After all, a mighty town's wealth was measured then not so much by its merchantmen and traders as by the collection of sacred shrines it could boast. Any city in Christendom needed to be a rich lectionary of holy relics and legends.

So here I was, pacing out every foot of the Thames, from

the Tower to Hampton Court, as though that tidal thoroughfare still carried on its back the kings, queens and traitors who'd once been its weighty cargoes; as I'd once paced out the route from Tower Hill to Tyburn, coming in the process to feel I could actually smell the entrails pulled steaming from disembowelled martyrs, as the traffic of Marble Arch buzzed relentlessly around me, in its riotous, entropic order. It was still there, the inquisitor's mighty and allusive question: history as self-incrimination, with your conscience duly scraped.

And as I walked back and forth, up and down Blake's chartered streets gridlocking the Thames, I started to believe, without any artificiality, that time was now indeed standing still, or had actually run backwards – this being one of the more occult properties of any pilgrimage – so as to lessen the distance between where, in the world of longitude and latitude, we stand and what we might in faith and truth come to apprehend. I was glad at last that I'd never learnt to drive, no longer embarrassed about it. After all, no one has ever unthreaded time's labyrinth like this from the inside of a car. You must touch the holy tracks for yourself. The truest pilgrims even take off their shoes and kiss the ground until their lips, along with the soles of their feet, start to bleed.

Pilgrimage. *Peregrinatio*. The soul in its wild wander, out on the roads in search of a home. *Pegrinus*: foreign. Here is no abiding city. We discover nothing for as long as we feel at home. The imagination is everywhere a stranger's kingdom.

I had moved the table over to the window so that I could sit there and work with the world beneath me, just as Ralegh and Hariot had done on the top floor of Durham House.

And now, fresh from my new training in the dark world of suspicion, I was at last ready for my task. Like the members of the School of Night themselves, I no longer accepted what tradition had bequeathed me. However venerable the legend, I now doubted it in its entirety. I'd become as dubious of the historical certainties I'd been handed as I was of the motives of every shifty, light-fingered employee downstairs. I had become, I suppose, my own black intelligencer. I had even started looking in the mirror at last, but with suspicion, suspecting a subterfuge, and I was right of course, for there was one. I was it. Dan's man. Dan's cryptic agent with the golden skin. Whoever was emerging out of that silver pool, it no longer looked like me.

Now at long last I had come to study in detail, and without prejudice, the darkest of all the rumours that have emanated from the School of Night, the one that might at last make sense of the crowding doubts that had been accruing in my mind through the years. Many accepted that Marlowe's hand could not be disentangled from Shakespeare's in the early works. Even the most orthodox of Stratfordians, including Sidney Lee, who had effectively invented the modern orthodoxy of the Bard, were in agreement that the following plays could not be settled between the young actor from Stratford and the young scholar from Canterbury: *Titus Andronicus*, *Richard II*, *Richard III* and all three parts of *Henry VI*. That's a fair bit of the corpus to be another questionable body underneath the accepted body. In fact there's no doubt that if Marlowe could ever have been viewed as a serious candidate for the true authorship of the works attributed to Shakespeare, that case would have represented the gravest threat ever posed to the

Stratfordians, but they have always had one simple and seemingly unanswerable response to this lethal enquiry: Marlowe had died on 30 May 1593. But had he?

I studied the evidence in detail. I went down twenty or thirty times to Deptford Strand and St Nicholas, as though proximity to the reported events might somehow let the truth leech into me out of the ground, out of the air. I became convinced, though I couldn't prove it, that this stretch of the river had provided these lines in *Hamlet*:

> *And duller shouldst thou be than the fat weed*
> *That rots itself in ease on Lethe wharf,*
> *Wouldst thou not stir in this.*

I became more and more convinced that Marlowe had not in fact died that night in Deptford in the house of Mrs Bull. That instead his friend and patron Thomas Walsingham had arranged for a drunken sailor of his height and build to be killed with a poniard through the eye, and to be dressed in Kit's clothes. A local inquest had been fixed and swiftly conducted. Promises had been made; money had changed hands. Strangely, no friend or relative of Marlowe's had been summoned to identify the body and where the corpse was buried has remained a mystery to this day. 'Nearby' says the plaque, hardly even taking the trouble to believe its own words.

This way Marlowe did not have to return to Star Chamber, and so did not have to talk of what had happened in the School of Night. He was spared the ordeal of incriminating all his friends under torture. He was spared and so, of course, were they. All three men in the room with him when he 'died' were in the employment of Thomas Walsingham, and all three were taken back into that employment without question after they were released from their perfunctory imprisonment one month later. Marlowe was undoubtedly Walsingham's favourite. It was at Walsingham's house that he mostly stayed. Some have even said that their relationship went far beyond mere friendship. It would have been a curious act to have taken Marlowe's murderers back into his employment so swiftly, so entirely without recrimination. So if Marlowe didn't die, then what did he do?

He was spirited abroad, under a false name, in some chartered vessel covered by the Kentish mist. He went to live in the north of Italy, there to continue writing plays for the rest of his life, plays of mystery and devastation, plays about murder and disguise, about how a human being is an exile even from himself. Plays endlessly concerned, obsessively and inexplicably concerned, with people who die but are not really dead, who come back after ten or twenty or thirty years to be met with tearful incredulity by those who thought they'd witnessed their demise. But there was a problem. If these astounding works were to be published, under whose name could that be done? Well, who better than another low-born theatrical character with gifts above his station, though nothing like Kit's, born in the same year, his father another leather worker, and with whom Kit had already collaborated, using the actor for his working theatrical knowledge while he provided all the intellectual substance? Who better than a man from Stratford desperate for coin, who knew his way around the London stage? They had something on him, in any case, for one of Kit's

discoveries in his murky work at Rheims was that Shakespeare was not merely Catholic, but had done some business
for the cause during his hidden years amongst the recusants
of Lancashire. This he very much wished to keep secret.

Thus did these inexplicable works of loss and desperation
come to be published under the name of the reasonably
gifted actor from Stratford-upon-Avon, whose first published
work appeared a few months after Kit's own disappearance
from the world. Thus did Marlowe, the divinity student and
translator of Ovid, provide all the material which could not
have been provided by the somewhat less sparkling intellect
of William Shakespeare, a man who left not a single book in
his will and spent his last years relentlessly pursuing matters
pertaining to his tithes. Not alchemy as Ralegh and the
Wizard Earl had done, not witchcraft, a subject that evidently
fascinated Marlowe and the author of *Macbeth*, but tithes.
Tithes and litigation. As though nothing in the world truly
mattered except for money. How many zeros might balloon
in mischievous vacuity behind a particular figure. This man,
a zero in his own right, was perfect. Tom Walsingham
arranged it and from then on Marlowe, already posthumous,
used the fellow's name, perhaps even his hand, but had no
need of his spirit, having substituted his own instead. Thus
did the dead speak through the living. And this would also
explain the curiosity, often remarked upon, of what appears
to be a considerable knowledge of continental Europe on the
part of a man who never seems to have journeyed south of
Bermondsey. It might also explain the kindly tone so often
employed in the collected works when the word spy appears,
for Marlowe had been one himself while he was at
Cambridge. It was the State, after all, which had employed

him to travel to Rheims, there to impersonate a Catholic at a Jesuit college to ensnare real Catholics and facilitate their imprisonment on their return to England. This might also explain the fascination with disguises that flows through the plays like a continuous and mighty river. And it explains the oddity of what I had so constantly noticed: that this man seems to know from practical and sinister experience something about murder and its accoutrements. Marlowe had killed at least one man and others had undoubtedly attempted to kill him. A whole state waited to do so, should it ever be revealed to them that he was still alive somewhere and writing.

And it finally explains that otherwise inexplicable peculiarity of language in *As You Like It*: 'When a man's words are misunderstood, it strikes a man more dead than a great reckoning in a little room.' How can anyone be *more* dead? One is either dead or one isn't. Comparatives don't come into the matter at all. Unless, of course, one is universally thought to be dead, while in fact continuing to live and write under another's identity. The dead man's fingers are holding the pen that signs the living name.

Banquo, the Marlowe figure in *Macbeth*, dies but does not stop acting; in fact he is more potent in his presence after his death than before it. Now he really does terrify the king.

And lastly it explains the desolation of the tragedies, though explain is here surely not the right word. Some things can never be explained. For what could be more desolating than to live a life as someone else, in disguise, displaced hundreds of miles from your country and your lovers; or to be the greatest writer of your time, perhaps of any time, and for no one but you and a few secret confidants, in another country, to know it? This is the desolation of being no one with no real body. This is hell, to know you are not out of it.

9

On this one particular day I simply kept walking. It was as though I needed to connect up the Tower of London with Hampton Court, as though to tread with my own feet the path between those two centres of power might in some way complete the circuitry, free the years that were flowing round my mind's topography.

And that was the only reason, I swear, that I found myself standing opposite Thames Ditton. I stared for a moment as I realised where I was, and then I took the photograph of Sally from my pocket. A fisherman was sitting on the towpath, his silently squirming yellow bowl of maggots at his side, a bright circle of yellow discontent, an antinomian inversion of the sun. Twenty feet away a heron stalked and stared into the water. Its manic watery eyes reminded me, with sudden vividness, of Becky Southgate. I started walking. As I passed Hampton Court I saw the geometric topiary behind the wrought-iron gates: that's a king's way with nature for you – discipline it into the pattern that most pleases you. There were red and yellow roses, like the ones that once grew on my grandfather's wall. By then King Henry was already trophied with the badges of his regal disease.

And twenty minutes later I was knocking on Sally's door.

'What do you do, Sean?' she asked me as she made coffee. 'You don't live with Dominique any more; you don't live with anyone any more. You have no woman, you have no children. What do you actually do with all your time? Or have you just become my husband's eyes and ears at the Pavilion?' She brought the coffee over to the table.

'Who do you think wrote Shakespeare, Sally?'

'I would have guessed Shakespeare, but I suppose that's far too easy.'

'Yes, that is too easy. One advantage of living alone and mostly at night, without children or women to take up your time, is that you can get into focus things other people stay blind to. A dead man wrote his works for him, I'm pretty sure of that now.'

'Isn't it a bit difficult, though, writing things from underground?'

'The dead sometimes control the living, or didn't you know that?'

'Well, they don't control me, Sean. And the living don't either. Not in that way; not even Dan, just in case that's what you've been thinking. I know a lot of people do think it. And they're wrong.'

We walked into the village talking. I carried her bags of groceries as we came back. Everything seemed easy and intimate as if all the years between us had simply fallen away. I suppose that's why I did it.

'No,' she said and lifted my hand gently from her breast, where I had just placed it.

'Dan wanted me to come, you know.'

'Maybe he did. I want you to come too, Sean, but not that

237

way. My husband may not be the faithful type, but I am, all the same. I live here on the proceeds of his various endeavours. You know, it surprises me more and more that you and Dan ever became friends.'

'Why?'

'Because you just take whatever life gives you and Dan never takes anything life gives him. Whatever life gives him, he takes something else instead.' I must have looked sad. She reached across and stroked my cheek. 'Those are my children playing upstairs as well as his, you know. And that's the greatest single compliment life ever pays you, Sean.'

'What?'

'A child's trust. I don't want to have to start lying to anyone. I certainly don't want to have to start lying to him. And neither should you. Anyway, you had your chance.'

'What do you mean?'

'You know exactly what I mean. What a lovely tan you've got.'

That night I went to the Oasis again. Found someone with blonde hair and Sally's build. White flesh in the darkness, a whiteness going deeper down through the well inside me than I knew was possible. I hadn't realised before that I went that deep. All paid for with Dan's money.

The next day I read this one line in Marlowe: 'See, see, where Christ's blood streams in the firmament.' Sacraments. I had been raised on them, after all, those threads providing a link to sacred possibilities. Transubstantiation of man and matter. I had never resolved to do without them and I suddenly felt their absence acutely. I walked through the streets to the place I had noticed so many times before during my wanderings. I entered the little church on Cadogan Street and knelt in prayer for ten or fifteen minutes. When a small priest entered silently to tend the altar, I stopped him as he stepped back down into the nave.

'Could I speak with you? I need to talk to a priest.'

'Is this something you need to do now?' The hair was cropped and beneath it the large eyes looked intently, with a mild smile, but an intelligent one. I would have said he was about sixty; I would have also said he was a little tired.

'Yes,' I said. 'I'm afraid it has to be now.'

He led me up the stairs to his room and once we were settled I said, 'I've been committing someone else's sins.' The priest seemed to bethink himself for a moment, then the smile returned as he spoke. 'They're seldom original, I suppose. I can't think of a newly minted one in thirty–five years of hearing confession. Goodness can always take one by surprise with its freshness, but sin I suspect was ever a little hackneyed. Or second-hand if you prefer it.' My eyes had been straying around the room. There were tiny crosses wedged into gaps in the bookshelves, icons, reproductions of Romanesque ivories: Christ in agony; Christ in glory; saints luminous in their aureoles. My sense of urgency made me lean forward in my chair.

'No, I don't mean that. I mean that I took over someone else's sins, accepted them as a gift. Took them on as a job, accepted them as a career. I didn't even decide to commit these sins, I simply inherited them.'

'The sins of the fathers, you know, are . . .'

'Not my father. He had one set of sins, but not these. These sins belonged to someone else. Someone closer to me than my father ever was. And I took on his sins as easily as putting on his overcoat.'

'And are you still . . .' He faltered.

'I'm afraid that I'll only stop if the opportunity disappears.'

'Are you sorry for these sins? You were the agent, after all, if not perhaps the instigator.'

'Yes, I'm sorry. But I'd be sorry if the sins were to go too. I'd miss them, I can tell you. One in particular.'

'You're not unique in that, of course.' He had crossed his hands neatly in his lap. He closed his eyes for a moment. 'St Augustine would often sit for hours lamenting the sins he'd failed to commit. They can undoubtedly seem most welcoming, in retrospect. But it is a necessary part of the act of penance to make a firm act of amendment. You must resolve not to sin again, even though the resolve may prove frail.'

And I did so resolve, receiving the words of absolution before I stepped back on to London's streets half an hour later, temporarily shriven and cleansed. The burden of sin had been lifted from me. For the moment anyway.

10

I was writing, silently, fluently, for everything was now in place. My thesis was finally ready for expression. I wanted to speak to Stefan again, to explain the distance I'd travelled since we'd last discussed these things. I was thinking that I might phone him and suggest we meet somewhere. Just the two of us. Without Kate; I couldn't face that. There was a knock on my door and then Jess came in.

'It's Charles Leggatt,' he said. 'You'd better do what you can to get him out, Mr Tallow, or there'll be a fight down there. Not that it would be much of a fight: given the state Charlie's in, he'd be lucky to hit the floor.'

'What did he do?'

'He told Eric Johnson that' – here Jess paused to make sure he'd remembered the words precisely – 'that the act of sexual congress with his wife was like coition with a dead fish.'

'I'm surprised he phrased it so delicately.'

'He didn't the second time.'

'Coition with whose wife? Charlie's or Eric's?'

'Eric's, I'm afraid, though Charlie's so drunk it's hard to tell.'

By the time I arrived down there, Eric Johnson was

already attempting to manhandle Charlie from his bar stool, but Charlie was resisting with liquid and inebriate manoeuvres of his arms and legs. Eric saw me approaching.

'Just get this creep out, will you, before I deck him.' And somehow I managed to reach my arm around Charlie and speak sufficiently soothing words to charm him into going downstairs with me. Once I had him outside on the pavement and we were making our erratic way towards Markham Square, I relaxed.

'Why did you have to insult the man's wife, Charlie?'

'I merely pointed out that making the two-backed beast with that particular lady was as pleasurable as coupling with a dead fish. I happen to know of what I speak.'

'You've had a dead fish then, have you, Charlie?' He stopped and stared at me with the exaggerated dignity of the truly drunk. The end of his red tie had somehow ended up stuck into the top pocket of his suit.

'Yes, since you ask, I have. A rather sizeable old trout, as I recall.'

'Was that with or without the boiled potatoes?' Charlie was lapsing backwards. I just managed to catch him before lapse turned to lurch.

'Did you see the wretched woman?' he said, permitting my supportive arm to grasp him round the back once more. 'With her gimcrack gewgaws over her tits, which she was flashing, Sean, let's be serious about this. A woman does not have to be quite so décolleté these days, unless she's a professional. There are plenty of alternative necklines for the bar-room attire of the fashionable floozie.' He stopped and turned to me with great solemnity. 'Am I getting old or are their breasts getting bigger?'

'That's not an either/or, is it – logically speaking?'
Charlie's face brightened under the street lamp.

'You mean, I could be getting older *and* their breasts could
be getting bigger?'

'I don't see why not.'

'So there is a God after all.'

We arrived at his flat. I helped him down the steps to the
basement and, after much fumbling with his key, he finally
let himself in.

'Will you be all right, Charlie?'

'I'll be all right, and I'm indebted to you. An Aristos
amongst the baying hordes of Demos. Good night, sweet
prince, and hordes of angels choir thee to thy rest. That's not
right, is it?'

'Near enough.'

And then one day the telephone rang. It was Dan.

'You'll have to get out, Sean.'

'How do you mean, get out?'

'By tomorrow the bailiffs will be in. Grab everything you
can, cash, anything, and go.'

'But I don't understand . . .'

'The whole thing's gone down, my friend. I've gambled
the entire company on this deal. You'll probably be reading
about it in the papers over the next few days. Gerry's already
in jail, where I have no intention of joining him. Which is
why I'm getting out of this fucking country by the back
door. Pronto. They've gone insane. Six months ago we were
heroes; now we're criminals. But I can't stop what's going to
happen at that end, and it will happen quickly, believe me.
Legally speaking, unless you've been very stupid, you don't

exist. Keep it that way. Don't hang around long enough for them to find you. Take whatever you can and then vanish. And keep well away from any investigations. I'll be lying low for a while myself. Nobody's going to know where I am. Or who. Do me one favour, will you, Sean?'

'What is it?'

'Stick a few hundred in little Jenny's hand. With my fondest regards.'

Then the phone went dead. For five minutes I sat there staring down at the road and its metal snake-back of traffic. Then I packed my notebooks and my clothes into my two bags and put the black steel box in there too. I walked downstairs with all the insouciance I could muster and a large brown envelope in my hand. I went round each till in turn and methodically extracted half the notes, making a great show of counting them and scribbling figures on to the envelope. When I'd collected everything I thought I could get away with, short of attracting unwelcome attention, I went and found Jenny. She was leaning against a wall in the kitchen, smoking.

'Jenny, could I see you outside for a moment please?' I said, in my most authoritative voice. She stepped out to join me and smiled, as though I'd finally had the sense to realise what I'd been missing all these months.

I pressed two hundred pounds into her hand. She stared down at it for a moment, then she looked back up at me.

'I can come up later. What time would you . . .'

'Daniel Pagett sends you his love,' I said and walked off.

Five minutes later I left the building, carrying two bags. For the first time in months I noticed Dan's Porsche in the courtyard, covered from roof to bumper in a fine layer of dust. How angry he'd have been if he'd known, but it didn't seem to matter too much now. With my grandfather's snooker cue angled jauntily over my shoulder, I set off up the King's Road in search of a new home.

Part Four

This thing of darkness I acknowledge mine.

WILLIAM SHAKESPEARE, *The Tempest*

1

It was part of the Orphic religion to utter the words *soma seme* – the body is a tomb. Similarly the alchemists believed that only once putrefaction had set in could the sacred spark trapped inside the material be released – the divine light that had fallen into darkness. The work, the opus itself, could now at last commence. Dan has surely started rotting, so maybe that's his free flame out there finally, igniting the darkness, and starting to dance on the water. But I think it's more likely to be dawn, come at last. The long night of memorial perplexity is over. The last sentence I read in the Hariot Notebooks was this:

If only the end of this school of ours heralded a dawn. But I fear there is merely a different darkness falling.

With my two canvas bags on my shoulders I walked away from the Pavilion towards South Kensington. I had often noticed a shop there with a window full of cards. I read them for the first time, made a note of one of the addresses and went round to see if the advertised bedsit was still available. It was.

'You'd have to give me a cash advance if you want to move in today,' said the middle-aged lady with the mop of white hair. I gave her the money and she seemed satisfied. Then, once I had placed my notebooks on the table and my few clothes in the wardrobe, I walked around the corner to Sol. A beggar squatted on the pavement. I dropped my pennies from heaven into the cap that lay between his legs. His head jerked forward automatically in acknowledgement, producing a little blizzard of dandruff.

There was still that sign saying: *Staff Wanted: Enquire Within.*

Malcolm had been losing a little weight. These days he was invariably dressed in a tracksuit. His life had evidently acquired a new régime.

'Do you want the facial or a bed?'

'I want a job?'

'Come again.'

'It still says *Staff Wanted* outside.'

Malcolm thought for a moment and then said, 'All right, I seem to have known you long enough. Let's try it for a week anyway. You'll soon get the hang of operating the beds and cleaning them. The only other thing is taking bookings and payments, but that's not too difficult. I'll be glad to get out in the fresh air during the day, to be honest. I've taken on a few girls down here, but it's never worked out. The men are always trying to talk them into joining them on the beds. The money's not brilliant, but it's cash in hand. I'm not interested in tax or National Insurance or any of that stuff. As far as I'm concerned you're nothing to do with me or my business, officially speaking. That suit you?' I nodded. 'You can start on Monday then.'

As I made my way down to the London Library I thought briefly of what Malcolm had said. The truth is I had never even thought about the matter since leaving the BBC, where all my deductions had been made automatically for me. Tax. National Insurance. All such things had disappeared from my life, not to mention pension funds, savings, building society accounts. I seem to have had a certain genius for never much considering these things, things that so many other people spend most of their working hours poring over. I felt the distant possibility of a migraine returning. Odd that, when I thought of it: I didn't seem to have had one ever since I'd started working at the Pavilion. So they really do go as you solve the problems; it had been something trying to get in, after all. Taxes and insurance. It seemed a bit late to be addressing the issue now. How was I supposed to explain what I'd been doing all that time at the Pavilion? Anyway, have no care for the morrow, that's what it says in the Bible, so it must be true. Such distracting concerns are one of the capital sins against time. Walter Ralegh had backed me up in 'Ocean's Love to Cynthia': *Hold both cares and comforts in contempt.* So I decided to forget all about it.

After I had been to the library that day I walked down to Trafalgar Square and went into the National Portrait Gallery, where I climbed the steps to the top floor. This Elizabethan display never failed to touch something inside me: so many grandees, spymasters, explorers; the eyes of the killers and the killed speaking with such silent eloquence of their power and their fear. Behind them all, magnificently mounted, was the queen herself, the milk-dab of her face a pearl set amid the spectrum of her grand brocade. The centre of the widening circle of the world. Bald as a badger, some said, though they said it in whispers, out of earshot of ministers of State, or any versifying flatterers on their way towards the court. Syphilis, contracted from her mother perhaps, but the tides still heaved towards her, as navigators looped out like ecliptics from Gravesend.

The following week I started. It didn't take long to learn how to switch the bed-timers on and off, and once I had settled into the routine I did it without thinking. Taking bookings, taking money, switching on fans and coolers, handing out lotions, chatting about the variety of skin types and the expected speed of tanning, wiping the sweat off the glass surface afterwards. There were occasional surprises, little murmurs rising just above the thrumming of the beds. The heat, I supposed. But mostly it was routine. I started bringing my notebooks down with me, turning the pages as I waited for the next phone call or the next customer. I threw away the pile of defunct motoring and gardening magazines to make shelf space for my few remaining books.

My view had by now become defined, dogmatic: the man from Stratford had not written the works attributed to Shakespeare. That doltish-looking maltster and usurer from Warwickshire, without a book in his will, whose daughter remained illiterate all her life, and of whom no mention was made at the time of his death as having written a single word, could simply not have composed this body of work more brimful with life and learning than any other that's ever been created. As early as 1728 Captain Goulding had spoken derisively of the army of chuckle-headed historians who would have been required to supply William Shakespeare with all his necessary data. He had once done some acting, certainly, and picked up a fair amount of the equity in one or two theatres. He had even assisted Marlowe in a few early pieces. But I could see more and more clearly that Shakespeare wasn't who he was supposed to be. It had confused many, at the time even the man's own contemporaries. Ben Jonson obviously thought he was the author of the works ascribed to him, but then, if the secret had been well enough kept, why shouldn't he have done? Jonson wasn't in the room with him when the plays were being written. After all, the queen had thought Anthony Blunt merely a scholarly and patriotic old curator until someone had whispered in her ear about his decades as a Soviet spy. She'd seen him more often than Jonson ever saw Shakespeare. People can be other than we think. This would also explain why the Warwickshire man didn't carouse much, but tended, by report, to stay alone at his lodgings most nights. Best keep yourself largely to yourself and thus keep out of danger from any detailed questioning.

No, it had been Marlowe all along. The dead man had written the words, using the living one as his mask. Thomas Walsingham had facilitated the deception and Thomas Thorpe of St Paul's Churchyard had been sworn to secrecy for his part in the production. And there were, of course, two other people who knew all about it: Walter Ralegh and Thomas Hariot. Now I found more clues whenever I opened up the Collected Works. I could seldom read more than six or seven lines without cryptograms starting to emerge. Here, for example, was one of the sonnets:

> . . . *nor that affable familiar ghost*
> *Which nightly gulls him with intelligence*
> *As victors of my silence.*

Whole books had been written trying to establish the identity of the rival poet mentioned here. But for the classically minded, as Marlowe undoubtedly was, there was another way of writing the word William: Guilliam. And that's the way it is written on the memorial in the church at Stratford-upon-Avon. Guilliam. The gull. Also the victor of Kit's silence, since he was the one who reaped the worldly rewards due to the other.

As I turned the pages of my notebooks, I realised that I had been edging towards this recognition for a long time, even when I'd had no idea where I was going. There was this entry from years before:

Hamlet's the first modern figure in drama or fiction for a very simple reason: the further he delves into the past the more of a catastrophe he becomes, the more he questions his own identity. His ancestors in the genre would simply have taken their cue for revenge and got on with it, but the burden of the past settles on to Hamlet's soul like a shrieking monkey. He takes revenge instead on himself; he finds it impossible to see how he could put things right. And he doesn't, does he? He makes things worse. He retreats into a labyrinth of self-examination. He damages everyone around him before he finally gets to Claudius, and a few minutes later almost anyone of any interest is dead. Then the stage is inherited by Fortinbras – about the nearest we get to a fascistic automaton before the invention of fascism itself.

But Hamlet's the first figure of modernity for another reason too: the possibility of suicide is the very condition of his thought. Self-extinction is the only clear exit from his dilemma. His own power, in other words, cannot resolve the fractured world he finds himself inhabiting; or it can do it only by turning against himself. Seconds after the poisoned sword has been poked into his flesh, it is in his hand being wielded against others – it's almost as though it was always in his hand, as though the others were vicarious exponents of his own search for an exit. He is liberated into action only by his mother's death, a death she has brought on by her own sexual infatuation. It is as though he has committed suicide by using someone else's hand.

The more he finds out what's really happened in the past, the more trouble Hamlet's in and the less sense he can make of it. Isn't the same true of the School of Night? Four hundred years on and we still don't know how or why Marlowe died in Deptford that day. Or even if he did. Some might say that it's hardly surprising we don't know: it was four hundred years ago. But this could be reversed. We've had four centuries to think about it and ponder it and weigh up the evidence. If we haven't come to a firm conclusion by now, what hope is there of establishing what went on a mere forty years ago? You can understand the judicial employment of torture, in a way. It's an aspect of the State's exasperation: will you, for God's sake or the devil's, just tell us what actually happened? If not, we'll have to question you to the full. The scraping of the conscience, it was called back then.

I bought the papers for a few weeks, something I had stopped doing since leaving the BBC. Maybe I'd felt a little let down by the news after performing such sterling service on its behalf for so many years. But now I scanned the headlines with my old expertise. The story about the collapse of Arborfield emerged first in the financial sections, but made it finally on to the news pages. There was much talk of junk bonds, of a change of mood in the US regulatory bodies, a new intolerance in regard to asset-stripping and high-yield refinancing. It was hard to divide the politics from the economics, but then I suppose it always is. Arborfield had certainly not helped its own case by the nature of its expansion into South America at precisely the time that the dubious logging industry down there was coming under scrutiny for its potentially catastrophic environmental effects. They had been cavalier in this regard, though, as far as I could see, no more so than most of their competitors. One or two of the papers carried a picture of Gerry, with a caption saying that after a few days in prison he had been released on bail. And there was an occasional mention of Gerry's partner, the English tycoon Daniel Pagett, who had also been guaranteed to make a fortune had their scheme actually come off. He, it was thought, had left the country, but no one knew where he had gone. His own companies elsewhere were all in liquidation.

During this news trawl I also noticed something else. Henry Willoughby, late of my Oxford college, had been charged with spying. It seemed that Henry had become so disillusioned with the British secret service, which he had served mostly in Northern Ireland, that he had toddled along to the Russian embassy in London one night and popped a list of his fellow agents through the door. He had been drunk: like so many famous English spies before him, he was an alcoholic. The Russians had been convinced that an attempt to contact them characterised by such blatant ineptitude had to be a set-up. They had complained to the British authorities and Henry had been caught the following week. Then it had also transpired that the figure I had known at Oxford had not been entirely what he'd seemed.

The Anglo-Catholic with the upper-class accent had a few years before been a working-class boy in a council house. He had, said the authorities, always had some difficulty in blending his different personae.

One evening I walked down to the King's Road. There were notices in the windows and on the door of the Pavilion, but it was still open; figures were walking in and out; I could even make out one or two yellow suits inside the foyer, but I didn't dare go in. Instead I went along to Markham Square and knocked on Charlie's door.

'Well, well, well, if it isn't Mr Tallow.'

'Hello, Charles,' I said. 'Keep your voice down, will you?'

'Ah, staying out of harm's way, are we? I did note your somewhat speedy departure from the scene. Come in and have a drink.' And as I walked through his elegant hallway, hung with watercolours, and into his kitchen, he turned to me and smiled.

'Keeping a low profile, Sean?'

'Exactly, Charlie. You have put it with characteristic succinctness.' He poured me a glass of chilled white wine and then he explained, with the expertise gained from his profession, how the receiver had evidently decided that the best way to attempt to liquidate the portion of debt accrued by Davenant's was to keep the business going, which they were endeavouring to do.

'They did drive off in Mr Pagett's nice sports car. Mind you, it needed a wash by then. Daniel was always so fastidious about it too. I did get the feeling they'd love to have a chat with you though.'

'I'm not here, Charlie, all right? I'm not anywhere.'

'I spend half my life pouring drinks for chimeras, so let me

refill yours. Do you remember the Dong?' he said meditatively, looking out of the French windows into his neat little
garden.

'The Dong?'

'He was a poet, so I'm told anyway. Used to sit over in the
corner of the Pavilion on a Friday evening. Nose glowed
with forty years' straight whisky. If there'd ever been a
power cut, he could have charged you lot utility rates. Had a
young chap there with him last week, a nephew or
something, who informed me he was about to go to Scotland
for three months. To stay in a remote castle, on some new
course of therapy specifically designed to discover the inner
self.

'I told him I'd discovered my inner self years ago, without
too much effort being required. Found it repellent, quite
frankly, a ceaseless whine of appetite and mawkish blather,
yearning for the womb all over again, so I reverted
immediately to the outer self, where I've been more than
happy to remain ever since. Why do you think people are so
hard on repression these days? It is, after all, the only thing
that makes life amongst us even halfway tolerable.'

'I never thought of you as particularly repressed, Charlie, I
must say.'

A photograph had caught my eye and I went across to
peer at it. Charles was standing in his morning suit outside a
church, and beside him in her bridal gear was a figure I was
sure I recognised from years before. I looked more closely.

'Yes, that's right,' he said, 'it's Becky Southgate.'

'And what are you doing there?'

'Marrying her.'

'You *married* Becky Southgate?'

'Oh, don't sound quite so disapproving, Sean.'

'You told me she was a hysteric and a liar.'

'You didn't see her at her best that evening. I mean, she could get a bit worked up from time to time, but to be fair she was never a liar.'

'So Comrade Protheroe and the Disciplinary Committee were right after all?'

'I think even Becky came to see that she'd overreacted to what is, when all's said and done, a pretty traditional way for a man to express his physical admiration for a woman. In some cultures it's the required first step in a courtship ritual. It's thought very rude if you *don't* put your hand there.'

'I wouldn't have thought that Becky would have been very keen on marriage.'

'She wasn't, but her father was. And Becky did love her old daddy.'

'So what happened?'

'She found after a while that she didn't believe in marriage after all. Well, not to me anyway. We got divorced.'

'Any particular reason?'

'Tell me something: does it strike you as a realistic condition of life, Sean, to ask a man to stick to one pair of breasts? I mean, you say "I will" on some misty Saturday morning and then that's it for ever. Just the one pair.'

'I don't know,' I said. 'How many pairs do you have access to these days?'

'None.' He pondered this for a moment, then looked at me intently, his bony features quizzical and quirky. 'Are you suggesting we should try to average it out? Decide if three pairs a year at one stage of your life really justifies having no pairs at all at another? Is that what you're getting at? A sort of statistical approach to the mammary question?'

'I don't know, Charlie, but I suppose it might be one way of looking at things, don't you think? How long have you had this flat, out of interest?'

'My old man passed this on, pausing only to pass on himself first. I should be grateful. In fact, I *am* grateful, believe it or not. What have you inherited, Sean?'

'A snooker cue.'

'Do you play snooker?'

'No.'

We walked out into his trim and tiny garden. The liquefying throb of a blackbird's song seemed to moisten the evening air.

'Do you know what that noise is, Sean?'

'Joy?'

'Territoriality, I'd say. Thank God the little buggers aren't armed.'

2

How quickly months turn into years. Come to think of it, I really didn't miss being employed by my old friend Dan all that much. I suppose I so easily fit in with the conditions wherever I find myself, not wishing to commit any of the capital sins against time or to push against rivers, but I did wonder now and then what had happened to him. For some reason I simply couldn't bring myself to call Sally. One day I walked along the towpath between Hampton Court and Kingston and stood opposite Thames Ditton. I knew, even before the new people stepped out on to the lawn, that the Pagetts didn't live there any more. Down in that cellar I tried hard to think things over, but nothing made much sense, so I simply kept on with my work on the Shakespeare mystery, following my tutor's priceless advice to spend the rest of my life studying the School of Night. At times I felt I was beginning to disappear inside my own cryptographia, which is perhaps understandable. Shakespeare's text, after all, is not a stable thing. The folio edition of *Henry V* says, unequivocally, in regard to Falstaff's death: 'For his Nose was as sharpe as a Pen, and a Table of greene fields', whereas today any edition will read: 'for his nose was as sharp as a pen, and 'a babbled of green fields.' Such being the present principles of emendation, which shift with vertiginous force from century to century. We've always changed the Shakespeare text at will to suit our latest preconceptions.

After the chemical wedding comes the dissolution of forms, darkness and eclipses. She's an elusive one, Lady Alchymia. I remembered once reading how Richard Pryor, while attempting to freebase crack cocaine in his basement, had suffered first-degree burns when his equipment exploded. Disreputable alchemists were still locked in their cellars searching for the veins of gold.

One night, as I was closing up after treating myself to an hour on one of the beds, I called Dominique on an impulse. I wasn't even sure if she'd still be at the same address.

'Where the hell did you go, Sean?'

'Not far.'

'You took your time letting us know.'

'I'm sure you all survived.'

'One of us won't survive much longer, though.'

'Don't understand.'

'Dan's sick, Sean. Very sick. Come over for dinner tomorrow and I'll tell you about it.'

The next evening we sat eating pasta and drinking red wine, as though the years that had passed between us had altered nothing. Except for little hints, italic lines about Dominique's eyes, flecks of grey scattered through the ringlets. She looked as though the transference had finally started working and now she really was receiving the sorrows of fractured hearts from the other side.

'You look better than I've ever seen you,' she said. 'You

should have introduced yourself to daylight earlier.' I didn't tell her that all my sunshine came from underground.

And then as we ate she spoke of Dan.

'He's had radiotherapy and chemo, but it can't be long. He's a sorry sight, Sean, to be honest. I can't remember the names now but there are three sorts of tumour that affect the brain and he's got the big one. He'd like to see you, I know that. But you'd better make it sooner rather than later.' And she gave me the address and telephone number.

'Ramsgate?' I said, baffled.

'Don't ask me. He's bankrupt, of course. The big house they had on the Thames was taken and Ramsgate's where they ended up. Maybe he'd put some money in his wife's name.'

'Sally,' I said quietly.

'That's right, Sean. Your old girlfriend, Sally.'

'You got quite close to Dan, didn't you?'

'He'd told me he was getting divorced. I don't make a habit of screwing up other people's marriages.'

'I thought you hated him.'

'No, I never hated him. It's hard not to be fascinated by a man like that, isn't it? You always were.'

'Was he a good lover, out of interest?'

'No better than you. Different, but no better.' I found it hard to believe her.

'You never told me I was a good lover.'

'You never asked. You never told me whether I rated much either.'

'You were the only one I'd ever had, so I didn't have anything to compare you with.'

*

The next day I called and Sally answered. Her voice was subdued.

'Nice to hear from you, Sean. We thought you'd vanished off the face of the earth. Dan's not too good today or he'd come to the phone himself. Could you travel down at the weekend? It's only a couple of hours on the train.'

I stared out of the window all the way from Victoria, and when I arrived I walked about for half an hour, along the coastal road, before I managed finally to direct my feet to the house. Ramsgate. Despite the new marina, the place felt as though out-of-season winds had blown away the heart of it some decades before. Like so many English seaside towns, it had lost the will to continue. The stucco that remained on its old houses was peeling from the walls and the facias of the new shops and fast-food dives were just as tawdry, newer maybe, but equally dismal. It felt like a place that no one actually came to any more; these days everyone merely passed through. It was a transit camp beside the grey, unlovely swill of the Channel. The few amusement arcades bleated disconsolately as unsmiling children rammed coins into their slots. What on earth was Daniel Pagett doing here?

It was on the East Cliff, a big white building with a curious little tower. There was a similar one further along. Presumably there'd been a vogue for turrets in Ramsgate some time around the 1920s.

I pressed the bell and Sally answered. She was older too, still attractive, but a little worn all the same. Some of the sunshine inside her had been put out. One or two shadows had finally started breaking through.

'Hello, Sean. God, you look good. Spending the winters in the Caribbean? You're positively glowing.' Her northern accent had not shifted by a single vowel. We kissed, awkwardly, and gave each other a gentle hug.

I was sitting in the living room looking out through the window towards the Channel when Dan came slowly into the room. His head had been shaved and there were mottled patches where I supposed they'd had to drill. He was wearing a short-sleeved shirt, the sort they wear in hospitals, and his arms were covered with blue patches, still sore where the needles had gone in. All of the old Dan had disappeared from his walk, which was painfully lumbering and unsure. And he'd put on weight. For the first time ever, Dan's belly was bulging. So quick bright things come to confusion. But there was still some of the humour in his eyes. I gave thanks for that as I stood up and walked across to him. I took him gently in my arms. I was frightened of squeezing anything in case it hurt.

'You look well, Sean,' he said slowly. 'The years are getting kinder to you at least.'

And then we sat down. Sally brought us some coffee and I asked questions which Dan could sometimes answer, sometimes not.

'It comes and goes,' he said. 'Sometimes I can remember things, but I can't remember what you just said. The only thing I can ever remember is that I'm hungry. No, there's the headaches, I remember them too. You used to be the one with all the headaches, Sean. How are yours now?'

'Seem to have gone, pretty much.'

'How did you manage that?'

'It was something trying to get in.'

'What?'

'I think the pain was the sensation of something trying to

get into my head, not out of it. Everybody got it the wrong way round, including me for a while. Some information needed to be transmitted, and now that it has been, the pain has largely gone away. Well, that's not entirely true. It still happens on big occasions.'

'Strange you say that,' he said, with a hint of the old brightness in his expression. 'My doctor says that no one really knows what pain is. So I said, I know what pain is, my friend; maybe I should wear the white coat around here. He carries on, my doctor. He says, pain: it's a form of information. He says, it's a way of moving messages around the body. The steroids, he says, send the information on, now what did he call it, a diversion from my brain. And some of this information ends up in my stomach. Which is why I'm so ravenous half the time. All the time, I mean, not half the time. I'm even hungry when I'm sleeping, Sean. I have these dreams. Never mind. Now I can't remember what I was talking about.'

'Weeks,' Sally said to me later in the kitchen. 'Maybe days. They're surprised he's lasted this long. This Monday he lost most of the sense from his left side for the first time, which is why he has to walk so carefully.' She looked at me and smiled. I remembered her sad smile from all those years before. 'He wants to talk to you, Sean. For some reason he was always convinced you'd turn up before he died. And he says he needs to have a talk with you. By himself. He's written some things down on sheets of paper. That's the only way he'd be able to remember everything he needs to say. And he doesn't want me there.'

'Do you know what it's about?'

'Probably.'

'You don't want to tell me anything about it?'

'No, love. Only this. You don't go and do anything you really don't want to. Do you understand that? We'll survive, you know, one way or another. We always have. Well, when I say we . . .'

She stopped then and she was gone before the tears came, and a few minutes later Dan came back in, clutching his sheets of paper. He spoke with difficulty and had to keep returning to the beginning of some of the sentences, but little by little it dawned on me what he was talking about. I wondered briefly whether the tumour had so mangled his mind that he had entirely lost any capacity for coherent thought. He *could* still think though, haltingly, fragmentarily, and with recurrent difficulties of expression. But he certainly could think. When he'd finished, he sat back exhausted and I looked at him in silence, pondering all that he'd told me.

'But what would I actually have to do, Dan?' He looked up, obviously weary with the effort of so much communication.

'The same as you had to do at the Pavilion, that's all. Just be here. Everything's set up, but she needs the company. She can't do everything by herself.'

'I need to go back to London to work things out, Dan. I can't answer your questions straight away.'

'You didn't say no.'

'I didn't say yes either.'

'But you didn't say no.' Then Dan was somewhere else entirely. Things he must have had on his mind.

'Funny how we're wrapped up in air,' he said. 'I saw this thing on the television about some of the other atmospheres out there. Little envelopes of dust. There's that gull again outside trying to shout down the wind. What am I talking about, Sean, do you know? Didn't you used to explain things to me.'

'Only once, I think.'

'And when was that?'

'On your wedding day.' He turned back from the window and looked at me with a bewildered expression.

'What did you explain?'

'That you were getting married. To the assistant librarian on the seventh floor.'

'That was very good of you, Sean. That was a good thing to do.' He fell silent for a moment and seemed to look around the room in sudden panic, as though he had mislaid the next word somewhere amongst the furniture. 'We did manage it once here since I came back from the hospital. I sort of stumbled into her. I reckon it must have been a charity fuck, to be honest. From Sally's point of view, that is. When I came, I remember there was this amazing rattling and shaking going on down there, like an engine blowing up on you on the motorway, but you know the odd thing was it all felt as though it was happening to somebody else. Felt I should get on the phone about it. Report it to the council. Maybe it *was* someone else. Couldn't have been you doing it, could it, Sean, cascading away inside her like that?' His old smile had returned again briefly. 'I seem to recall you did have a couple of my women back there, didn't you?'

'No, Dan,' I said quietly and then felt sorry at the confusion that returned to his face as I said it. 'You had a couple of mine.'

'Ah. Well, I knew it was something like that. Just remind me, what was it they kept behind those soft doors, Sean?'

'The soft room, Dan. The softest room.'

Then Sally let the doctor in. A small thin Indian, with a ready smile and a pair of enormous steel-framed glasses on his delicate nose, he nodded to me then turned to Dan.

'And how is Mr Pagett today?'

'One day closer to not needing your services than he was yesterday,' Dan said, with his eyes still closed. 'But thank you for your curiosity.'

On the train back I finally opened the paper I had bought at Victoria that morning, and reading automatically as you do when your mind is elsewhere, I saw the item about the newly discovered Hariot Notebooks and where they were exhibited. I've just deciphered another sentence:

Sir Walter's ravaged face: how badly death must desire the sons of men, to be filled with such an unholy passion to possess us.

3

When I got back to London I phoned Malcolm from the station and told him I wouldn't be able to work that week and perhaps not for a while. He sounded taken aback. I suppose he'd grown so used to having me around. The next day I travelled by tube to the exhibition of the Hariot Notebooks. That's when I transcribed what was written and took it back to my bedsit to start the decoding. That's when I made out the words 'the School of Night'. And the next day I made my decision.

I called Sally from the pay-phone in the hall downstairs.

'Are you sure? Absolutely sure?'

'I'm sure.'

'So when will you come?'

'Tomorrow.'

The train was delayed by half an hour and I found myself thinking again about the recent crash at Paddington. I had read all the accounts in the papers of how the trains had screamed into one another, steel splicing steel, the carriages swerving wildly and turning over, flinging their cargoes about like clothes inside a tumble-dryer, except that these clothes had actual flesh inside them, soon to be torn, severed and scorched featureless by the flames already eating them. Acrid smoke blackened their insides.

Within minutes the scene had fallen silent except for the cries and the hissing of metal, a much greater noise now coming from the sirens shrieking their way through London's traffic. And then it had begun, the curious bleat of lamentation, the mobile phones scattered throughout the wreckage with their ceaseless wails of 'Greensleeves' and 'Eine kleine Nachtmusik', digitalised musical phrases, activated by the wives and husbands, the mothers and sons of those missing commuters. For hours this bleeping had continued, until one by one the batteries inside each compact plastic device went flat and the noises died. Then the people on the other end of the line, accepting at last that all day they had been sending messages to corpses, crumpled to their knees in the fading light of their hallways. Now finally they could weep without let or hindrance.

Soon enough I was on the train, remembering once more the photographs and the interviews with the bereaved. How quickly the curious pornography of grief had begun, legions of counsellors swarming and buzzing over their latest carrion. And then I saw a tiny item at the foot of the page, about Miller's Peas being withdrawn from the supermarket shelves. Someone had been poisoned. How things do come around.

Sally met me at the door.

'Dan's lying down upstairs. Come and get a coffee and then go up to see him.'

When I entered the bedroom I realised what death smelt like: it seemed to be eating away at the air in there, gradually vacuuming its potency.

'I knew you would, Sean, I told Sally you would. I said,

now that he knows he'll never invent a dog that doesn't shit . . .' But he'd lost his thread. He seemed too weak to move much and I lay my hand on his arm, cratered and bruised from all the needles that had gone in.

'Go down and talk to Sally. She can explain things better than I can. She's been the strongest one round here for a while. And when you've done, come back up and see me. All right?' I nodded and went downstairs.

We sat together in the front room on the sofa, both staring out at the mist gathering over the water. I only took in certain phrases as she talked.

'The usual line has been English cigarettes from here to Andorra, where there's no duty,' she said and took a sip from her mug. 'You take them out lawfully, duty-free, then it's just a question of getting them back in without the excise boys noticing. That's the scam down the road in Dover. Dan, as usual, had a good look at the rest of the world and then did otherwise. Everyone else is functioning out of Dover; so he decides we'll have to come to Ramsgate. Who'd have ever thought that Daniel Pagett would end up living in Ramsgate?' She laughed quietly to herself.

'So we bought this extraordinary bloody house with its tower and its two-foot white perimeter walls. And Dan then made friends with a funny little man in the bonded warehouse.' She looked up again and out towards the sea. It was beginning to be grey and bleak now on this December day. I followed the line of her eyes and found myself staring at the ferry leaving port and heading out into the Channel. A muffled bell made a dim sound.

'If goods land in this country for trans-shipment and are

put into the bonded warehouse, as long as they're properly sealed and that seal remains unbroken, then they haven't landed here at all, or not so as to incur any of the normal duties anyhow. All the paperwork says is that the goods go into the bonded warehouse for trans-shipment. And if you can arrange for that same paperwork to accompany lots of bona fide goods going out to where they say they're going, while still keeping enough of the original stuff here . . .'

'You pocket the difference.'

'Well, you and the nice man in the bonded warehouse share the difference between you. With a big trailer moving three times a week, it's quite a big difference, believe me.'

I did a few swift mental calculations from the figures she'd mentioned. Thirty times ten thousand. There were too many noughts on the end, it couldn't be right. So, I did the sum again more slowly, but it came out the same. So many zeros. As she had said, it was a big difference.

'As you can imagine,' she said, 'the Customs boys don't like it one little bit. Which is why Dan's been so keen we should complete our schedule according to plan and with no change of personnel. Except for the one, of course, the one that couldn't be helped. Another few months of what we're doing and we'll own the house and have some put away for the future as well. Can't think of any other way of getting it now. He'd hoped to have the whole thing settled before he died, but it does look as though, just this once, he's got his timing wrong.'

And then I went back upstairs.

'All sorted?' Dan said.

'Pretty much.'

'There's one more favour you can do for me, Sean. I know you won't let me down.' He managed to gesture for me to lean over him, and whispered in my ear.

'No,' I said, 'I can't.'

'You can do anything now.' He gestured me down towards him again and whispered something in my ear, something so terrible that I nearly hit him.

'Do it,' he said. So I did.

4

At first you think maggots are silent, but they're not. If you sit in the room with them long enough you'll start to hear their sound – a tiny sound, the sound of thousands of white-blooded bodies the size of a baby's fingernail, crawling and flexing over one another. This sound grows by an infinitesimal amount each day, until suddenly it goes completely silent. Chrysalis stage. Then you forget all about them for a week or so. Not a murmur. Suddenly there's a black buzzing like something waiting to explode. A shifting bomb in a bag.

As my grandmother used to say, if you want to hear God laughing just tell him your plans for the future.

When I arrived back in London a few hours later there was a note stuck in my door. Please Phone Mrs Pagett in Ramsgate. Urgently.

I went slowly down the steps to the pay-phone in the hall and called the number.

'He's gone, Sean. An hour or so after you left I went up to see him. He must have died in his sleep.'

'It's a blessing.'

'You haven't changed your mind?'

'No.'

'So when will you be down?'

'The day after tomorrow,' I said. 'I have something to do first.'

The next morning the wood yawned and splintered, making the loudest sound I'd ever heard in my life, and I took those notebooks out of that old Victorian case in the museum. Then I went to the church in Cadogan Street.

The priest listened to what I told him and tried not to look astonished at the things I had just done, but I knew that he was. Then I explained to him what I was about to do.

'You can't absolve me for sins I'm intending to commit though, can you?' He thought for a moment.

'Do you feel sorry about them?'

'I'm sorry that it has to be done.' He paused again and then looked down at his hands, which were crossed as usual in his lap.

'Do you sincerely wish to be reconciled to God?'

'Yes.'

'You wish to be in communion through the sacraments?'

'I need it now more than ever.'

'Then I must, as far as possible, enable you to do that. It is of course the case that one of the conditions of making a good act of contrition is to make a firm act of amendment, but one accepts that very often a person leaves here to continue with the selfsame sin he has just come in to confess. We are fallen, one and all. It was the sinners and criminals Jesus came to forgive, not the just and the righteous. This crime of yours, the one you are about to commit, have you inherited it, as you have so many other things in your life?'

'Yes.'

'But the original perpetrator is now dead, as I understand

it. So why is there still a necessity to continue?'

'His wife's not dead.'

'And you love his wife?' The question was so straightforward and unexpected that I didn't have time to think about it.

'Yes,' I said.

'So the crime, although objectively bad, is being committed out of love. Who is the victim?'

'The Customs and Excise, I suppose. They'll be missing out on some of their importation levies.'

'There is no violence?'

'No.'

'And you will promise that this crime will cease as soon as whatever necessity is presently impelling it has passed?'

'Yes. I don't want to do it at all. And neither does she.'

'Then I will give you absolution. Perhaps only the grace which the sacraments provide will be able to bring the matter finally to a close.'

So it was that when I took the train back to Ramsgate, I felt cleansed once more. Spiritually cleansed in readiness for what was shortly to become my third major felony.

Now here I am in the Ramsgate dawn. And this history is finished at last, because what's happening now isn't history any more. The day has finally arrived, and I'll have to note things down as we go along.

16 December

At eight the bell rang while I was standing in the kitchen. I went and opened the door, and stumbled back briefly, convinced now that I was in a Jacobean tragedy after all, as I stared at the face of Daniel, unspoilt by the passing years or the ravages of that last disease. Only as the young man held out his hand and introduced himself did I realise, by the difference in his voice, that this must be Dan's son, aged twenty-one, and newly flown back from Australia. I tried to explain who I was as we walked through the house, but I'm not sure he was really interested. Why should he have been after all?

'Uncanny, isn't it?' Sally said later.

We sat in the big black cars and motored slowly to the crematorium. I was surprised at the Catholic priest who was there to conduct the service, particularly when he said, 'Daniel lived outside the faith for most of his life, but made his peace with God before the end.' That confused me so much I had to be prodded by Sally when the time came for my reading.

She had asked me to choose something for the brief ceremony. The only thing I could think of was this passage from Thomas Lovell Beddoes's *Death's Jest Book*:

> *'Tis better too*
> *To die, as thou art, young, in the first grace*
> *And full of beauty, and so be remembered*
> *As one chosen from the earth to be an angel;*
> *Not left to droop and wither, and be borne*
> *Down by the breath of time.*

Beddoes had been at my Oxford college in the early

nineteenth century, the college Dan never quite made it to, so busy was he by then selling perishable goods. The poet had studied there before changing to medicine, like his father before him, who had apparently performed human dissections in front of his children, thereby hoping to inculcate in them a proper scientific interest, but all he managed to instil in Thomas was a lifelong obsession with death and putrefaction. Everything maggoty held him. His teacher in Germany, a formidable man called Blumenbach, kept an enormous collection of skulls, which ceaselessly fascinated his English student. Beddoes poisoned himself in 1849 at the age of forty-seven. Dan never got to be so old.

Dominique was there, dressed in black. She looked beautiful, though very forlorn. Her face, which had so often appeared to me to be sleeved in glass, had now shattered entirely into the shards of her tears. I realised how much she must have loved him and for some reason I was glad. She asked me how I felt as we sipped our drinks back at the house and I told her I was fine.

'Migraines?'

'No. I was sure there'd be one today. But nothing.'

'Maybe you've finally cracked it then, Sean. Head cleared up; all the information from the outside finally got in.'

'Does that mean my hidden desires have at last been set free then, Dominique?'

'I don't know what it means. I suspect I know a lot less these days than I did when we used to live together.'

I smelt a familiar smell. The smoke from a menthol cigarette.

There she was, Dan's mother, wandering about. It seemed to me that she had barely aged. She was accompanied by a younger man, who had driven her to the funeral.

'That bitch gets other people to do her dying for her,' said Sally, in the first unkind comment I'd ever heard from her lips. 'Dan always said she'd see him in the grave. First her husband, then her son. If I were that chauffeur, I'd watch out.'

Evening. A gibbous moon and the same gull gallowing outside, maybe the one Dan used to listen out for. Sally started to tell stories of Dan's younger days. How quickly grief can be overlaid with laughter, without in any way ridding you of the mourning.

17 December

Unusually for Hariot, the second half of this second notebook is dated. I suppose this was because of Ralegh's impending execution. Hariot observed the days passing with the same gravity as his patron, perhaps a little more, for Ralegh was capable of swoops of gaiety until the very end. It is still a laborious task decoding this writing, even though it is hardly a complex cipher, merely a series of displacements of letters of the alphabet, according to their numeric sequence. These strange reported utterances from Ralegh:

> Then the mare's belly grows mighty and the foal drops.
> That's the field of the world.

The foal grows to a stallion and soon has the globe spinning beneath its hooves.
At the end they bring it back to this small field, so it can gaze over the wall, and see the world it once cantered over so freely.
Now its grey head is lowered and it quietly crops grass.
Soon enough it will be axed and fed to the hounds.

I know that he still broods on that last trip.

We went far enough up the Orinoco into Guiana, he said, where the seams were ored with pure gold. I knew that all we had to do was hack deep into the earth's belly and we'd bring out enough of it to blind the king with riches, however wide and greedy his eyes.

He knew well enough that his crew on that voyage were the scum of the earth, and he has said so to me again today: drunkards, fornicators, blasphemers, he calls them. Some being the sort of men who would kill a child and then hold up its mangled body before its mother's weeping face. For himself, he would not have chosen to entrust a dog to their mercy. Not one he loved anyway. They were the sort for whom one could only find night employment.

He mused for a little, and then looked up smiling as he spoke:

> *His desire is a dureless content*
> *And a trustless joy.*

I think he was pleased that I could complete his quatrain:

He is won with a world of despair
And is lost with a toy.

He looked out of the Tower to see a bird, pecking about on the roof.

A maggot pie, he said with an unexpected delight. How pleasant to see a little white glistening among the executioners' hoods of the ravens.

I reminded him how I had once seen the eclipse over the Atlantic, the time I sailed to Virginia without him. The two Indians we had on board had been afraid; they had deemed it a portent of evil times to come. I had explained to them how the moon had interposed its body between sun and earth, so that through a certain trajectory the moon's shadow had brought an uncalendared night. My explanations were listened to with a wonder tempered, it seemed to me anyway, by their native scepticism.

In Virginia, the men had stood about with six-foot bows of witch-hazel, twitching the firing threads on and off, as I demonstrated the very latest sea compass, the one designed by Doctor Dee. I held up a Bible, explaining that it contained all the potency of the sacred word, how its truth could heal damaged and fractured mankind, even though everything in it might not be literally so.

One of the naked women, handsome with firm breasts and dark tattooed skin, took the book from my hands and performed a makeshift dance with it, drawing it over her breasts and through her legs, then rubbing it gently over her belly to make herself fecund. I had given her a word and she had accepted it; only with the birth of the metaphor are we all of us turned into sceptics.

I reminded him how many had said that their dark skins and tattoos undoubtedly put them at a further distance from God, when we published our account of Virginia. Their souls could hardly be as large as those of the sons and daughters of Europa.

We on this planet are all the same distance from God, Sir Walter said. Between God's hierarchies and man's, God always provides the more generous dimensions. Then he spoke again with reverence of the fishes and their sharp liquid prayers, timed to perfection.

Finally I looked up to find that it was dark already. The night had fallen on the waters between here and France, without my even noticing. There's a single boat out there festooned with lights. A whole Christmas tree of winking lights. As though all the stars from the sky had snagged in its rigging.

18 December

The boys leave today, one back to Germany and the other to Australia. They had both offered to stay on, but their mother wouldn't have it. You have work to do, she said. Anyway, Sean's here. Your father's best friend. Maybe the only true friend he ever had, for all the thousands of fine-weather companions who swarmed around him when he was riding high. Never saw any of their faces down here in Ramsgate.

And Sean promised your father to look after me before he died.

After they left, the house seemed suddenly vast and empty, and I couldn't face sitting in that turret room decoding Hariot's Notebooks. I might be afraid to find out how many years a dead man can go on living.

In my dream a swirl of life and colour had scattered through a void, like one of the photographs from the Hubble Telescope, or a painting by John Hoyland. Such a swarming splatter of cosmic energy. I woke and thought I heard her breathing in the other room.

19 December

We finally receive the visit Sally had warned me was bound to come, sooner or later. They'd had them before, apparently. She told me only to remain calm whatever was said.

The detective inspector sat in the living room, at a chair by the table, with his notebook laid beside him, and talked of the business of cigarette and alcohol smuggling, and how no one should be under any misconceptions about how seriously it was taken by the authorities. A joint investigation was presently being conducted, involving Customs and Excise and the police. Of course, for those who came clean there might be the possibility of a very light sentence indeed. Probationary really. Effectively an amnesty. Sally heard him out and then replied.

'Neither of the two people you are talking to has ever committed a crime, Detective Inspector. Oh, I might have parked on the odd double yellow line, and I suppose he might have spat on the pavement from time to time. But we're not criminals, either of us, so what right have you to talk to us as though we were?'

'Simply being in receipt of smuggled goods is a criminal offence.'

'But we're not in receipt of smuggled goods.' The policeman bethought himself, and shifted about on his chair.

'Being in receipt of any proceeds from smuggled goods . . .' he started, but Sally was aflame, or was pretending to be. It intrigued me. I had never seen her like this.

'When you get your nice fat pension, Detective Inspector, a fair chunk of it will presumably come from crime.' The officer bridled.

'Now what precisely do you mean by that? If you are implying that I . . .'

'Oh, I'm not suggesting you've been doing anything wrong, or picking up bungs on the side. How would I know which of you fellows do? For all I know, all your activities have been clean as a policeman's whistle, but the better part of your pension will still come out of other people's taxes, so they tell me, and we can presumably assume that a fair amount of that, maybe ten per cent, has come from dealings that weren't entirely above board. I'd have thought that's a conservative estimate myself. So would you give it back, then? If it could be proved? If it could be shown without question that ten per cent of your entitlement was coming out of funny money, would you accept a cut in your pension of the same amount?' She turned and pointed to me. 'He worked at the BBC for twenty years, before they decided they no longer required his services. Tell us, Sean, did they have somebody there to vet the money coming in from all the licence fees, to make sure it was all free from contamination?' She didn't bother waiting for an answer. 'It's just that when I go down to the post office to pay for my own licence, I haven't noticed anyone holding the money up to the light to see if there might be any fingerprints on it. From the gypsies – you know, the ones I brought in under cover of darkness in my little boat. No one seemed to bother at all.' The policeman had been sitting perfectly still, but his face had gone a flesh tint pinker during her tirade. I couldn't work out whether it was anger or embarrassment. Then she was off again.

'If one of your lot is caught leaning too far in the other direction, he's suspended on full pay for as many years as it takes for everyone to forget about it. And if they still haven't forgotten by then, he retires on a full pension, owing to ill health. Very sickly lot, you police. All right for some, isn't it, Detective Inspector? My husband was never extended the same courtesies when he hit a spot of bother. And now you come round here, fishing. I won't have it and neither will Sean.'

'You seem very close,' he said, in his copper's tone of sinister intimacy, 'you and Mr . . .'

'Tallow,' she said, matching his quiet intonations with her own low northern confidentiality, 'Mr Sean Tallow. And we are very close, since you ask. Maybe you have a problem with that. In which case, let me give you a bit of advice, speaking as a woman, you understand. Try not to play the inquisitor with your ladies, because we don't like being taken by inquisitors – never entirely sure if they might change their minds in the morning and decide to burn us in the village square after all. It's not all that long ago, is it? Anyway, thank you so much for coming round to pass on your condolences. It's such a help with the grieving process.'

Detective Inspector John Marney stood up then and left the house without another word. And for the first time in my life I knew I was definitely on the other side of the law.

In the notebooks I found myself staring at a complex drawing of a set of parabolic curves. After a while I realised that they could only represent the trajectories of missiles. Curious how many scientists, even Einstein, that peaceable and unworldly Jew, seem to become involved in devising surer and surer ways of blowing humanity to bits.

21 December

We walked down to the harbour. It was windy but dry. Sally took my arm as we stared out at the waves. They were beginning to rise. She spoke slowly, on our way back to the house, of Dominique's affair with Dan. It was, she said, the only one of his many liaisons that had ever seriously threatened their marriage. She seemed to know all about it and assumed that I did too.

When we returned I read more of Hariot:

Sir Walter spoke of how birds have the whole of the heavens inside them; only thus do they understand the relationship between stars and time. How else could they navigate with such precision and seasonal aptitude? This is the primal transaction by which the vastness of the heavens passes through the tiny globes of the eyes and into the only slightly larger globe of the skull. They must swallow the world entire to understand it, he said, just as we do. By the time we die, we have each of us eaten a universe.

22 December

Now I go each morning to the church on the hill. It's a dark enough place, all mortar and flintstone, though the ribbed bands of Whitby stone inside do lighten it. Pugin built it after he'd finished with the House of Commons. It was here in Ramsgate that he used to set out on stormy nights in his fishing boat, alarming even his professional sailors. Then his mind went entirely haywire and he ended up in Bedlam. His wife finally brought him back here to the house he'd built, but his wits and his spirit were already gone for good by then. He died soon after.

I attend mass and receive the sacrament, trying to prepare myself as best I can for what's to come, intent, as I now appear to be, on a life of crime, however brief. The reading was from John: how the light shone in the darkness and the darkness comprehended it not. On my return Sally gives me a sceptical look.

'Not going to die on me, are you, Sean?'

'I hope not. Why?'

'It's just that Dan only took up with God again just before he went to meet him.'

First new shipment arrived at dawn. Sally says everything was blessedly uneventful.

23 December

Second shipment. The beginning of a routine. I suppose anything you do often enough becomes either liturgy or routine. In the evening after dinner, I climb back up to the turret room, place the snooker cue over my shoulder as though in propitiation and start once more to decode. These cipher books from the London Library are now three years overdue. I wonder briefly which was the last address I gave them. I worked for a few hours and was about to go down for a last drink when I turned the page and saw the words. I have grown sufficiently used to the code by now to recognise certain clusters of characters. And there they were, all in the space of a single paragraph. Shakespeare, Marlowe, the School of Night. Here then is that new source which had seemed impossible even to hope for; here at last is the solution to nearly twenty years of work. I walked to the window and stared out into the night. I won't be sleeping between now and dawn.

The clumsiness of urgency. In my desperation to decipher the words I make twice as many mistakes as usual in the transcription. But piece by piece it comes together. I stare at what I have written, startled.

I had brought him Shakespeare's quartos and prompter's copies over the years. At first he had seemed to us no more than Marlowe's apprentice, but after Kit's death it was as though he had taken all the other man's strength and then added that of others too.

'How can this man, given who he is, given who he isn't,

gather so much into his work? He has made a whole world there, a bigger one than any of the rest of us.'

'Remember the experiment we did with the light?' I replied. 'The way one glass shape drew all the different beams and made them a single colour, but the other we devised took the single light and rainbowed it.'

'He's a rainbow man, then? Is that what you are saying? That the light goes into him at one place and comes out everywhere?'

'And everyone,' I said.

'Did he deliberately cultivate that air of being nobody, a little nobody with tiresome aspirations for his own coat of arms?'

'He liked to be invisible, I think; all things to all men.'

'And what did he once call us in that play of his?'

'The School of Night,' I said.

'Well, so many of our number have since gone into the dark, maybe he saw something under his rainbow that we were all blind to.'

I went back to the window. Stared intently into the black shroud of what I couldn't see. So it wasn't a dead man using him, after all. He'd known the dead, all right, for he could never have found his thousands of voices without them. But he'd not been controlled by them; instead they'd been resurrected inside him. He had taken his fire from their flames. And because he had been a nobody, the man from nowhere, he had been able to become everyone. Shakespeare was Shakespeare after all. So who was I? I pulled the Collected Works out of my bag and started turning the pages of *Love's Labour's Lost*, where all of this had first begun, and I realised that in paying so much attention to the words and the myriad clues they might contain, I'd actually missed the plot. For what Shakespeare – and I could use that word at last without qualification – what Shakespeare had written of was a group of men, all highly intelligent, who had decided to eschew women and daylight and human company so that they could find the truth. And all that the plot showed, with its wry twists and turns, was that they had lost it entirely in the process. These men in their dark studies had merely stumbled about, blinded by every need they could not acknowledge. All of the proofs I had found in Shakespeare's text had simply shown its inexhaustibility; how it could be interpreted in an infinity of ways. It only yielded as much truth as the living could bring to it.

24 December

Christmas Eve. Sally has put up a tree. Twinkling away in the bay window. She prepares a real dinner for the first time since I've been here, as I try to come to terms with what I read yesterday in the notebooks. How many years has it been since I first started pointing in the wrong direction? I feel numb, realise at last what a fool I am.

We are drinking wine. Then later she brings out the brandy. For some reason we start to talk about Dan's early days up north. I am still so startled by my new discovery, I can hardly bring myself to speak of it.

'It's the living,' I begin, but break off again. She looks at me and smiles. She starts talking again. She is a little drunk.

'I think the only thing Dan's mother taught him was that

anything he was permitted to have probably wasn't worth having, if you must know. I'm only surprised he didn't turn to crime before. Or maybe he did – it seems to be a pretty thin line in a lot of businesses these days. What I mean is, if there was anything she was prepared to give, his darling mother, then there couldn't be any pleasure in it anyway. The world existed only to disgust her. Emotionally speaking, he'd always had to steal whatever he really wanted from those closest to him.'

'The way he stole you.'

'He hardly stole me, did he, Sean? When he came back from seeing you in Oxford during your first term, the message I was given was that you wanted to leave it all for a year. You had other things on your mind; there were other people you might meet. Some of them female.'

'What?' I had a strange sensation of sinking underneath the surface of something I'd managed to keep my head above, but only just, for many years.

'Oh, come on, what difference does it make now? He's gone and you're still here.'

The rough wool of her skirt helped abrade the memories. Then my fingers alighted once more on cashmere. Obviously her favourite.

'Always were scared of him, weren't you, Sean?'

'Weren't you?'

'Not in the way that you were.' I had the curious sensation he was willing me on: I was after all in his house, with his wife, and he had placed me there. Perhaps it was his vagrant spirit that prompted me moments later into the bedroom. White bodies in the dark. The electric charge of memory.

And then we are in bed together and a whole lifetime of

something inside me has come pouring out. And I tell myself that this is life, and this was the secret I'd been searching for all that time: that the dead, finally, do not control the living. Which, for the living, might not necessarily make the days to come any easier to endure.

He says those words in my ear once more: 'A maggot's life, Sean, is it really worth it? Must you always be a coward in the playground?' I press the pillow down hard on his face then, not with love but anger, all the years of anger that have erupted in this one focused moment, as he probably knew they would and there is a brief struggle, but it's the struggle of a body, not a mind. It is merely flesh protesting that it still has air to breathe, food to eat, love to make; that it is surely too early to be asked to leave this place. But Dan doesn't have much strength by now and this is what he has asked me to do, begged me to do, taunted me into doing at last, and so I press on, press down relentlessly, as though to prove that I'm neither a maggot nor a coward any more, and as the greater strength of my body overcomes the lesser strength of my old friend's, the jerks and spasms of his limbs grow fainter and less frequent, until at last there is no movement left in him at all.

The body has fallen silent. I lift up the pillow then to look at what lies beneath me and as my hand reaches down to touch his cheek, still warm but already dead, my fingers are now only inches from that face as I suddenly jerk forward in the bed, heart racing and forehead damp with sweat, shrouded in the dream of the final thing I did for Daniel Pagett while he was on this earth.

Sally lies beside me, sunk deep in sleep, so I stumble out of bed and go downstairs. I stand for a moment at the window, staring out into the witching howl of the weather. I stare and stare as though some message might be written on the night's pelt. Then I walk around from room to room. Don't ask me what I'm looking for, but even in this blind gloom I feel they're staring back at me.

Soon the dawn will arrive to deliver its own grey visibilities. These household mirrors are blind as bats now, dark lakes drained temporarily of all crime and possibility. Come dawn, they must resume their daytime jobs as witnesses. Lucid and lethal witnesses.